Waiting for HARPER LEE

LEA DALEY

2013

Bella Books, Inc.
P.O. Box 10543
Tallahassee, FL 32302

Printed in the United States of America on acid-free paper.

Editor: Katherine V. Forrest
Cover Designer: Sandy Knowles

ISBN: 978-1-59493-342-4

About the Author

When Lea Daley first read *Silences*, she didn't dream that she'd experience the disruptions in creativity that Tillie Olsen described so long ago. However "real life" quickly absorbed most of her energies, just as Olsen predicted. Daley has written in short bursts while raising two children; claiming a lesbian identity; earning a BFA in painting; teaching preschoolers and college students; narrowly surviving the death of her only daughter; and heading a nonprofit agency that serves low-income working families.

Waiting for Harper Lee is Daley's first novel. She lives in St. Louis with her longtime partner and a very opinionated poodle-shih tzu mix. A hard-core liberal, Daley follows politics and enjoys animated debates at the dinner table. Because baking is a passion, her freezer almost always contains at least one heavenly homemade dessert, and she's happy to share her recipes with anyone who asks.

For Jaycie—how could it have been otherwise?
And for Gale, who's been there ever since.

With thanks to Katherine V. Forrest—
not once, but twice.

CHAPTER ONE

Much later Charles Dunnevan would accuse me of using music to seduce his wife. And looking back, I have to agree with him. Still I would plead innocent. It seemed perfectly natural to offer a spare concert ticket to a pianist. But I didn't know then what I do now. It never occurred to me that music was the only thing Alix couldn't resist. If my motives had been less pure, I'd have been a lot more careful. But she wasn't just married—her marriage was a living legend. So I was too open with her, caught off guard. Almost before I noticed it, the damage had been done.

By local standards I was a newcomer to Alix's community. Eighteen months earlier, I'd set up shop in Quillan's Crossing, a small Missouri village with increasing claims to gentrification. I wasn't the only city slicker who'd migrated fifty miles west after discovering that pristine setting and the Victorian architecture that was just begging for reclamation. Tension hadn't yet begun to develop between longtime residents and newbies like me. Back then we were welcomed, seen as fresh lifeblood for the old town, which had been hollowed out by a string of big-box enterprises on the highway a few miles beyond the Crossing. Not a single hardware store, bakery or stationery shop had survived the invasion.

I'd rented a dilapidated building on the central square and spruced it up a bit. The front had a small showroom but most of the real estate was devoted to the ceramics studio I set up in the back. From that base, I could produce far more pottery than I expected the locals to absorb. Much of my income would derive from sales to the galleries and consignment shops in metropolitan areas where I'd already established a credible reputation.

Although I couldn't have guessed it at first, that little storefront would become the leading edge, one of the early, trendy boutiques destined to transform this sleepy town into a thriving arts center. As more and more artists established studios, we began to attract attention. To our surprise, crowds of St. Louis shoppers would soon descend on the Crossing in search of rural charm and deep discounts on handcrafted work. Quaint inns—mostly the bed-and-breakfast type—weren't far behind that curve and a highly regarded summer arts festival would follow. But I hadn't been seeking fame or fortune when I opened my doors to the public there. Truth be told, I'd simply been running away.

Locating a space for my studio had been a piece of cake. Lots of empty spots on the square could be rented for cheap in those days. My living requirements were unique however, and couldn't be satisfied by just any residential neighborhood. So I purchased an old farmhouse well beyond the town's outer limits, a quiet, private place, with a wide front porch that overlooked a vast, wooded valley. But the real draw was the level ground out back as far as the eye could see, mostly planted with corn and soy. I owned three acres of that land, which was perfect for erecting a huge stoneware kiln, so essential to my work. And the hard manual labor of building that kiln would be a welcome distraction, part of my survival plan—in more ways than one.

* * *

Once the kiln was up and running, it hadn't taken me long to locate the only outcrop of activism in the area, a tenuous women's group that was just taking shape. The membership met once a week in the dank, cement-block basement of an Episcopal church. I liked those ladies for the most part. Their intentions were noble and the very existence of the group was remarkable in that redneck county. Still their timidity frustrated me almost beyond endurance. The nominal goal was the establishment of a women's community center for the area, but that seemed overly ambitious to me. Because *these* ladies were as badly in need of help as anyone. Each proposal struck at least one member as too radical. We couldn't offer a workshop on female sexuality—that would alarm the general populace. We couldn't sponsor services for abused women—the security challenges were insurmountable. We couldn't offer reproductive counseling—we'd discredit ourselves. Each Tuesday night, from sevento nine, I watched this circumspect deliberation with detached amusement. Every idea was deflected. The circle always closed itself around emptiness. When I talked about the meetings with friends in St. Louis, I described the action as "Feminism-Lite."

Even choosing a name for the organization had taken weeks. We'd finally agreed on the Abigail Adams Alliance—the Abbies, my new friends called it. As in, "I'll leave dinner in the oven for you tonight, Bill. The Abbies are meeting." Though the nickname made me retch, it sounded harmless—which was precisely the point.

I kept trying to push the envelope. But I'd nearly undone the Abbies the day I'd taken them to the county fair to collect signatures supporting passage of the Equal Rights Amendment. "Their husbands wouldn't let them sign," I was told by more than one member as they'd turned in mostly blank petitions at the end of the afternoon. Jesus *god*, I'd thought, it's *1980*! Nineteen—*fucking*—eighty! What's *wrong* with these people?

Time seemed to have stood still in Quillan's Crossing. It was more like the sixties there—the *early* sixties. Before the civil rights movement made waves. Before Vietnam. Before the assassinations of two Kennedy brothers and the Reverend King shocked us to the core. Before *The Feminine Mystique* sparked millions of heated discussions. The town was startlingly homogenous. White, conservative, Christian, straight, untouched by dozens of things that seemed perfectly ordinary in the city I'd abandoned. Gay bars and vegetarian restaurants. Feminist bookstores and womyn's coffeehouses. The annual "Take Back the Night March." And only outsiders like me had rescued it from certain death.

Of course, in that setting, I was the oddity. Since attending my first meeting where I'd introduced myself as "Lynn Westfall, your friendly neighborhood dyke," I'd gotten a lot of mileage out of being the lone lesbian. Six months in, titillated by their own daring, the membership appointed me to chair the meetings. My function quickly became obvious: I was there to fling outrageous propositions into the genteel debate, recommendations that would be quickly dismissed. But surely I'd provoke somebody into offering workable alternatives sooner or later?

That was nearly the only fun I had until Alix Dunnevan joined the Abbies. From the first moment, she caught my attention. Arriving at the last minute one night, I spotted her leaning against the table that housed our laboring coffeemaker. As an artist, I'd been trained to observe, so I did. She was petite with short, dense, glossy black hair and deep-set dark eyes. That fine-grained skin would tan easily, and her mouth seemed made for laughter. Hard to tell under bulky winter clothing, but she struck me as strong yet somehow delicate—high-tensile steel in a fragile sheath. Slender fingers were wrapped around a Styrofoam cup for warmth, and she looked totally at ease.

When I approached the coffee machine, she moved quietly out of my way only nodding a greeting. I checked my watch. It was time to call the meeting to order. Setting my coffee on the table, I pulled copies of the agenda from a folder and began to distribute them. The new woman crossed the room, draped her down jacket over the back of a battered chair and settled herself for the evening. Before we got down to business, I asked the members to introduce themselves to our guest. As I'd learn afterward, much to my chagrin, I was the only person present who hadn't recognized her instantly.

There was an air of calm about Alix that our unproductive antics failed to disrupt. She sat without comment through the entire discussion, though it seemed at times she was watching me intently. I found myself playing to her, determined to make her participate in the dialogue. I never broke through, and at last the meeting wound down. As usual, we'd renewed our liberal credentials while failing to identify any practical outlets for action. We were still safe.

I shook my head in despair, wondering whether I ought to resign. This group had nothing to offer anyone, much less me. I could be equally ineffectual on my own. They've put the horse before the cart, I thought. They should have begun with consciousness-raising. Because until they figure out who they *are*, they won't be able to articulate what they hope to *change*—much less fight for it. Trying to conceal real irritation, I jammed files and books in my backpack, then went to fetch my coat from the dim hallway. While stuffing my arms into quilted nylon, I noticed Alix at the exit. She opened the door to leave, then paused, those alert eyes measuring me.

"See you next week," she said.

And I knew I'd return.

* * *

So it began with this randomness—with Alix reading a press release about the Abbies in a throwaway newspaper on a day when her husband was out of town. If a dog had carried off that paper, if it had landed deep in drifted snow, if she'd spread it under her children's dripping boots, we might never have met. Is that what they mean by fate? This loosely woven curtain of possibilities that parts to reveal the inevitable? When I think back to that icy day, retracing our crisp, pale footprints, I cannot regret one minute.

* * *

Almost immediately, Alix and I formed an unbeatable coalition at our weekly meetings. She had an uncanny ability for finding connecting points between competing factions, then using them to forge consensus. And because she was so well respected, her support lent instant credibility to my propositions. Once I recognized that, I began tailoring my suggestions to fit the fabric of reality in the Crossing. We could *educate* women about the Equal Rights Amendment, leaving flyers at Laundromats, beauty shops, the health clinic—maybe then a petition drive would be successful! We could sponsor a camping trip for the local Girl Scout troop! We could hold bake sales to purchase women's literature for the public library! Probably only Alix Dunnevan recognized the delicious subversion of that proposal. Suddenly months of wrangling were at an end. The organization came to life under our hands. Yet there was nothing between Alix and me but unacknowledged intuition.

If we talked about ourselves, it was while lounging near the coffeemaker after meetings. In abbreviated form, we'd exchanged some basics about our lives. Alix had seemed fascinated to learn that I was a potter. I was awed when I heard she was a musician.

She'd laughed. "It's not necessary to genuflect. These days I'm really a housewife moonlighting as a piano teacher."

"Come on—Kate told me you were trained for the concert stage."

"Past tense," was all she'd say.

"And I've heard that you sing?"

"Some," she'd acknowledged, pointedly dropping the subject.

Other people told me plenty though. Alix occupied an elevated position in our little world. She was the only child of Caldecott Edwards, a high-profile physician and tireless self-promoter. Cal Edwards had single-handedly transformed a substandard nursing facility in the boondocks into a famous research hospital. Belmont Medical—BelMed—was now a mammoth enterprise. Each year over a hundred thousand patients received a wide range of care there. Cancer treatments.

Sports rehab. Mental health support. And during her father's tenure, he'd grown unaccountably wealthy. *The St. Louis Expo* regularly reported on the doctor's latest activities—a land grab of acreage for a new hospital wing. A hostile takeover of a chiropractic school. A million dollar home built with donations that might have been meant to provide medical services. Over time, he'd become a big deal in politics too—a steamroller of a guy who fancied himself a kingmaker. "And he's a real *bastard*," Alix would say if people sounded overly impressed.

About her husband she was more reticent, but that didn't stop other people from talking. I tried to tune out the gossip, yet couldn't help taking in a bit of detail. Apparently Charles was ungodly attractive—the Crossing's answer to Robert Redford, if rumors had any merit. He was a politician of some sort in Jefferson City, our state capitol. The kind of guy who might one day become a wholesome hero on the national scene. Their two young daughters were bright and beautiful, the family apparently without flaw. If I thought there was a melancholy edge to Alix, some darker side, I ignored it. One learns to look at the married ladies only peripherally. I limited conversation with her to the most superficial of topics, and refused to analyze my conviction that those brief encounters were somehow significant.

* * *

One frigid night, Alix came early to the church hall. She was glittering with snow and had her husband in tow. Charles needed their four-wheel drive for an errand, she explained as she introduced him all around. He expected to return for her about the time our meeting broke up.

As I shook Dunnevan's hand, I assessed his fabled magnetism. The man *was* strikingly handsome. The rising wind had tossed his sandy hair into appealing disarray, which I suspected he knew. His eyes were so blue they verged on indigo, his skin suspiciously tan. And his easy, boyish smile had an intimate quality that would take him far. Dunnevan was tall and well-built, his clothing slavishly observant of prevailing trends in menswear. Calvin Klein, unless I missed my guess.

Breaking away from that hypnotic grin, I glanced at Alix. She pulled off a stocking cap to shake free her short hair. Fine gold hoops pierced her ears. Under a flannel shirt, she wore the requisite thermal top. Threadbare jeans were tucked into serious hiking boots and a knapsack hung from one shoulder in place of a purse. Still busy introducing her husband, she was unaware of my inspection. I reeled with disbelief—no wonder she'd stood out amid all those pastel pantsuits!

Because alongside her big, buff husband, Alix resembled nothing so much as an improbably-married dyke. I could only suppose she didn't realize she was sending conflicting signals. Watching closely as she said farewell, I had to laugh at myself. The Dunnevans were like any other couple busy negotiating a complicated scheduling dilemma—his errand, the estimated time the Abbies would adjourn, a babysitter who'd need to be driven home. Refilling my coffee cup, I concluded that this was one instance where appearance and actuality parted company.

* * *

Our session ended early that night. Accumulating snow had prevented several women from attending. The others weren't sure they'd been wise to brave the worsening weather. Long before Dunnevan was due back, members began to trickle out in twos and threes. But I'd agreed to lock up, so Alix and I were still at the table, delving deeper into "classism," the evening's discussion topic.

"I suppose everyone knows that my family's wealthy," Alix sighed. "And while I understand their hostility toward rich people, I wish they understood that affluence isn't always an unmixed blessing."

"I can't imagine never having to worry about money," I said, recalling a youth of minor deprivation. "What's that like?"

"I can only speak for myself," Alix answered grimly. "But in my case, it was a lot like being a child prostitute."

"That bad?"

"Would I lie to you? As soon as I was conscious, I realized that money was all that mattered to my father. So there was no way dear old dad wouldn't use me to enlarge his holdings. I was a piece of window dressing—a prop he could manipulate to get another grant or endowment for that damned hospital."

"Maybe poverty has an upside, after all."

"Not sure we want to go public with that concept," Alix quipped. But she still had one foot in the past. Her voice dropped into a lower register. "My father's appetite for power and influence is insatiable, to put it mildly. So my earliest memories are of being fondled by old men, of having to smile at them till my face hurt."

She must have noticed my appalled expression. "I don't mean anything sexual, Lynn…at least not overtly. I just understood that my primary obligation was to stay cute, to bring in more donations. I guess I've always hated my father for it, but I can't help blaming my mother too. How could she have let him do that to me?"

I pressed her hand briefly. "I suppose it depends on how badly he'd damaged her before you came along."

Alix nodded. "You're right, of course. Poor woman—she's done *her* share of smiling. It's her only marketable skill. She couldn't have survived without my father."

"Sometimes I think my old man's disappearing act was the best thing that ever happened to me," I confided. "I've always known that women can make it alone because I watched my mother do it. She didn't have it easy but nobody owned that woman's soul. It never crossed my mind that I couldn't cope without a man or that some guy had a right to call all the shots."

"Consider yourself lucky," Alix muttered.

Just then the door swung open and Pam came rushing into the room again. "Lynn—I was halfway home when I remembered something. I won't be able to make it to that concert. My grandmother announced that she's coming into town the same night. Do you think you can unload my ticket on such short notice?"

"Not to worry," I assured her as she dug the oversized rectangle out of her purse. "The concert's a sellout. I might even make a profit."

"Great," she said. "I'll be sorry to miss it."

"Yeah. It's the event of the season for us alternate-lifestyle types," I cracked. But looking at her retreating back, I wondered if she was actually relieved. Our youngest member, Pam was studying deaf education at the community college. She'd only wanted to observe a professional interpreter in action. Maybe a gay get-together wasn't her ideal venue for that particular learning experience.

When we were alone again, Alix turned to me, eyes sparkling. "*What* concert?"

"Oh, Holly Near. Do you know her?"

She shrugged. "Tell me."

"Let's see: she's a lesbian-feminist-pacifist-singer-songwriter."

"Is that all?" Alix laughed.

"Far from it, smartass. She's also a political activist. This is a benefit for an assortment of radical groups. It should be a wonderful night—terrific music and all the freaks you could ask for."

Alix looked tentative. "I don't want to put you on the spot if you know someone who needs the ticket, Lynn, but I'd like to buy it. I'd see that you made a profit," she teased.

"I don't need to be paid," I told her. "Just make a generous donation to one of the causes that night."

"Works for me," Alix said.

I handed over the piece of colorful cardstock, hoping I wasn't making a mistake. "Sure you're up for this?"

"You forget," Alix said. "I was a music major."

But I hadn't. Not really.

CHAPTER TWO

For all my bravado, there's a part of me that quakes whenever I take a straight person into the gay world. I cursed myself for giving that ticket to Alix. And I'd compounded the error by agreeing to ride into the city with her. All afternoon I agonized about the time we'd spend on the road. Would Alix be tense on the drive up, then shocked on the trip back? Would she expect me to explain or justify? There's a lot I don't like about the extremes of gay culture, plenty of things I don't associate myself with. I'm not an apologist for certain forms of behavior, but I didn't intend to discuss them with someone who could never understand.

As I waited for Alix that night, I tried reminding myself that heterosexuals don't assume responsibility for the weirdoes in *their* ranks. Of which there are bajillions. But I was only slightly reassured. By the time she knocked on my door, I'd drunk four cups of coffee and was a nervous wreck. I'd have to piss every twenty minutes. Jesus!

At first, Alix concentrated all her energies on negotiating the slippery streets leading out of town. She was, I could see, an excellent driver who managed the intricacies of stick shift and clutch without fanfare despite the treacherous conditions. Sitting beside her, I was mostly silent, thinking that we were probably the only people in the county who'd travel fifty miles over ice to hear a lesbian performer—though undoubtedly there were dozens who'd go twice as far to hassle a homo.

By the time we reached the highway, I'd begun to relax a little. And not just because the snowplows had done a fair job of clearing the interstate. There was a kind of ease that emanated from Alix. If she were comfortable, why shouldn't I be? Suddenly the evening looked more promising and speech began to seem possible. I decided to tell her a little about feminist performances so she'd know what to anticipate. But I gave up almost immediately.

"Nuts," I said. "I don't have the vocabulary to explain what I mean to a musician. And I hate discussions about the arts anyway. You'll just have to see for yourself."

Alix grinned. "Can't wait."

* * *

The cavernous lobby outside the concert hall was already mobbed when we arrived and the atmosphere was electric with optimism, with purpose. An endless crush of women hawked T-shirts, passed out pamphlets and signed one another's petitions. The noise was deafening. Impossible to hear your friends after fighting valiantly to reach them. It was just as well, though. I could see the questioning looks as I introduced Alix—the speculation and the approval. I could only hope she was unaware of the innuendo. Elbowing our way to an ornate staircase, we sat on gritty marble to survey the crowd.

"Looks like a fucking bazaar," I shouted.

"Is that spelled b-i-z-a-r-r-e?" Alix asked, but her laughter was accepting.

"Honey, you ain't seen nothin' yet," I promised. "Let's go inside and find some seats. The noise is really getting to me."

Within the hall, the scene was less hectic. I tried to guess how it must look to Alix, but I didn't know her well enough to predict her reactions. What did she think when Tamara Feingold greeted me with an enthusiastic kiss? On the lips. How did she feel about the careless display of female power, and that sea of unfettered breasts? There was scarcely a bra in the place. What about the gay men, arm in arm with one another, oblivious to the masses of women? And our clowns—those poor refugees from the sixties who'd lost all but the trappings of an era? What did she think as they flaunted themselves so proudly, feathers billowing and beads glinting through gypsy tatters? How did they look? How did we look? How did *I* look to Alix?

As always, the concert started late. And began in the usual way—with announcements, program corrections, protracted introductions. When the opening act appeared at last, the hall quieted. But when Holly Near crossed to bow at center stage, the crowd went wild. Come what may, Alix was on her own now. It was a relief to forget about her, to focus on the fluid movements of the interpreter, to lose myself in the music. I let the feeling of community wash through me, floating on it, welcoming it. Engulfed in a sense of belonging, I was wondering why I'd strayed so far. Wondering how I could have hesitated to share this beauty with Alix.

Much too soon, the lights came up for intermission and she blinked at me. "You doing okay?" I asked.

"*Oh*, yeah," she sighed contentedly. "When's the best time to buy albums—now or afterward?"

"Wait till later," I advised her. "The stuff will still be on sale and you'll know what you want."

"Idiot! I want it all!" she told me. "But I can wait."

* * *

The overhead lights faded again. I sank down in the seat, at peace with myself. I sang favorite tunes under my breath and closed my eyes through new pieces, trying to really hear them. Then, for her final number, Holly Near asked us all to link hands and sing her trademark anthem of unity. "Regardless," she said, "of your sexual orientation."

Alix reached for my hand shyly. The sound of her voice was drowned out by the ecstatic crowd. Her smooth, warm fingers left an imprint on my palm that was still there after I'd applauded through two encores. Deep inside me, a voice said fiercely, Don't even *think* about it!

* * *

A lot of luck came our way at that event. We had just left the sales table with a pile of albums when Alix gestured excitedly. "Lynn, that's *her*!" Ten feet from us, the fresh-faced singer was exchanging greetings with people in the slowly thinning crowd.

"Want to say hello?" I asked.

Eyes glowing, she nodded. We edged forward until we stood in front of the performer. Alix extended her hand. "I just wanted to thank you for tonight," she said. "It meant a lot to me."

With a smile, Near reached for the top album in Alix's stack. "What are your names?" she asked, pen poised above the cardboard sleeve.

Alix began to spell, while I made a small negative gesture. But I was too late. The scrawling dedication had already begun to appear on the fuchsia cover of *Fire in the Rain.* It read, "To Lynn and Alix, in sisterhood, from Holly Near." I threw back my head and laughed. Who was I to argue with an omen?

* * *

I couldn't help myself—I was still chuckling as we backtracked through city streets. But Alix had become very quiet, worrisomely quiet. At last she spoke.

"Lynn, did she think we were…*lovers*?" Alix said the word softly, as if it were unfamiliar and she wanted to get it just right.

Here we go, I thought. But aloud I said, "Yes, my friend, like almost everyone else you met tonight, she assumed we were a couple. I owe you an apology. I should have warned you in advance, but, stupidly, it didn't cross my mind. If it's any comfort, remember you live fifty miles from everyone you saw this evening—it's unlikely that word will get around back home."

"It's not a big deal," she assured me. "I just wanted to know."

Silence strung out between us, gathering weight and intensity. We'd covered several miles before Alix said, "I suppose you get tired of talking about it?"

I considered pretending not to understand her, but decided against it. I knew what she meant. "Sometimes," I answered. "With some people. Do you need to know?"

"I'm interested, curious—hell, maybe I'm just nosy."

"Who isn't?" My voice sounded tired, almost rude. Embarrassed, I relented. "Okay, Alix. I'll answer two questions—provided you realize that asking them is dangerous." I'd tried to say it lightly. Did she pick up the undertone of seriousness?

"Cheater," Alix laughed. "I suppose I have to use one of my questions to find out what the risk is?"

"No, I'll play fair. The risk is that once people start thinking about homosexuality, they can't rest until they figure out where *they* fit into the picture. Do you see what I mean?"

"Maybe not completely." She seemed subdued. "I still want to discuss this. I'm just searching for the right approach…"

She drove on a little, before asking from the darkness, "Do you *have* a lover?"

"Oh, god!" I gasped. "Not *that* one! I can't answer that one!" I was choking on the pain, on tears so unexpected.

"Christ, Lynn, I'm sorry! I'm so, so sorry!" said Alix, apologizing without even knowing what line she'd crossed.

When she pulled off the highway, her car bumped over mounded snow on the shoulder. She flicked on the emergency flashers. We sat there in the winter chill, alternately shadowed and neon green. Alix didn't know what to do for me. I sensed her need to soften the blow as keenly as I felt nails gouging my palms. But something inside me was so doubled over that I couldn't rescue her. At last she pulled my head down on her shoulder and patted me awkwardly while I struggled to suppress my sobs. We didn't move until our feet began to feel numb.

"The awful thing," I told Alix, as I straightened up, "is that there's no easy exit from a situation like this."

"Sure there is," she said. "We simply signal and pull out."

So we did.

CHAPTER THREE

One good thing about being self-employed: it allows you the freedom to break down, if necessary. After I got home from the concert, I stayed up even later to water my houseplants and pack some gear. Shortly after dawn, I loaded a duffel bag, backpack and some snack food into the station wagon. Then I called my cat and lured him into the front seat. Long before the little coffee shops opened in the Crossing, I drove through town. At my studio, I stopped to post a sign on the door: *Closed For Vacation.*

Back behind the steering wheel, I turned my car toward the highway. The only friend I wanted to see lived four hours south. I knew I'd be welcome even without notice and right now I really needed Mattie. Under the circumstances, no one else would do.

* * *

The sun was riding high when I pulled into the long, rutted driveway that led to Mattie's cabin. By the time I turned off the engine, she was waving on the front porch. I walked toward her at first, then gave it up and ran. Wooden steps creaked underfoot and suddenly I was enveloped by Mattie's strong arms.

"I've come to dig clay," I said into her warm neck. Of course, she knew that was bullshit. The ground would be too hard for months. But Mattie understood—she always has.

We unpacked the car, liberating an indignant cat, and hauled my stuff into her small cabin. I've never surprised her. No matter what time I arrive, Mattie's living room has an expectant air. The book on the coffee table seems to have been chosen for me and some enticing smell promises homemade delight. I've seen wood fires try to outshine Mattie but nothing ever has. Sometimes, our history aside, she feels like my mother.

She'd been stacking cordwood when I arrived so I followed her back out into the cold noon light. We worked for an hour, almost without speaking. I'd heave a length of wood to Mattie, she'd catch it and place it with great precision on a stack beside the door. Darting between our feet, rubbing against our jeans, Sol did his best to disrupt us, but we persisted. I was tired and sweaty when we finished, yet happier somehow. I don't know why it's so easy with Mattie. Leaving her, returning to my other life, never seems like the right thing to do.

After we finished the dinner dishes that night, I pulled a large flat package from my duffel bag and handed it to her. "I brought you a piece of springtime."

Mattie peeled back the tape carefully then smoothed the heavy brown paper. I knew she'd fold it later, setting it aside for another use. Finally she turned her attention to my gift, a black-and-white photograph in a simple silver frame. When she slid it from its bubble-wrap envelope, she was staring at herself.

Mattie, outdoors, squinting into April light. My lens had caught her well and truly—her long, thick hair bound back and topped off by an ancient tennis hat. Her weathering skin and considering eyes, the faded work shirt, that incredible smile she wears in her garden. Mattie rendered in the richest light and shadow.

"Oh, I wish Diana could have seen this!" she said in her soft country drawl.

"Heart-stopping, ain't it?"

"I believe it's very good," she pronounced, still studying the image.

"The best I've ever done," I assured her. "It's part of a series—the last stuff I printed before Sarah packed her enlarger. Working on it was the only thing that kept me sane just then."

And since that was what I'd come to talk about, Mattie nodded, rocking more slowly. We had the whole night ahead of us.

* * *

Mattie was out and about when I woke the next morning, a bit stiff in my sleeping bag. She'd left coffee warming on the counter next to a loaf of whole wheat bread and a jar of wild honey. I carried my plate into the living room and took inventory while I ate. The woman was nothing if not eclectic. Seashells, rocks, feathers and driftwood shared space with one or two of my ceramic pots, her books and a crazy quilt. I smiled fondly at the latest addition to the collection—my photograph had been given a position of prominence on her slate mantel. I could only take that as a tribute, if temporary. Mattie would be uncomfortable about being on display and the picture wouldn't stay there long.

The cabin was very quiet. Only the occasional sound of a branch brushing against the tin roof broke the silence. Last night's embers still gave off heat in the fireplace and sunlight made a patchwork of windowpanes on the old pine floorboards. The peace was almost palpable. No wonder Mattie had so much to spare for her friends. Suddenly, I felt like drawing.

My sketchbook was in my backpack—an act of faith really. Though I'd tried to deny it, I'd been in the doldrums for a long time. Ever since Sarah left, my work had been repetitious, predictable. Strictly speaking, that wasn't all bad. Replication is the backbone of production pottery, and my very life depends on it. So many matching mugs to purchase groceries, so many nesting canisters to cover utility bills. Sets of dessert plates pay for my khakis, and salad bowls buy my sneakers.

But my luxuries—mental as well as material—have always rested on those exhilarating moments when clay rises up under my fingers to assume a unique presence. Those are the show pieces, the pots I enter in competitions, the creations that entice discriminating customers into my shop. Occasionally one of them takes on special meaning for me. I'll overprice it on purpose so I can live a little longer with its challenge, its reassurance. And if it sells at an elevated price, so much the better.

Like anyone else, though, I spend most of my days doing routine and difficult work. There are no shortcuts in ceramics. It's an arduous process. You begin at the beginning each day. Once, in frustration, I'd bitched about that to Sarah.

"A printmaker can pull hundreds of pieces from one engraved plate, but potters have to have a personal relationship with every goddamned mug and planter!" I'd wailed, wanting empathy more than a solution.

Leaning back in Mattie's rocker, the sketchbook open on my lap, I could still hear Sarah's response: "Why don't you just make molds from your best pieces and pour duplicates of them?"

Her question had rubbed me the wrong way. "Barbarian! How could you suggest such a thing?"

"It seems perfectly reasonable to me," Sarah had said. "It would still be your work, after all—your designs, your marks on the clay, your glazes."

"Over and over again? With no variation or refinement? Gross! In the future, woman, get your coffee cups from Walmart!"

Sarah had looked patient enough, but I'd known her a long time. I recognized the patronizing tone when she replied. "Calm down, okay? Maybe you haven't noticed it, but you've just reversed your position. Anyway, working from molds was only a suggestion."

I was irritated by that subtle undercurrent of superiority. "Well, I have a suggestion for you, Sarah—why don't you just tape your lectures and play them back for the next five graduating classes?"

"Damn it, Lynn, that's not the same thing! There's always additional material to incorporate—sometimes I've had a new insight or I need a new approach. And every class is unique. The students push me in different directions. I push back, based on what they can handle. There are a thousand variables."

I'd stared at her, astonished. Hadn't she been paying attention? "God, Sarah, you're so smug! Do you think there are no variables in *my* work? Every batch of clay is different, every firing. How I feel, what I need or can give, changes every day. I visit a museum and come home with a dozen new ideas. Shall I calmly and efficiently pour fifty old ones?" I was almost out of control. "Jesus, you make me mad!"

Sarah gave up on me. She put on her reading glasses with an air of finality, saying, "All right, Lynn! All right! Let's just drop it."

Knowing I'd been shut out, feeling abandoned, I'd stood beside her seething. At last I said, "Sometimes when you drop it, Sarah, it breaks."

The sketchbook slid from my lap, jolting me back to the present. I was gathering scattered notes and scribbles when an image started forming in my mind. A good one, the kind that floats to the surface fully realized and dares you to catch it before it dissolves. I thumbed through the book hurriedly, seeking blank pages.

Totally immersed in drawing, I didn't know Mattie had returned until she touched my shoulder. I leaped up, wondering what time it was and whether I should have begun making lunch. Mattie just laughed at me. "You're a sight," she said. "Charcoal all over your face."

"Who are you laughing at, woman? You're so covered with burrs and pine needles, it's a wonder a jay hasn't nested in your hair."

"I had a fine morning," Mattie acknowledged. "Guess it shows."

"Why don't you clean up while I fix something for lunch?" I suggested.

She gave me a quick hug. "Best offer I've had in ages."

* * *

I spent a week and then some with Mattie, letting her do her magic tricks on my aching psyche. We roamed the woods and fields till only fear of frostbite sent us in. We talked late into the night. Mattie listened when I needed her to and asked no questions otherwise. One evening she pulled an old six-string guitar from her closet saying, "Wonder if I still know how to play this thing?" She did. No doubt about it.

I have no gift for music, except that it moves me. But her voice is low and warm and healing. We sang until the fire died down. Just before I fell asleep, I called through the shadows, "Mattie…I've met a musician I think you'd like." Then I realized that I could be home for the weekly women's meeting if I left in the morning. By sunrise, I'd be on my way.

We stood in slushy snow beside my car, the horizon just emerging from the dark. We'd been hugging and saying goodbye for five minutes. As I said, leaving Mattie never feels right. Finally I took hold of her arms. "I'm actually going to go, my friend, but first there's something I want to tell you. I know you don't like speeches, but don't interrupt anyway." Mattie nodded and squared her shoulders.

"I just want you to understand how much you've helped me. This is the first time I've been able to talk—really talk—about Sarah and I feel a lot better. You've made me see that I've been afraid to deal with her. I've been fighting so hard to hold in the pain, I was never going to be free of it. Now I think I can let go. I want to thank you for that—for everything."

Mattie gripped both of my hands. "I only gave back what *you've* given me," she said. "Take care of yourself now." Then she hustled me into my car and shut the door firmly.

CHAPTER FOUR

Even after driving for several hours I felt wired. When I arrived home I dumped my stuff in the living room and put out fresh food for Solly. Back in my car again, I headed for the shop, hoping like hell the clay hadn't dried out in my absence. I'm usually careful—even anal—about things like that, but I'd left so impulsively that I couldn't be sure. I parked out front then made a sudden decision not to open to the public that day. I was invigorated by those new sketches and wanted time to throw without interruption. I drove around back, entering the shop through the rear. Before I'd shed my jacket, I'd begun to take stock in the studio. My clay was cold but in good condition.

I took a moment to get my hair out of the way—it's thick, fine, straight, strawberry-blonde stuff that people have fussed over since my childhood and I guess I'm too vain to cut it. After I pinned my bangs to one side, I worked a loose French braid down my back, something I'd learned to do with lightning speed when I became an art student. You can't be a potter unless you have damned good coordination.

I rolled up my sleeves and began to wedge air out of several heavy slabs of clay. As a cocky college student I'd found this process boring, mechanical—nothing more than a necessary prelude to the fun stuff. But in my years as a professional I'd come to recognize that wedging has an intrinsic value beyond its primary function. Now I think of it as a transitional technique, a way of crossing from one mental state to another.

The action is almost Zen-like in its monotony and mindlessness. Moving rhythmically, using my whole body to knead the clay, I not only released air bubbles that could explode in a superheated kiln, I also set aside a hundred daily tensions. My hands explored the material, gauging its plasticity, knowing how to use it. Soon I'd shaped the clay into five crude cones and I was at the wheel, feeling eager yet tranquil.

I worked until my studio went dim, then cursed the madman who'd wired the place. The only light switch in the long, narrow building was in the showroom at the front, a situation that frequently caused customers to believe I was open at all hours. Arching my back to relieve tired muscles, I left my wheel to flip that switch.

It had been a good afternoon. My shelves were full of plaster "bats" that supported new bowls and pots. Each soft, wet form was a welcome departure from the stale work I'd been producing since I'd come to the Crossing. I'd almost decided not to break the spell, to throw on right through the meeting time. Kate, our excellent vice chair, would pick up the slack again if I didn't show.

Then, in the first bright flash of illumination, I saw a note on the floor of the showroom. For a week it had lain by the front door gathering dust. The edges were slightly curled from dampness. I bent to pick it up. In bold strokes Alix had written, "I was here. Where were you? Hope to see you the next time the Abbies meet."

I tapped the paper lightly against my palm, calculating. If I didn't bother to change my clothing, I could get there just as things got rolling.

* * *

Most of the group had assembled before I arrived. After a week with Mattie, I'd forgotten how strange my work clothes would look in contrast to all those tailored separates. But that didn't seem to matter. Several women greeted me warmly, saying that they'd missed me at the last session. Jenny patted my back and whispered, "Glad you're here tonight, Lynn. Maybe now we can cut through some of the bullshit." Smiling back at her, I had to appreciate the changes. Not only could Jenny actually *say* "bullshit," she'd learned to *recognize* it, as well. And if she and the others had gotten tougher, I'd become a little softer. Perhaps anything was possible, given enough time.

All the while, of course, I was waiting for Alix. Just when I'd given up hope, she walked through the doorway. In my brief time away, I'd almost forgotten how captivating she was. I couldn't stop staring at her, couldn't quit smiling. I moved to my chair and started shuffling papers, hoping like hell I could concentrate on the business at hand.

I called the meeting to order. Minutes were approved and reports were made. Questions were asked and answered. Objections were raised. Consensus was reached on some items, while others were tabled for later consideration. Yada yada. Finally, I was able to adjourn the meeting. But Kate had engaged Alix in conversation as they gathered up their belongings. Still talking, they left together with only a perfunctory wave goodbye.

Shaking my head ruefully, I locked up and drove home. My headlong dash from Mattie's had been pointless—I hadn't even managed to say hello to Alix, much less spend time with her. Consider that a *good* thing, Lynn, I told myself sternly.

* * *

It was one of those days. Nothing going right. I'd cut my thumb slicing an apple for breakfast, which would make wheel work unpleasant for a while. Too bad, because I really needed to make up for lost time. I'd driven to the studio with a plan to sidestep the injury—instead of throwing, I'd do some hand-building. But when I parked my car, I noticed a slow leak in one tire. On a Sunday, natch. Both of the Crossing's repair shops would be closed. I thought I could probably nurse the station wagon home, and drive back in the morning. If not, I'd hit someone up for a ride. But then the car would need to be towed to town, because—sadly—I knew my spare needed repair too. The downside of being more optimistic than organized.

The hand-building was going well, at least. I'd trimmed thin slabs of clay and shaped them into six free-form boxes. I thought I might glaze them as some kind of series. The details TBD. I'd let the possibilities percolate for a while before proceeding. Setting the boxes aside to dry, I decided to break for lunch. Except.

"God*damn* it!" I said aloud. "What a day!" My little refrigerator was empty, which meant that my tuna sandwich was still on the counter at home. Except that it wasn't, of course. Because by now, Solly would have leaped up, dragged it down, shredded the wrappings and smeared tuna around the kitchen. If I were lucky. If not, I could slip on a lettuce leaf when I entered the front door. Not to mention other unlovely possibilities.

I grabbed my backpack and flung myself out of the studio. On the square just opposite my shop was a local gathering spot, the Quillan Café and Grill. The soups weren't bad there, and with luck the traffic would be light. Everyone else would be at home with their families for Sunday dinner after church. I hoped. I just wanted to get in and out quickly, then find a way back to my house.

I called out a greeting to the owner who appeared to be working solo on a slow day. Draping my coat and backpack over the frame of a booth, I went to the restroom to wash my hands. When I came out, someone had slung a leather bag on top of my stuff—a case for binoculars, maybe. Nervy, I thought, as I approached the table. And entirely unnecessary, since the place was virtually empty. I was cranky and prepared to be snappish. Until.

I could see over the top of the booth now. Dark, shiny hair. A small, beautifully-shaped head. Alix Dunnevan.

All my irritation fell away and nothing could hold back my smile. Cool it, Lynn! I warned myself. But when I slid into the booth to face her, it was with naked delight at the surprise.

"Hi," I beamed. "This is the nicest thing that's happened all day."

"That's the nicest thing I've heard all day," she replied, grinning back.

A little silence fell. Anything I might say felt fraught. And Alix wasn't helping. In fact, she was studying the menu now.

At last I said, "Binoculars?"

She closed the plastic folder and set it aside. "Yep. I'm headed to the dam to watch the eagles. It'll be even colder on the river, so I wanted to take something hot with me—coffee, cocoa, whatever. When I came in, I saw you headed to the back. I didn't think you'd mind if I joined you for a minute."

Not if you keep flashing that dimple at me. Not if I can make you wink just once. "Eagles?" I asked. Sharp as a tack, that's me.

"You know—raptors? Symbol of our great nation? They winter on the Illinois side of the Mississippi?"

"Give me a break, smartass. I'm new in town."

"Umm...I forget," Alix murmured. "Seems like I've known you forever."

My heart skipped a beat. "Ten weeks," I said before I could stop myself.

"But who's counting?" she teased.

My face flushed. "The meetings," I told her. "The first one you came to was just before Thanksgiving, so it's easy to track."

She hadn't meant to embarrass me. Now she was embarrassed. "Sorry, Lynn—I'm a bit off-kilter today. Call it early spring fever. I'm hoping a long drive will mellow me out."

Spring fever, hmm? Better take a pass on *that* one. "So, explain the birds," I said. "I'm totally clueless."

"You know the locks and dam? In Alton?"

"Only in the vaguest sense. Even when I lived in St. Louis, Alton wasn't on my radar screen."

"Okay. About this time every year, a zillion bald eagles migrate from Canada and settle there for a few months. It's a nesting spot, ideal because of all the fish that come through the locks. I'm on the board of a river preservation group and we work hard to keep the area attractive to the eagles. Part of a plan to increase the population. I always go check on them two or three times in the season."

She was dressed for it, I saw. A turtleneck under a fisherman's sweater. An oversized denim jacket lined with sheepskin. Warm boots. A woolen cap on the table next to the menu. She could stay out all day dressed like that. What she *couldn't* do was stay indoors much longer. Her face was already pink. Tiny beads of sweat had blossomed on her forehead. And she was still adorable.

Peggy was alongside the table now, her pad and pen in hand. Alix asked for coffee and chili to go. Then she turned to me. "Want to double the order?"

"Go *with* you?"

"Sure. If you don't have anything better to do."

I didn't. And it had been such a crappy day. But spending time alone with Alix would violate a bedrock principle. She was looking at me quizzically, waiting for my answer.

Screw the rules—I'm going! I smiled up at Peg, feeling much better about the afternoon. "I'll have what she's having," I said. "But would you throw in some extra crackers?"

* * *

We talked about everything and nothing on the hour-plus drive to the Great River Road. The chances for passage of the Equal Rights Amendment. Our never-ending amazement that so many women had been persuaded to oppose their own inclusion in the federal Constitution. The intensity of the winter. Our hopes for an early spring. The breadth and depth of the river. Whether snows up north would raise the water level, flooding the road beneath our wheels. And books we were reading, movies we'd seen. I didn't care what the topic was, or how long the journey took, as long as I could sit alongside intoxicating Alix Dunnevan while she steered me into unknown territory.

Upriver the bluffs were steep and austere against a gray sky. Bare trees crowded small islands. The water glared back at a white winter sun. On the narrow shoulder of the road, cars were parked in clusters. Small knots of people stood beside them, binoculars up, scanning the clouds.

"Let's go a little farther," Alix said. "Too much human activity can really screw up the cycle. Last year, we had several abandoned nests. We were able to relocate some of the babies before they fledged, but we lost at least six birds."

"So, you're like an expert on this stuff?"

Alix laughed. "No way. But I'm a real water baby. Belmont—where I grew up—is on the Lake of the Ozarks. So I know a little about sailing, love to swim, water ski, all that stuff. When I moved north, I transferred my watery obsessions to the Mississippi. And then I fell in love with the eagles. The preservation work was easier to manage when we lived in St. Louis, though."

"Why'd you leave?"

She rolled her eyes a little. "Charles decided that owning a home near the capitol would 'enhance his political profile.'"

I puzzled that out. "A man from the heartland?" I said in a voice just this side of snarky.

"Precisely."

I paused for a moment before I decided to risk the question: "Did *you* have any say in the matter?"

"If you're thinking that Charles usually gets his way, you're right," Alix said, impressing me with her insight. "I *do* have a long history of giving in to him. But there wasn't much point to resisting the move—mostly because the Crossing's a pretty good place to raise children. My only caveat was that the girls and I would actually live there. So Charles rents an apartment in Jefferson City for all the time he has to be away, and I get to keep things simple for Beth and Cindy. They deserve to do everything I did when I was a kid. Making mud pies and weed salad. Blowing dandelions. Bouncing on grapevines. Stuff you can't really do in a city."

That sounded a lot like my own childhood. "Snow forts," I said. "Splashing in creeks and jumping in piles of autumn leaves."

Alix nodded appreciatively. "Yeah. Of course, we have to backtrack to the river—or go home to the lake—for most of the water sports."

I shrugged. "Out of my league."

"How so?"

"I grew up poor, remember? I've never even learned to swim. Which is really stupid, because I love water."

"What's poverty got to do with it?"

I looked at her in surprise. "Swim lessons cost money, Alix. Pools charge admission. And don't even get me started on sailing—that's totally a rich person's sport."

"I could teach you how, you know."

"What?"

"I could teach you to swim—I'm certified."

And *I* was *certifiable*. Because now I was visualizing her in a little-bitty bikini. Seeing myself lying in her arms as she taught me to float. Feeling our bodies separated by only the thinnest skin of water…

"Thanks," I said, clearing my throat, "but if I'm going to humiliate myself, I think I'd better do it with an instructor at the Y. At least they're paid to put up with people like me. I'll get there someday—it's one of the things on my bucket list."

"Well," she said, "the offer's open-ended. Just in case you change your mind."

Alix had pulled off the road while we talked, stopping in a small clearing near an overhanging bluff. As we got out of her car I looked up at the immense wall of limestone looming overhead. Then down at the field of fallen rock around us. No boulders smaller than a basketball, I noted. And a lot that were larger—much larger.

Gesturing at the rubble, I said, "Interesting choice, Alix. A person could get killed."

She laughed and took my hand. Pulling me into a deep recess at the base of the bluff, she said, "It would take an earthquake to bring *this* slab down on us. And we can see the eagles without being seen."

A good thing, because, standing beside her in that cramped space, I could imagine a number of things that should only be done in private. *Jesus, Lynn! Get your libido under control!*

Alix was pointing at the sky now, passing the binoculars. "Look!" she cried.

Two huge eagles, talons locked, were plummeting headlong toward the river. And then, faster than I could see, they were soaring through the skies separately. "Mating ritual," Alix said, retrieving her glasses.

"Incredible!" I breathed. "But I can think of *safer* ways to flirt." *Stop it, you moron!*

Alix, who was searching treetops on an island directly across from us, took my remark at face value. "They can die if they don't time it just right," she confirmed. Then, "I'm trying to find a nest to show you. It's too soon for babies, but the aeries alone are knockouts. Some literally weigh tons, depending on how long the pairs have been building them."

"So they're monogamous?"

"Yep, and they usually return to the same nest each winter. Oh, there's one!" Alix passed the glasses again and gave me a clue about where to point them.

"Got it," I told her, as I zeroed in on the mass of interwoven branches. "My god! It's *enormous*!" And it made me think new thoughts about how clay could form a very different kind of bowl—more of an irregular, openwork basket, really. I'd try that out tomorrow, since I still wouldn't be able to throw on the wheel.

Several eagles were aloft now, sailing high above us with a grace that lifted my heart. When I swiveled to make sure Alix had seen them, I caught an unguarded look on her upturned face. Some wrenching combination of awe and sorrow and yearning. Something that had nothing to do with the birds themselves, it seemed, but only what those extraordinary creatures evoked in her. Or something to do with early spring fever. Or both. But *definitely* something too personal to probe into.

"Coffee's gonna get cold," I told her, and left to go back to the car. When I returned with our sacks from the café, Alix was in a different mood, smiling and holding out an eager hand for her cup.

We sat on a boulder while we ate. Just barely enough room to keep our hips from touching. Just barely enough clearance to sip coffee without brushing against her arm. Then Alix checked her watch. "I'll have to leave for home soon," she said. "The girls will be back from my parents' house before dark."

"Can I ask a favor? Another favor?"

"Shoot," she said, without hesitation.

"If you have time, will you drop me at my house? My car's got a tire with a slow leak and it would be great to leave it in town overnight. I'll find a ride to the shop tomorrow."

I could see her doing the mental math. "If we take off right now, that'll work. And I'd be happy to pick you up in the morning, Lynn—it's really no trouble."

"Only if you'll let me repay you at a later date," I said, suspecting it was easier for Alix to extend a hand than accept help for herself.

She looked into my eyes and saw that I meant it. "Deal," she promised. But when she kept staring at me, I said, "What?"

"Your eyes are *exactly* the color of the river," she pointed out. By which she meant a changeable greeny-gray. "And how'd you score dark brows and lashes with light hair, for god's sake?"

Her scrutiny was unnerving, but I tried not to make too much of the moment. It was hardly the first time someone had commented on my coloring. "I have my dad's eyes," I told her awkwardly. "It's my mother's hair."

"I'm all my mom," Alix laughed. "The two of us must have the most common coloring on earth."

I wanted to say, "You wear it well," but every now and then I actually manage to keep my mouth shut. By the time I'd succeeded in suppressing the thought, Alix had shifted her gaze to her watch again—it was time to get the heck out of Dodge.

Since I could breathe once more, I helped her gather trash from our lunch and we climbed back into her car. All the way home we talked of nothing but eagles. How it would feel to ride the wind. How astounding that the birds found their way to the exact spot each year, after migrating hundreds of miles. Their brief sojourn in Illinois. The challenges and rewards of rebuilding their numbers. Alix, I learned, was not just *part* of the river restoration group—she'd *started* the organization with money she'd inherited from a grandmother.

"These days, though, I'm just chairing the Eagle Committee. I've handed off a lot of the responsibility to other volunteers, and we've used Grandma's legacy to hire a part-time executive director. Because now I have Beth and Cindy, not to mention a dozen piano students."

"And the Abbies," I pointed out.

"That too."

"And you hate doing anything halfway." A statement, not a question.

"It's a curse."

"For you, maybe. For everyone else, it's a blessing."

The drive was over far too soon. And I was getting in much too deep. By the time Alix dropped me at my house, I felt like *I* could fly.

* * *

But before long, I crashed on the rocky shores of reality. It was beyond dangerous to spend time alone with a woman like Alix. I didn't dare increase the risk by letting her pick me up in the morning. Right after dinner, I telephoned my nearest neighbor and arranged for a lift into town. Coward that I am, I was relieved to hear an answering machine pick up when I dialed Alix's number. I left a message, saying that I'd found another ride to the shop and thanked her for her generous offer.

That night, I dreamed Alix and I were floating on a slow-moving current in a broad, sunlit river. I still didn't know how to swim, but that didn't matter at all because she was holding me, holding me…

* * *

When I arrived at the church for the next gathering of the Abbies, Alix was already in the thick of things. She was chatting with Jenny, so she missed my grand entrance. There was something in her hand—a stack of cards, I thought—and her eyes were scanning the room. Certain somehow that she was seeking me, I started toward her. The second our eyes met, she broke away from Jen and rushed across the room. Something warm began to unfurl at the center of my being. No, no, *no*! I chided myself, while I did my best to wave casually.

"Hi, Lynn," Alix said, handing me an envelope. "This is for you." I looked down. My name was written on the front in her strong, original script.

"What is it?" I asked, as she turned away.

Over her shoulder, she said, "It's a party invitation, goof—open it."

I watched her circulate, passing out the damned things to new arrivals, and I knew I was in big trouble.

We worked our way through the agenda with uncharacteristic economy. Jenny and Nadine reported on three women's centers they'd visited. We formed a committee to educate the public about our goals. Kate browbeat us about fundraising, yet again. The meeting ended before I'd caught even a glimpse of Alix's dimple. I kept telling myself that I should know better than this. *She's off-limits, Lynn! Get a grip!*

As soon as we adjourned, I scurried to the parking lot, trying to evade Alix. But her car was in the slot next to mine. How had I failed to notice that earlier? Before I could fit my key into the lock, she was there, barely visible, on the far side of the station wagon.

"You must have worked late again," she called over my luggage rack.

"Yeah," I answered, glancing down at my clay-encrusted khakis.

"I've never really seen any of your stuff—only what I could tell through your shop window."

"We're even then. I've never heard *you* sing," I replied. *Only at a concert, your voice obscured by eight hundred others.* God, I was shaking from more than the cold, and *she* wanted to chat.

"No great loss," Alix laughed, her breath making foggy accents under the stark streetlight. "Can you come?"

"What?"

"Can you *come*, Lynn? To my party?"

I scooped some snow from the roof of my car, wadded it into a lump, and hurled it at a stop sign. It missed. "No," I said harshly. But I couldn't stand the bewilderment in her eyes. Giving up, I walked around the end of the station wagon and went to her. "It's too complicated for tonight, Alix. Have lunch with me tomorrow and I'll try to explain, okay?"

She nodded, swallowing hard. "The café again?"

"Quillan's?"

"Why not?" she asked.

Very public, I told myself, very safe. "See you there," I agreed. "At noon." Then I slid into my car and slammed the door. All the way home I drove like a fool.

* * *

See what celibacy gets you? I thought, as I tossed and turned that night. You're so desperate these days that you think you're in love with the first cool woman who's crossed your path.

I counted backward through the months I'd been alone in Quillan's Crossing then added all the months before when Sarah had maintained a careful distance from me. I arrived at a number that made me whistle with surprise. It had *definitely* been too long since I'd slept with anyone. But I'd never been attracted to the empty comforts of casual sex. Getting physical with strangers, or even good friends, wouldn't solve my core issues—that damnable loneliness, the ache to be cherished again.

So suddenly I was looking for love in all the wrong places. A small, ultraconservative town. The world of straight women. Why hadn't I considered these critical constraints before I'd pulled up stakes and left St. Louis? Dykes were a dime a dozen in some neighborhoods there, a prospective partner on every street corner. But when I'd fled, I hadn't factored in the limited potential for romance in the countryside. You were still in love with Sarah back then, I reminded myself. Still hoping she'd come to her senses. Being sexual with anyone else was simply unimaginable.

Now even the briefest contact with Alix Dunnevan could turn me on, leaving me frustrated and edgy. I shifted my position against the pillows, relaxing my legs a little, deciding to address that problem with my own capable fingers—and with far more certainty of satisfaction than any stranger was likely to provide. A pleasant, if meaningless, diversion on a sleepless night. Hopefully, I'd be a bit more mellow during my lunch date tomorrow. Which would be a very, very good thing…

Letting both hands roam the hills and valleys of my restive body, I transported myself to a blessedly mindless place. Twice. Just before I finally drifted off, it occurred to me that I'd taken a quantum leap forward. Because, at some indeterminate point in time, my imaginary lover had gone from ash-blonde to dark, and acquired a slow, sexy wink that took my breath away…

CHAPTER FIVE

Alix phoned my shop before nine the next morning. She had a sick child. Could we eat lunch at her home, instead of the café? Stupidly, I said yes, and then tried to get back to work. I was too distracted to throw that day. I couldn't even concentrate enough to mix glazes. So I passed the time wrapping and crating pieces for shipping. The morning dragged, yet I wasn't looking forward to the afternoon. It was always a problem, knowing how much to say. And under stress, I have a regrettable tendency to say far more than necessary.

Just before leaving the shop, I emptied paper clips and rubber bands from a delicate porcelain bowl on my desk. After rinsing it, I wound it in tissue then tucked it in my coat pocket. If it meant something special to me, Alix didn't have to know that.

The Dunnevans lived a mile or so outside of Quillan's Crossing, at the opposite end of town from my place. It wasn't hard to find their house, but the ice-covered driveway plunged down from the road at a daunting angle. The proverbial slippery slope, I thought as I brought my car to a halt on the shoulder.

Alix had warned me to park at the top of the hill and walk its length—easier said than done. By the time I arrived at the halfway point, I'd given up worrying about breaking the porcelain bowl. Keeping *myself* intact had assumed primary importance. I felt ridiculously triumphant when I reached the bottom in an upright position. Now I just needed to keep from smashing anything else.

Alix met me at the front door. "Jesus!" I said. "You can *navigate* that hill in this weather?"

"The four-wheel drive," she reminded me. "With it, all things are possible."

I handed her the small package while I was taking off my jacket. "An early thank you for lunch, Alix."

Sitting on the couch, I watched her unwind the wrapping until the bowl tipped into her hand. She rotated it thoughtfully, then turned it upside down to examine my mark.

"It doesn't weigh anything," she announced.

"Thank you," I said. "That was the goal."

"You know, of course, that it's beautiful."

I caught myself in time, and only smiled in return.

* * *

How did we make it through that meal? I don't know. I guess there's enough trivia in the world, and who knows better how much gossip? The child slept on undisturbed, although Alix tiptoed upstairs to check on her every so often.

At last we were back in the living room—a light, airy place she shared with her husband—surrounded by all the tasteful things they'd chosen together. I tried not to take it in, didn't want to retain a single memory of that space. We sat on the couch, facing each other over too great a distance. Doing her best to look severe, Alix said, "Now, to the purpose of this meeting: Why won't you come to my party, Lynn? I warn you—no feeble excuses will be accepted."

I was fighting flashbacks from last night's fantasies and couldn't meet her eyes. "I won't guarantee the quality of my explanation, Alix. But the decision is final." Staring at my knees, I asked, "Have you ever been friends with a lesbian?"

"Not that I know of," she answered cautiously.

I raised my head, hiking a sardonic eyebrow. "Pretty good for an amateur—candor and political correctness in one neat package."

She looked like she'd been slapped and I saw I'd have to apologize. "I'm sorry, Alix. It ain't easy being queer."

When she reached out to pat my hand, the space between us was too wide. I leaned forward and squeezed her fingertips briefly. Withdrawing again, I said, "Let's see if I can do this by analogy…Once upon a time, a Happily Married Lady met a lonely Lesbian. Now the Lesbian and the Happily Married Lady were sure they could be friends. They spent a lot of time together and learned—or so they thought—to be quite comfortable with one another. Then suddenly, they were no longer on speaking terms. The Lesbian claimed that the Happily Married Lady had come on to her. But the Happily Married Lady told a different story. She said the Lesbian had simply *misunderstood* her open, accepting nature. Of course, everyone believed the Happily Married Lady. Never questioning her innocence, they swept her into their warm, protective circle. Which, predictably, left the Lesbian out in the cold—and lonely once more. The End."

I'd been avoiding Alix's face the whole time I spun the fable. Now I looked directly at her. None too gently, I said, "The moral of this tale is standard wisdom in the circles I travel: stay away from straight women."

Alix sat unflinching under my gaze, but she was pale and still. "Did that happen to *you*?" she asked quietly.

"Does it matter? It's commonplace."

"I just wondered, that's all."

"No. It was a friend of mine. But it could happen to me. Anytime. Now even."

"Lynn, do you think I'd *let* it?" Her voice was heartbreakingly earnest.

Rubbing my hands over my face, I tried to find a painless way to tell the truth. "Look, Alix, I know the rules in your world—I have to—but you don't know them in mine. I do what I can to minimize my involvement with heterosexuals."

"The eagles," she pointed out. "You went to see the eagles with me..."

"Poor judgment on my part."

She bristled. "Funny. You *seemed* to be enjoying yourself."

"Exactly. That's the problem. That's why I can't accept your invitation, Alix. Do you understand?"

"No!" she said vehemently. "It's just a party."

"Alix," I sighed, "to you, it's just a party. To me, it's a big deal. Let me get more specific, because I can see that this matters to you. Will there be dancing at your party?"

"Probably. We'll have music. People usually dance."

"Okay. I like to dance. I am, in fact, a fairly good dancer. I suppose it's the only outlet I have for my feelings about music. So, who could I dance with?"

Now she couldn't meet my eyes. "I'd like to be real open and say 'bring a friend,' but I can see that would just complicate matters."

"Yeah. We could be the entertainment. Freak show at nine."

Her eyes went wide and a hand fumbled for mine. "Lynn, you're not a freak!"

"I *know* that, baby, and I do my best to remember it. It's just harder in some situations than in others."

I was tired, but I wanted to make a clean sweep of this thing. "Listen, Alix, I'm not a lesbian because I have to be. Like many of my friends, I've had experiences with men. I simply *prefer* women. If you don't have to bed down with the opposite sex every night, you can afford to be honest about them. After a while, it's maddening to spend much time in the company of men—or with the ladies whose lives depend on humoring them. Here's an example: Did you hear Faith say she'd left her kids with a neighbor last night because her husband had 'refused to babysit them' during our meeting? His own children?"

Alix swallowed hard but nodded acknowledgment.

"Okay. I have trouble keeping my mouth shut when I hear garbage like that, but straight women are uncomfortable if I question it."

"I just don't see why there has to be such a separation—such an emphasis on labels."

"Then let's get back to specifics about your party. Will some man tell a string of ugly jokes about women once he's had enough to drink?"

Alix winced, but I continued. "Will some guy argue about the ERA, insisting that women already have *enough* rights?"

"That's a possibility," she admitted.

"And after I leave, will somebody suggest that one good fuck would change my life?"

Her head was lowered as if I'd been attacking her. Maybe I had. "Yes, I see," she whispered. "But I *like* you, Lynn."

I moved closer, took her by the shoulders and shook her lightly. "You don't make anything easy, do you? I like you too, Alix. I like you too much. I'm *afraid* of liking you."

I let go of her and retreated again. "You must have guessed that I'm still recovering from something unbelievably painful. I can't afford the special brand of hell you're offering me. I don't have the resources right now."

Then I decided to use a little shock treatment. Or maybe I was just being self-indulgent. "Alix, think about what it means to be a lesbian. Besides the lifetime commitment I've made to women politically, I notice them *physically*. Some women are very beautiful to me. And some I've taken to bed. When I look at you, you're not just a face and a pair of feet with some clothes in between. I have expectations—I can imagine how you look, I can guess how you feel, I know what it might be like to make love with you. And you want me to set all of that aside—to just be your friend?"

She was shaking on her own now, and those dark, dark eyes were flashing. "How the fuck do *you* know what I want?" she yelled. Then she began to sob.

I wrapped my arms around her, not really allowing myself to react to the cascade of feelings that roiled through me as our bodies met. I was patting her back gingerly when a small voice at the top of the steps cried, "Mommy?"

"I have to go," Alix said.

"So do I. I'm sorry—I keep making a mess of things. But I'm right about this, even if I'm clumsy."

I watched her climb the stairs toward her daughter and then I let myself out.

CHAPTER SIX

During the next two meetings, no one in the Abbies could discuss anything except the party that Alix had planned. Suddenly this would-be radical crowd was reduced to the most banal of topics: what to wear? what to take? who was going? At first, I dodged the questions then I took refuge in the tired excuse of a previous engagement with other friends.

Once I'd said that, I realized I didn't want to stay home that evening envisioning Alix dancing with Charles. It would do me good to spend some time in laughter and distraction with my own people. I called college classmates and arranged to meet for dinner in St. Louis.

But, wonderful as it was to see them, in the beginning I found conversation with Deb and Susan difficult. My mind was elsewhere and I seemed to be losing a private battle with depression. By the time our food arrived, I was so far gone that I welcomed Debra's question.

"Who were you with at the Holly Near concert, Lynn? I didn't catch her name."

"Alix Dunnevan," I answered gratefully. All night long I'd been afraid the litany in my head would spill out into sound. Now it was legitimate. "She's a member of that feminist group I'm working with."

"Very attractive woman…" Deb noted, clearly fishing for details.

"And extremely married, my dear."

"Oh, come on!" Susan protested. "I almost took you seriously for a second."

"Might as well. It's true. She's a musician—she was only along for the ride."

"What a loss for our team!" said Deb.

"C'est la vie," I answered brightly, and we all clinked glasses.

After dinner, we adjourned to Deb and Susan's loft downtown where we discussed everything from politics to literature into the wee hours. Deb described her latest series of paintings. Susan did a long riff on women in sports, beginning with Billy Jean King's rout of Bobby Riggs and ending with her unabashed adulation of Martina Navratilova. I mostly listened, confessing nothing, never mentioning Sarah, nor my precipitous flight from the city, nor the risk I'd run by isolating myself professionally. And I did my best not to think about the Dunnevans' party, not to wonder what I was missing, not to imagine Alix in her husband's arms. They talked me into staying overnight, and showed me into a sweet little guest room.

When I left after breakfast the next morning, Susan followed me down to my car. "Take care of yourself, Lynn," she said solemnly, as she hugged me goodbye.

"I promise to drive carefully, Mom."

"I was talking about something else," Susan told me, a worried expression on her face. This, I thought, would be worth hearing. Suze O'Neil was a computer analyst, rational and practical to the core. It often seemed she was the only thing that kept airy-fairy Deb from floating off the planet.

"I want you to be careful with that Dunnevan woman," Susan continued. "She looks downright dangerous, Lynn. I'd hate to see you get hurt." *Again*, she meant, though she was too tactful to say so.

I closed my eyes, took a deep breath, and admitted the truth. "She's hazardous to my health, Suze. But I'll work through it."

"I hope so, sweetie. Straight women equal double-trouble, you know. Just a friendly reminder."

I smiled with genuine affection. "Thanks. I need all the help I can get."

I drove the hour to my studio, knowing before I unlocked the door that my day would be a total loss. I was too tired to work, too down not to. I flipped through Saturday's mail first thing. Sandwiched between kiln catalogs and utility bills, a postcard said simply, "This H.M.L. feels secure enough to befriend an L."

Every cautionary word Susan had spoken only an hour earlier evaporated as I studied Alix's unexpected note. Newly energized—*idiotically* energized—I reached for a stack of announcements just back from the print shop. I tore the wrapper and peeled one off the block—an invitation to the opening night of my next exhibition. Across a sepia surface I wrote, "Your reputation will be ruined." I meant to send it out with the other cards in a day or two. Instead, I took it to the post office that night after work.

By return mail, Alix answered, "I'd be honored."

* * *

Was she actually flirting? I was exhilarated—for about five minutes. Then sanity reared its ugly head and I started beating myself up. I really *was* a self-indulgent jerk. In spades. I was right—and I knew I was right—when I told Alix that we were in a dead-end situation. Nothing had changed—except that I'd sent that damned invitation. And I wasn't *just* being self-indulgent, I was being *irresponsible*. Even a mild flirtation had the potential to wreck her happy home. Not to mention my own self-respect and peace of mind.

Furious, I ripped the lid off a galvanized trash can packed with clay and wrenched out big masses of the stuff. I hurled the heavy chunks against the canvas-covered surface of the wedging table, slamming them down again and again—another, more violent, way of dislodging air bubbles. After half-an-hour of strenuous activity, I was worn out, but far from calm. I stored the prepared clay in a can by my kick wheel, ready to use the next day. Then I clanged the lid on the container with a grating, metallic finality. The deed is done, I told myself. The die is cast. You can't withdraw the invitation.

There was nothing to do but treat Alix like every other guest on opening night, then back away slowly.

* * *

That next month was filled with frenetic activity. Exhibitions are awful. Receptions are worse. I can never figure out why I agree to them. The nightmare fades, I suppose, then the owner of some gallery pounces. When asked, I always feel flattered, but as soon as I have to select work for display, I realize that I've never produced anything good enough to show, and probably never will. Frenzy becomes a way of life. I give away dozens of decent pots to anyone who happens by, and break a lot more with my trusty hammer. When the madness subsides, I know the pieces that survived are the special ones, the ones that even I couldn't bring myself to destroy. A simple selection process, though wasteful.

Naturally, this psychological state isn't conducive to civility. I alienate suppliers and irritate friends. I antagonize the gallery owner, castigate his lighting system and agonize over the display cases. Finally the syndrome runs its course. By the time we're dismantling the show, it's started to look pretty good to me. Every time I go through that cycle, I vow it's my last exhibition. Until the next one. Artists are crazy—you heard it here first.

* * *

All alone in the big city—except for the illuminated cases lining the gallery. Still in a sardonic frame of mind, I paced the floor, waiting. I was alternately afraid that guests *would* attend, and terrified they *wouldn't*. I kept hoping my supply of bullshit was adequate for the demand.

Do lay people understand that fancy dancing is the principal stock-in-trade of any artist? Pity the poor soul with nothing but brilliant work to offer. Far better to be mediocre, but articulate, able to frame your product in a hip narrative. Extol the significance of your art with sufficient force and critics are likely to spread the rumor. Sadly, the biggest blowhards are often taken the most seriously. And, truth be told, I can bullshit with the best of them. I'd just rather not.

I was doing my version of animated chatting that night when Alix appeared. She was solo, thank god. I watched covertly as she studied the catalog then made the complete tour. For what it was worth, she stopped longest at my favorite pieces. When she'd finished, she sought me out. Her eyes were sparkling and she was extremely complimentary. But, as I'd told her once before, I *hate* talking about art—too fucking ephemeral, too subjective, too phony. I waited until she'd wound down, then tried to divert her.

"Nice dress, Alix," I said. And it was. A slender, backless little scrap of a thing that rose well above her knees. The heels were hot too. I tried, but failed, to push away the thought: she looked *just* like a lipstick lesbian. Minus the makeup. Which she didn't need.

Alix assumed I was teasing her out of some dykely superiority. She colored and started to defend herself. "Give it a rest, you creep! I only dress up on state occasions. I haven't worn this thing since the last shindig for the Bar Association."

It was my turn to be thrown off track. Alix read my puzzled expression and explained, "You know—the American Bar Association? Charles is a member, of course."

My hand went to my throat. "Charles is a *lawyer*?" I gasped.

"Well, sure. What's so funny about that?"

"Just one of life's little jokes...I thought he was some kind of politician."

"Close," Alix answered. "He has been. And may be again. Right now he's the General Counsel and Director of Policy for the Lieutenant Governor."

I grimaced, embarrassed by my ignorance. "Sorry. Except for ERA stuff, I've been out of the loop for the past few years..."

Alix did her best to downplay the faux pas. "It's not a big deal. Almost no one knows there *is* a General Counsel, much less who he is. Charles was in law school when we married. He was planning to become a public defender, or to work with a group of storefront advocates back then. Something excruciatingly noble and poorly paid."

"I can hardly wait to hear what happened."

"Oh, my *father* happened—what else? Not a sparrow falls but that he knoweth. About five minutes after Charles passed his bar exam, St. Louis County's Prosecuting Attorney dropped dead at the courthouse. I'm not sure Dad didn't arrange his coronary. Anyway, in a *most* unlikely turn of events, Charles was appointed to serve out the term of office. Pissed off quite a few more deserving lawyers."

"And put an abrupt end to the grand plan? Farewell to those altruistic ideals?"

"Quite." Alix nodded, wrinkling her nose. "But attorneys are trained to revere both sides of the legal system, so Charles managed a speedy accommodation to his new role. *And* he made a concerted effort to be useful to anyone with influence in state politics. At the same time, my father smoothed lots of ruffled feathers—much juicy meat was cast into the arena for everyone else. I'll spare you the details."

"I probably wouldn't understand them anyway," I interjected.

Alix dimpled. "Lucky you. Charles won the next election in his own right. Over time, he's developed a network of high-powered contacts all his own. And dear old dad's made it clear that Charles is the heir apparent—no advantage to holding any grudges against him. Now my beloved husband's in cahoots with the lieutenant governor and probably hopes to succeed him one day. I try not to think about that." She set down her champagne flute and looked at me sharply. "I hope you're not impressed."

"Hardly," I told her. "White male politicians are pretty low on my list."

Just then, someone touched my shoulder from behind. I turned to respond and nearly dropped my wineglass. Sarah was there, elegant as ever. Tall, slim, cooler than cool. Black wool sheath, handcrafted jewelry, a hopeful smile on that unforgettable face. When she leaned forward to kiss my cheek, the familiar scent of her ash-blond hair swirled around me. "Lovely show, Lynn," she said warmly. "Your best yet."

I could scarcely speak. "Will you excuse us, Alix?" I stammered. Drawing Sarah aside, I steered her toward a quiet corner.

"What are you doing here?" I demanded.

"I saw the announcement in the *Expo*. I knew you wouldn't send me an invitation, but I thought I might be welcome anyway."

"I'm not ready for this, Sarah," I said, cursing the tremor in my voice. "I don't know how to play it. I need you to leave—I'm sorry."

"No, *I* am, my dear. I just guessed wrong. Be well," she said. And she disappeared, taking my fragile façade of composure with her.

There was a storeroom behind the gallery, with a door that opened on an alley. I fled to it, flinging it wide. Stepping into the bitter air, I tried to slow my pulse and steady my hands. I don't know how long I hid out there before Alix found me and coaxed me inside again.

"People are looking for you, Lynn," she said, as she chafed my frozen fingers. "Are you all right now?"

"Sure," I lied. "Just a momentary breakdown."

"Something to do with that gorgeous woman?"

"Seven years' worth of something. She used to be my lover—before I moved to the Crossing."

I could see Alix struggling to make sense of that information. Sarah does *not* look like your average dyke.

"I think we need more wine," Alix said finally, and she led me back to the gallery.

For the rest of the evening, she ran interference. If people wondered who she was, I didn't care. Coping was beyond me, but Alix kept me from looking like a fool. She stayed nearby until everyone had finally left. When we walked out together, I thanked her. "You're quite the diplomat, aren't you?"

"Daddy's darling daughter," she called, as she picked her way down the sidewalk in her insanely high heels.

* * *

The following morning, I stayed in bed late with a stack of news magazines, trying to catch up on events in the larger world, but I wasn't able to concentrate. I kept obsessing about the night before. I had an uneasy feeling that I'd obligated myself to Alix—that sooner or later I'd have to explain Sarah. There was nothing very interesting to tell. I'd been dumped. It was the least original story on the face of the planet. Maybe that's why I minded so much.

Without a doubt, I'd had a setback—seeing Sarah had opened a door on an enduring misery. After she left me, I'd bailed on the city, desperate to avoid constant reminders of my life with her there. But even though she'd never crossed its threshold, this rural farmhouse reverberated with her absence. I regularly reached for objects that Sarah had claimed in the Great Divide—the quirky pair of scissors that could cut through anything, our garlic press, the address book we'd compiled. They now resided with her and her new lover in a pricey suburban neighborhood an hour away. And each time my hand came back empty, remembrance assaulted me.

You break up a household and try to recall who brought what. You divvy it up. If you're fair, or generous, some things that are rightfully yours depart with the other woman, who's developed a greater affinity for them. In the process, you more than halve your belongings. But when you're done being absurdly scrupulous, when the last carton is carried out the gaping door, you're still left with too many possessions.

For everything that remains is a repository of pain, each object an avatar of memory. The basket that contained her mail as well as yours. The couch where you made love. Books she chose for you. Open a kitchen drawer to find the flatware she left behind, or the corkscrew she wielded with enchanting élan. Launder linen that once she shared, and smooth it on your empty bed.

Even your closet betrays you—is there a shirt she embroidered, or jeans that were hers? Did she borrow the belt you're wearing or give you the robe you slip on each morning? All this and more—I could make a fucking catalog. So I'd learned to play tricks on myself, to wear mental blinders, to function in the material realm without really feeling. Sometimes I thought I'd be willing to trade the entirety of my worldly goods just for relief from those persistent associations. Everything of mine for everything of yours, no questions asked.

Clearly, I shouldn't spend this day at home. But I'd worked so hard preparing the exhibition that I'd forgotten how to live my ordinary life. I couldn't think of a single thing to do with my time. The studio was a mess, of course, but I didn't want to face it just yet. Go to the cinema? Nope. They've given up making movies for adults. And hanging out with friends would expose me to questions about Alix—not to mention more cautionary words about the perils of socializing with straight women. As if I couldn't already write a book on the subject. Suddenly deciding, I packed a quick sandwich, bundled up and raced Solly to the porch. Maybe I could quiet my mind outdoors.

The sun was strengthening, the snow finally melting. Poised between winter and spring, the valley below my house beckoned. It's a wide, deep, wooded bowl grooved by narrow troughs where water runs at the thaw. There's a huge meadow at the bottom, and an old quarry on the far side. You can walk all day in splendor and never lose your way. To return, you just climb upward toward the treacherous, winding road that circles it.

The best thing about the woods that day was how little they reminded me of Sarah—she was strictly tennis-court material. I didn't have to think of her at all as I slogged through soggy leaves or pushed my way past tangled grapevines. Sol and I shared lunch on a mossy boulder and left crumbs behind for the squirrels.

When we got home, I had that satisfactory tiredness you can get from time outside. I ran a long, scalding shower and came out purified. My material possessions had lost their potency. Nothing mattered as much as sun on birch bark or the scent of slowly warming earth. I put Meg Christian on the stereo and lay with my head near a speaker, totally surrounded by the sound of women's voices. When the last song ended and the record player clicked off, my house filled with a deep, calm, unbroken silence.

Lying there in the fading light of day, I made a mental list of things to relinquish. Sarah and pain and bitterness. Blame and self-doubt and despair. Lethargy. Sorrow. Second-guessing. But sleep overtook me before I could add Alix Dunnevan's name to the roster, and I think I dreamed of chasing eagles.

CHAPTER SEVEN

Suddenly, I was overwhelmed with work. Not only had most of the pieces in my show sold, I'd picked up some major commissions. The largest order was for a complete dinner service with a tricky glaze and a tight deadline. In the studio, I pushed myself as hard as I could, only coming up for air on nights when the Abbies met. Occasionally, Alix's face flashed through my mind, piercing me with a sharp sweetness. But more often, my attraction to her felt illusory, like a fairy tale I'd told myself. Impossible to believe I'd almost fallen in love with a straight woman—and a married one, at that.

I could sustain that sense of incredulity right up to the moment when I actually saw Alix again. Then I found her irresistible. Every molecule of my being was pulled toward her magnetic north. Whether she was lounging in improbable comfort on a metal folding chair, or deeply engaged in debate, she never failed to breach my defenses. But the more she drew me, the more I renewed my commitment to keep the barricades in place.

I learned to maintain a distance from her. Arriving at the church late and leaving early helped. The seats near her were usually filled before I entered the meeting room, and I made sure we didn't have a chance to talk privately afterward. If Alix appeared distressed, if I saw pain flicker in her eyes, I refused to acknowledge it. I kept reminding myself that she didn't know the rules of the game or understand how high the stakes were.

Still, we don't completely control our destinies, and sometimes there's relief in giving up the fight. The night that Alix and I were drafted to develop a performance piece about women's history, I tried to resist. At least I *tried.* I pleaded overload.

Kate brushed away my protests far more easily than should have been possible. Because I really *was* too busy to take on anything new. But I acquiesced when she said, "Hang it up, Lynn. Everybody's overcommitted. It's the American way of life. And everyone knows you've got the best background—not to mention you *still* own more feminist material than our public library. If we're going to do this at all, we need you."

Then Alix got conned because she'd done a lot of theatre work in her college days. She would understand how to add drama to the stark historical framework that I'd develop.

Bowing to the inevitable, not really reluctant, I held out my hand to Alix. "Partners?" I asked.

"Damned straight," she replied. Then she blushed to the roots of her hair.

I couldn't help it—I had to laugh. It was our first authentic moment of contact in a long while and it felt fabulous, almost surreal in its intensity. After the others left, we stayed long enough to nail down a date for Alix to look over my books. But I made myself bolt from the church before she sensed the ripple of anticipation that was spreading through me.

* * *

What fool turns down the chance to spend time with a beautiful woman? Certainly not I. Still, when Alix pulled into my driveway that night, my heart was pounding. Hoping I had my act together, I invited her in. Did my best not to notice how good she looked in a cream-colored turtleneck and tight jeans. Offered her a drink and snacks. Then we sat on the living room floor, surrounded by stacks of books, uncertain just how to begin.

My cat flounced around the place, ostentatiously annoyed by the unaccustomed clutter. I ignored him for as long as possible. But when he toppled a pile of books by leaping for a higher perch, I rapped him lightly with a rolled pamphlet. "Damn it, Sol! Play with your own toys."

He found refuge in Alix's denim lap. She looked from me to the ebony animal. Clearly mystified by his name, she ventured a guess. "Midnight sun?"

"More like a black hole, if you'd see my bank balance," I answered, busily stacking books.

But her curiosity was not so easily deflected. "Short for Solomon?" she hazarded. "A very wise cat?"

"Short for—*some*thing," I acknowledged, shooting a look meant to forestall further questions.

Alix got the message. Stroking his head, she said, "He's a beauty. Have you had him long?"

"Ever since I moved here," I ground out, wishing I'd lied, hoping she'd miss the coincidence.

But Alix had finely tuned instincts. She'd recognized touchy territory, I saw, and needed help backing off. So I gestured at Sol who'd just staked out a spot on the couch behind her, his neon eyes on the same plane as her brown ones.

"Do you know 'Sita and Sarita?'"

"I don't think so. What is it?"

"Survey of Art, 101. Subtopic, Minor Painters—that's *male* jargon for *female* artists." I reached for an oversized volume. After flipping through it, I held out a full-page reproduction of Cecilia Beaux's painting. The striking woman in white. The coal black cat crouched on her shoulder. The sensual linkage between them.

Alix's face lit with pleasure. "Oh, do *we* look like *that*?" she wanted to know.

I longed to say she looked both wilder and more wonderful. Instead, I answered, "Almost."

The conversation had made me restless. I pushed myself to a standing position and asked if Alix preferred silence or music while working.

"Take a guess—and make it something beautiful."

"I seem to be obsessed with Meg Christian right now. I think you might enjoy her...assuming lesbian lyrics won't make you uncomfortable."

"I think I might survive the experience. After all, I made it through the concert, and I play my Holly Near albums nonstop."

I kept the volume low and we began our research in earnest, but every so often, Alix would pause to listen intently. "Good stuff," she sighed once or twice.

As always, we worked together with genuine ease. We quickly agreed on an approach and structure for our program. Choosing specific speeches was a different matter. Knowing we had to suit the script to our conservative community, we selected standard writings by historical feminists. Then we rounded out the classic material with moderate essays from recent times, choosing humorous pieces whenever possible. It was almost midnight before we finished that first phase.

"Now," said Alix, who was reclining with her head on a stack of Charlotte Perkins Gilman, "all we have to do is edit the speeches, write the narrative, cast the show and schedule the rehearsals."

"Nothing to it. Another eight or ten meetings like this and we'll be in good shape."

"No argument here." Alix smiled and lifted her empty can. "Could I have another beer?"

"Sure," I told her. On my way to the kitchen, I turned up the sound on my stereo system. When I came back, Alix was reading the album jacket, studying photos of Meg Christian. "You should hear her in person," I said, regretting it immediately.

"I'd love to—she has an incredible voice. Where did you see her?"

"A lot of places," I answered awkwardly, trying to put the topic to rest.

Alix looked me in the eye. "This is a Sarah taboo, isn't it?"

"I suppose that's stupid. It's just that I can't keep from crying when I talk about her."

"Is crying another taboo?"

"No, just a bore. And my nose stays red for hours."

"Come on, Lynn—why don't you give it a shot?"

"Guess I still owe you two questions."

Alix thumped her small fist against the floorboards. "You don't owe me a damned thing, but I care about you and I'm a good listener!"

I covered my eyes with my palms for a second while I searched for a dispassionate tone of voice. "Sarah and I were graduate students—and lovers—when Meg Christian announced a tour. She'd be performing near our university and we could actually go see her. It was an incredibly important event for me." I was silent for a few seconds, lost in reflection.

"The concert itself was fantastic. And it was the first time I'd been in a room full of women I knew were lesbians. There were old women holding hands, so strong and beautiful. There were young women with their arms around each other, so brave and dazzling. Sarah and I were a *part* of all that. The excitement was nearly more than I could bear. I suppose it seemed like coming out, in a way. A declaration about our commitment, something momentous."

I drained my can and set it aside. "At least, that's how it felt to me. Sarah was a tad tense back then."

"And now?"

"Oh, that's something I'm bitter about, I guess. When we became lovers, Sarah was such a closet case, so insistent on secrecy. She had all these rules—lists and lists of things we couldn't do or had to hide. That was tough on me. I like who I am, and I'm too damned lazy to lie. But Sarah planned to work in academia after graduation, and was afraid she'd be blacklisted, or something. Then once she *had* a job, she was paranoid about being fired. I tried hard to accommodate her, to respect her feeling of vulnerability." I shrugged wryly and said, "So much for sincere effort."

"Where is she today?"

"She's living openly with a woman—they teach at the same university now. Greer has been out forever, but I gather that hasn't hindered her climb up the academic ladder. Apparently, she's a raging success. In some ways, I'm proud of Sarah for finally being honest about herself. Still, I'm dealing with a lot of anger—why wouldn't she live that way with me? And why did I surrender so much control over my own life?"

The turntable shut off with a loud click and the room went deathly still. I rose to flip the record. Sitting across from Alix again, I said, "This is so dumb! Everything I say about Sarah sounds negative, but she's a fine person. You know she's beautiful, but she's also bright and eloquent and funny as hell. We'd been best friends forever, long before we became lovers. Breaking up wasn't my idea—we had jokes about our declining years, for god's sake." The tears wouldn't stop flowing, but the pain wasn't as bad as I'd expected. "I just *miss* her *so much*!"

Alix dug in her pocket and produced a crumpled tissue. "Not used," she assured me. She would have wiped my face, but I took it from her and mopped myself up.

"Was it sudden—the breakup?" she asked gently.

"Yes…no…*I* don't know. It just happened. Sarah's college sent her to a conference on the Psychology of Women. When she returned a week later, she was really strange—she could hardly talk about her time away. I only knew that she'd met someone interesting, had even told her new friend about us, which was unusual. But I was too dense to understand what that meant."

I blew my nose and cocked my head at Alix. "Am I putting you to sleep yet? I can't seem to shut up."

A look crossed her face, something like compassion. She made a small motion as if to sweep aside the interruption. "Keep talking, Lynn."

"Well, anyway, that conference was a two-part deal. Everyone attending had several months to develop a project. Then the group was scheduled to meet again to discuss their work. I knew Sarah and Greer had been in contact, consulting each other about their presentations. Still, I didn't begin to get the picture until after the second session. Mail started arriving for Sarah."

I swallowed hard, remembering those damnable letters from Greer Barclay, so charming and witty and original—the perfect lure for an English professor. Sarah had shared every last one with me. I thought.

"By the third letter, I was anxious as hell, but Sarah denied that anything was changing between us. I tried to ignore all signs to the contrary. I thought if I gave her some space, things might improve, so I began to work very late." To avoid those awful moments when I could see Sarah forcing herself to go through the motions. To avoid the deadly charade that she still loved me, still wanted me...

I picked up my beer can and crushed it. "These things just happen, I guess. You can't fight chemistry."

Then I heard my own words, hanging in the air, reverberating. Saw Alix register what I'd said. Felt the room grow warm. Or maybe it was just my face.

She met my eyes unflinchingly, but steered the conversation back to Sarah. "Can I ask what finally ended the relationship?"

"Oh, all hell broke loose. Sarah and I were at a concert—" I paused and mustered a little smile. "A lot of significant events in my life have taken place at concerts. Anyway, we were just sitting in the hall, waiting for the performance to begin, enjoying the crowd. Then suddenly Sarah got all stiff and pale and weird. She was like a bird dog. I could actually follow her line of sight. A woman was coming toward us in slow motion. I knew without knowing that she had to be Greer." I stopped for a moment, chuckling.

"What's so funny?"

"An expression came into my head. I was mortally certain I was watching doom approach, and all I could think was, 'Holy shit! Executive Dyke!'"

Alix laughed too, but said, "Tell me."

"You know the type: very, very tailored. A three-piece, pin-striped suit, if you can believe it. Extremely short, razor-cut gray hair. I kept looking for the pipe and briefcase. Quite a change of pace for Sarah…"

I shrugged then took mercy on Alix. "Surely you don't want to hear more of this?"

"I'll listen if you'll talk."

"Well, the next part does have its amusing side…*now* anyway. It was funny and horrible at the same time. Greer finally got to our seats and Sarah stood up. She was so excited she was practically giddy. Then she forgot my name."

"She *forgot* your *name*?"

"Yep. Can you believe that? She was trying to introduce me and she just went blank. I made a joke of it—told Sarah if she couldn't remember who I was, she'd have to walk home—and I introduced myself to Greer. But that was really all she wrote. Two months later they were living together."

"What can I say, Lynn?"

"Not a goddamned thing, honey. Why should you be different from everyone else?"

"What does *that* mean?"

"Just that our breakup shocked all of our friends. Nobody knew what to say. Sarah and I…we were considered pretty solid. There's plenty of bed-hopping in the gay community, although it's the men who make a fetish of it. But not Lynn and Sarah. If there was one certainty in the universe, it was that *we'd* go on forever."

"That's a terrible burden to carry," Alix said. "Everyone counting on you to prove that perfection is possible. I know—I've been there."

My entire body went on red alert. Was she hinting at trouble in paradise? I did my best to sound casual when I said, "Rumor has it that *your* marriage was made in heaven."

"No one's relationship is without its stresses, Lynn—we all just learn to play the game."

I let myself look at Alix—really look at her—maybe for the first time that night. Her lovely face was tired, and something more. Wounded? Stoic? Resigned? I couldn't be sure, might even be imagining that troubled expression.

Standing abruptly, Alix picked up a stack of books. "It's late. I'd better go."

I walked her to the door, then collapsed on my couch, letting exhaustion have its way with me. My head was a jumble of memory and emotion. I tried to play back the events of the evening, but couldn't hold anything in place.

Glancing at my watch, I hauled myself upright. It was past one now, a brand-new day. Maybe sometime I'd actually get around to installing that pet door I'd bought—you never know. But since I hadn't, it was time to track down Solace for a brief interlude outdoors. I found him asleep on the window seat, curled atop Alix's forgotten scarf. I carried him to the lawn and set him down. He vanished into the shadows while I stood under a cold crescent moon, contemplating distant stars in a vast night.

At last, Sol and I went inside and I climbed the stairs to my office. Rummaging through the desk for paper, I realized that I was a little drunk. I wrote a cheerful, disjointed note to Mattie, telling her that I was well and working hard. I only mentioned Alix twice. Not bad, considering. Because something inside me was singing.

CHAPTER EIGHT

Spring had finally arrived. There was a corresponding thaw and bloom in my spirits. Some hard, constricting husk seemed to have fallen away, leaving me expansive and joyous. I had the unreasonable conviction that I glowed. My work was alive again, rife with new ideas. I could throw endlessly and never tire. Firings were unusually consistent, my sales the best ever. And after work there were rehearsals. At rehearsals, there was Alix. With Alix there was ever-increasing pleasure.

How much of this did I admit to myself? Sometimes I denied it completely. Sometimes I was frank about my feelings, only ignoring their looming, inevitable consequences. You know how it is—we all do. When it feels good, you think you can pay the price at some later date. Stupid springtime games.

I told myself that I could afford a little fantasy if I didn't act on my impulses. *More* idiocy: in my best moments I can acknowledge that I lack self-control. Still, I began to live from one rehearsal to the next, suffused with such irrational optimism that I was blind to everything else. I'd hardly even noticed how nicely our historical program was shaping up. After refining the script, Alix and I had turned it over to a production committee for casting and direction. Publicity had been arranged, high schools throughout the county had guaranteed captive audiences, our premiere was almost upon us and I'd be with Alix at every performance.

* * *

Costumed in calico, hands in apron pockets, I leaned against a wall at the back of a borrowed stage, waiting for dress rehearsal to begin. The rest of the cast was still changing, but I'd hurried into period garb and made my way to the auditorium in record time. Grateful for the solitude, I felt my shoulders finally relax. There's nothing quite like being the only lesbian in a dressing room full of straight women. It was hard to decide who'd been more self-conscious about my presence there. Even if *I* hadn't raised anyone's pulse rate, I knew most of those ladies would be wondering if they'd turned *me* on. They wouldn't be able to help it—it's just human nature. Or, at least, it's human nature in a homophobic society.

Ironically, the only woman who might have made my heart pound had yet to appear. Alix was preparing for the rehearsal at home and for the most part I was glad. I'd become so responsive to her that I wasn't sure I could undress in close proximity without making a fool of myself. And I was nervous enough about performing as it was.

Given my excitable state of mind, I was relieved that Reader's Theatre productions didn't require memorization. For my role, I'd clipped several excerpts from a frontier diary to the leaves of an old, leather-bound book. By turning its pages slowly, I could suggest a passage of time between entries. The journal I'd chosen was wrenching—the personal history of one Amelia Knight, who'd traveled from Iowa to Oregon in 1853, bearing her eighth child on the trail. When I multiplied each hardship she'd endured by thousands of women, I was torn between pity and awe for those indestructible pioneers. They seemed so very different from us, their undeserving descendants. These days, their brand of resilience was vanishingly rare. Had their endless expenditures of fortitude depleted some finite supply?

The muffled thud of the lobby door broke my pensive mood. Suddenly Alix was in the theatre, gliding down the aisle toward me, hoop skirt swaying. A stiff-brimmed bonnet concealed her cropped hair and framed that exceptional face. Surely Lucy Stone had never been so stunning? I raised my hand in greeting, then realized that Alix couldn't make me out on the dim stage.

She drew closer, quietly reciting her opening line, "All my life I have been a disappointed woman…"

Refraining from comment at that moment demanded all the discipline I had. "Hi, Alix," I called, stepping slowly into the light, trying not to startle her.

Even so, she gasped a little. Then she nodded approvingly at the costume, and at my hair, which was twisted into a heavy knot at the nape of my neck. "Lynn, you look perfect—a foremother incarnate! I can't *wait* till Charles sees you."

That damned door banged again and there he was, weighted down with video equipment, looking like something straight out of Hollywood. Alix explained: "Charles offered to tape the dress rehearsal so we can see how we're doing."

We're doing *fine*! I thought angrily. We don't need male confirmation or criticism. But the rest of the cast was unlikely to share my hostility. And no doubt I was being unfair to the poor bastard. Because it wasn't his fault that I was in love with his wife.

As women emerged from the dressing room in groups of two or three, the stage began to fill. Nadine's clever costuming and Melanie's expert makeup had transformed us all. Our own Abigail Adams was talking with the Grimké sisters, while Susan B. adjusted Margaret Sanger's cape. The colorful juxtaposition of fashions from several centuries was a visual delight and I wished for my sketchbook. Even without it, I could occupy myself with a comparison of line and detail in the costumes—a useful strategy for ignoring Charles Dunnevan.

No one else was trying to blot out his presence though. In fact, he and his equipment were attracting a lot of attention—and I don't *only* mean the AV gear he was busily organizing. Charles was just as tan, just as fit, just as mesmerizing as he'd been on first acquaintance. His powerful presence injected a brittle artificiality into the environment. Grown women were striking poses and giggling inanely. Sexual tension crackled like subliminal lightning. I stood apart from it all, despairing. I had little doubt that this would be a bad rehearsal.

It certainly got off to a poor start. We'd chosen Carla to narrate because her voice was clear but low-key, mellow, and yet it carried. For the program to truly succeed, her delivery had to be both the best and the most understated. Until that night, she'd always read every word with faultless emphasis. But in front of the video camera—in front of *Dunnevan*—she began to reach for big effects, pausing too long, stressing the wrong syllables. I could have cheerfully strangled the lieutenant governor's right-hand man with his own extension cord.

I could think of nothing to alter the predictable course of events. We were losing this last chance to refine the production, rushing through practice so we could admire ourselves on the screen. And once Charles was running his tape for us, he'd be running the show.

He didn't prove my suspicions unfounded. The moment rehearsal concluded, Dunnevan began to fiddle with gadgetry, wearing an important air. Every eye was on him, as if only his opinion of our hard work counted. Had he been married to anyone but Alix, I'd have dispatched him with thinly disguised irritation.

"I hope no one feels that I've intruded tonight," Charles began. *Is he looking straight at me?* "I consider it a genuine honor to have been your first audience. It's remarkable that groups like this persevere, even in the face of public indifference..."

Stealing a glance at Alix, I saw that she was uneasy.

"In just a moment, I'll play the tape I've made, but perhaps you'll forgive me for sharing a few objective observations with you first." Dunnevan paused to tamp tobacco into a pipe.

Really? I thought. *Really*? What a *pompous* son of a bitch! When Charles began to speak again—pipe in one hand, the other poised suggestively over his controls—I could feel Alix's discomfort change to mortification.

"Of course, you may not have time to incorporate all of my suggestions," he said, "but your program, while quite entertaining, is a bit static."

Just then, Paula got up and quietly left the theatre. I might have thought she was just hurrying home to her family, if I hadn't noticed how angrily she flung her shawl into a prop box on her way out. Longing to join her, dying to divest Dunnevan of this chance to grandstand, I still remained seated. I was preparing to defend our efforts. And I couldn't abandon Alix who now sat, bonnet bowed, staring at her hands.

"In the courtroom," Charles continued, "we recognize the importance of well-timed movement." He riffled through his notes for a few seconds. "I've identified some places in the script where I believe you might work in a little blocking to good effect…"

I shot a covert glance in Alix's direction. My mean-spirited little heart lifted when I saw she'd turned away from her handsome, self-absorbed husband.

Just then, there was a stir to my left, a rustle of taffeta petticoats. Kate had stood and was speaking with exaggerated courtesy. "Excuse me, Mr. Dunnevan, perhaps you're unfamiliar with the format we've chosen. Readers' Theatre is a relatively new approach that purposely reduces movement. Since it eliminates the need for scenery, and solves the problem of entrances and exits for so many characters, we felt it was an appropriate match for this production."

Kate was trembling when she sat down, but she'd turned the tide against Charles. The man wasn't totally without sensitivity. He felt it too. Probably an essential political skill—gauging the shifting mood of a crowd. Setting aside his legal pad, he said, "I see. That's a different matter then." And without further comment, he cued up the tape. In the subdued light, I threw Kate a congratulatory kiss.

To his credit, Charles's camera work was competent and the strategy was helpful. After viewing the video, we all modified our performances somewhat. But Dunnevan's presence changed the atmosphere in the theatre. As we stared at the screen in uncustomary silence, I thought about how much fun we'd have had watching that tape without him. Alone, we'd have been raucous, irreverent, *ourselves*. It wasn't the first time I'd been angered by one man's ability to inhibit many women—and *we* were supposed to be the liberated ones. What was life like for everyone else?

I couldn't wait to get away from Charles. When the playback ended, I practically ran to the dressing room. I changed clothes hastily, ripped the bun out of my hair, decided against braiding it, then strode toward the exit. But Kate caught me just before I stepped outside. "Beer and pizza at Signorelli's, okay?" she said in a low voice.

Nodding, I turned back and slipped into the auditorium again. I wanted to go out with the gang, to compare notes, to put a better finish on the evening. But there was a matter of some delicacy—I wanted Alix to go too, and I was sure Kate meant to exclude her. Because if she joined the party, it would be impossible to gossip about Charles. What the hell…I can play dumb as well as the next guy. I decided to invite Alix myself.

She was still on the stage talking with her husband, still in costume. Too late, I realized that they were arguing. There was no graceful way to retreat, so I kept walking toward them. Alix stopped in midsentence to watch me bridge the gap. I fought to keep my expression bland and my tone conversational. "Some of us are going for pizza, Alix. Can you come with us?"

Dunnevan laid a constraining hand on her shoulder. I'd never seen him touch her before, and I didn't like it. I didn't like it at all. He overrode Alix's enthusiastic response with a reminder: "We only brought one car tonight, Al."

She broke free from his grasp, bending to tie a shoe. "That's all right. I'll get a ride home."

Then she lifted her skirt a little and sailed down the brief flight of stairs, her hem floating out behind. I trailed after Alix, following her to the dressing room, feeling light as chiffon. I waited in the hall until she reappeared, looking like herself again in corduroys, a crewneck sweater and a bomber jacket. In the parking lot, only my car remained. Charles, it seemed, was long gone.

Signorelli's was like most small-town pizza parlors—crowded and noisy, overhung with plastic lamps that even the drunkest couldn't mistake for stained glass. Our friends had already shoved some tables together and ordered the first round of drinks by the time Alix and I arrived. There was a momentary lull in the conversation when we sat down, a heavy, watchful stillness. Alix reached for a pitcher and poured two beers with a steady hand. She shoved one toward me.

"Apologies, everybody," she said lightly. "All I agreed to was a cameraman. I didn't realize we'd get a goddamned theatre critic, as well. This round's on me."

I could feel the hostility draining away as she spoke. Surging in behind it was a rush of warmth and tacit understanding. Soon the little redneck restaurant rang with our laughter. Some of the regulars looked apprehensive, but that suited me fine. I'd been uncomfortable in their world often enough. We talked politics with the pizza, exaggerating our radicalism for good effect. I was having a stellar time being a shit disturber.

As soon as the server appeared with our check though, I offered to drive Alix home. "I'll practically pass your house on the way to mine."

She rose immediately and reached into her pocket for a handful of cash. Counting out her share of the tab, she stacked the bills on the vinyl tablecloth, then weighed them down with a shaker of grated cheese. I held her jacket as she slipped into it, vibrating all over when her hair brushed the back of my hand. Nobody seemed to notice, thank god, least of all Alix.

We walked over crumbling pavement to my car. I cut across-country toward her home, driving more slowly than usual. The house was completely dark when I parked at the foot of that steep driveway. If I'd expected Alix to say a hasty goodnight, I was wrong. She made no move to leave. We talked in the station wagon for a thrillingly long time, one topic flowing seamlessly into the next. And I deployed every strategy at my disposal to extend that idle chatter, from offhand humor to an amateur critique of Teresa Trull's latest album. The connection between us felt so complete, it seemed ludicrous that we had to break it.

Suddenly a lamp snapped on inside her house, spilling light over my dashboard. I thought I heard Alix sigh as she reached for the door handle.

"Goodnight, Lynn. Thanks for the ride."

She started toward the front porch, then doubled back to tap at my window. I rolled it down and Alix flashed that dizzying smile at me.

"We did a good job on our script," she murmured. "We're quite a team."

* * *

Quite a team. That's what she'd said. She'd made my evening with three short words. Quite a team. And we might be, if circumstances were different. But I'd better rein myself in, faster than fast. Because, I reminded myself for the thousandth time, Alix was straight and she was married. I could only be the big loser in this drama. Lying in bed that night, yearning for the impossible, I knew I'd been a first-class dolt.

If Alix and Charles had their differences, if they were headed for hard times, that was their problem. Not. My. Business. In the unlikely event that Alix decided to sever ties with Dunnevan, a dozen men would leap at the chance to date her. And one of them would undoubtedly become her next husband. I knew that—had always known it. Why did I persist in torturing myself with a fantasy?

It was time to get real, I told myself. *Past* time. Surely I have places to go, people to see, things to do? Right? And if I feel like I'm ready for love again, aren't there some other fish in the sea? Fish who are swimming in the same *direction*?

I spent a few moments thinking about Tamara Feingold, my CPA and longtime friend. She'd made it more than clear that she'd be glad to hear from me. Anytime. Anyplace. She had a fine mind, a great sense of humor, and we always had fun together. I could make contact with Tam, try harder to feel something romantic for her, see whether anything developed between us. But I rejected the thought almost immediately. Unfair—despicable, in fact—to lead her on, when there was actually only one person in the whole of humanity that I longed to reel in.

* * *

"About my husband…" Alix began.

We'd just finished our final performance and hugged the entire women's group goodbye. Now Alix and I were driving back to the Crossing, with cartons of costumes, props and leftover programs stacked in the back of my station wagon. As I tracked the curves of the road, I'd been thinking how lucky—and how *dumb*—I was to be alone with Alix, even for this brief ride. Thinking about how much I'd miss all the extra time I'd had with her during our theatrical production.

"…Charles…" she said, apparently having a hard time getting started, "Charles…"

"Yeah?" I prompted warily. "What about him?"

"He can be a real jerk…" she blurted.

"No argument here," I said, more brusquely than I meant to. The memory of that damned dress rehearsal was still too fresh.

"Well…I guess I just want you to know that he wasn't always like that, Lynn…When I married him, I mean. I wouldn't have, otherwise…"

I didn't want to hear about their glory days—didn't, in fact, want to hear a single positive thing about Charles Dunnevan. But I didn't want to short-circuit Alix either. Especially on this last night.

"Let's stipulate that he was once a fine fellow," I replied. "What the hell happened?"

Her voice shook a little as she spoke. "Some unholy combination of need and greed and my father, I suppose. Charles grew up grindingly poor. When we met in college, he was on full scholarship, just scraping by. I think he truly related to the underdog back then, sincerely meant to serve disadvantaged people in some way."

"Admirable," I said dryly, thinking how far he'd strayed from his mark.

Alix caught my meaning and looked for a second like she might reflexively defend her husband. Instead, she shook herself a little and returned to her explanation. "Anyway, the first time I took Charles home to meet my parents, he and my dad just clicked. They seemed to recognize something elemental in one another. Charles wanted—no, he *craved*—what my father had. And my father instantly saw in Charles the son he'd always dreamed of. The son who'd idolize and emulate him."

"How'd that feel to you?"

"A little like I was a pawn in one of their games. I'm not sure I'd have been *allowed* to marry anyone else," Alix joked weakly. "From the beginning, they were always planning a triumph or plotting a coup of some kind. Gradually, Charles and my dad became the real couple—and my father truly *is* a dangerous prick."

"So, if you pointed that out to Charles, what would he say?"

"First, that would be a futile undertaking. But if I had to guess? Charles would pat my head and accuse me of being melodramatic."

Alix continued to consider my question for several seconds, lost in thought, running both hands through her glorious hair. I was mesmerized by the sight, could almost feel that texture myself. Pay attention, you dweeb! She's trying to tell you something important!

"Anytime I'm too critical, Charles starts ticking off all the good work that's done at Belmont Medical—Dad's hospital back home. He reminds me that my father made BelMed the powerhouse it is today."

"And if you mentioned that old Cal Edwards has profited very handsomely from his labors?"

"They're labors, just the same, Charles would argue—why shouldn't he be rewarded?"

"Depends on how many skeletons are in his closet, Alix."

"Too numerous to count, I'm guessing. But frankly, I'm afraid to ask. And so is everybody else." Alix sighed. "Daddy Dear just keeps getting richer and richer, and more and more powerful. No one dares challenge him—and Charles wouldn't see any reason to do that. He's only too happy to have been sucked into my father's orbit. He adores being the fair-haired boy."

"Where's this leave *you*, Alix?"

"Charles is fond of listing all the comforts and privileges in my life…the security the girls have…"

"You're dodging the question," I said, sneaking a peek at her. That dark head was tipped back a bit and she was looking into the distance. Turning my attention to the road again, I remembered the last time I'd seen the pose. She'd been watching eagles in flight, an indecipherable expression on her face. Now I thought I understood what that look meant—Alix wanted to be free, to soar, but she'd been tethered to the earth so long she was terrified to fly. Watch out, Lynn, I warned myself. Not your job to cut the bonds.

After a telling pause, Alix turned somber eyes in my direction. "You're right. I don't have any answers. I just wanted you to know…Charles wasn't *always* an asshole."

"Duly noted," I told her. "Let's change the subject, okay?"

"Gladly," she agreed. "I was stupid to bring it up in the first place."

CHAPTER NINE

Clay was growing effortlessly into elegant upward arcs when the shop bell rang. "Damn! Wouldn't you know it?" I growled, losing the flow. I wiped both hands on my pants and made my way to the front, crashing into a slurry bucket as I passed by. Murky water sloshed over the rim, drenching my cuffs, soaking my sneakers. So I was a mess when I found Alix in the showroom, a wide-eyed daughter on each arm.

I felt my scowl do an about-face, turning into a helpless grin. Maybe I could disguise my pleasure with sophomoric banter and a lousy Cockney accent. "Good morning, madam. 'Ow may I 'elp you?"

Alix choked back a laugh and joined in the game, gesturing grandly at the display window. "Would you be so kind as to show me that turquoise vase with the forsythia in it, miss?" she asked in a far better accent than I'd ever produced. "My favorite cousin is marrying again and it may serve as a wedding gift."

I broke character and put both hands on my hips. "I'll have to remember this trick. You're the third person who's wanted that pot today, and all because of a little forsythia. Just think—if I put gladiolas in it, I could probably get the funeral trade too."

"Brat!" she said. "Is it really sold to someone else?"

I nodded. "Sorry. He's picking it up later today. When's the wedding?"

"Three weeks," Alix told me.

"Time enough to do a commission." Rubbing my hands in a servile manner, I added, "And just for *you*, lady, a special price."

The little girls' eyes got even rounder. Alix bent down to their level. "We're only playing, you guys," she assured them. When she stood, she placed a hand on each daughter's head. "Cindy," Alix told me. "She's almost six." Pretty, with fair hair, I memorized.

"And this is Beth, who's four." Adorable, with dark hair and eyes so like her mother's.

Taking a cue from Alix, I stooped lower too. "My name's Lynn. Do you like to play with clay?"

The children looked blank. "It's like play dough," I told them, "only *much* cooler."

Now the girls seemed excited. "If your mom has time, you can come in the back room and try it out."

Alix shook her head. "Not this morning, sadly. I have an appointment in twenty minutes. Could we have a rain check?"

The older daughter—Cindy?—was on the verge of tears. I thought fast. "How long will you be gone?"

"About an hour, I suppose. Then I'm done for the day."

"Why don't you leave the kids here, and we'll all go out to lunch afterward?" Because where's the harm? We'll have built-in chaperones, won't we?

The smile that broke across Alix's face lit her eyes and set that dimple in motion. "I'd love that, if you don't think they'll be too much trouble."

"Terrific," I told her. "You hit the road. We have important things to do." I took the girls by the hand and led them into my studio.

* * *

When Alix returned, right on time, her children were covered with ghostly streaks of sculpture clay and both were silly with pride.

"Look what I made, Mama!" Beth hollered, exhibiting a shapeless rabbit. "And guess *what*?"

"Bethie, you hush up!" Cindy warned. "You're gonna ruin everything! Don't let her *tell*," she begged me.

I lifted Beth and looked her in the eye. "Remember," I said, "it's a secret."

She wriggled free. "You'll find out soon, Mama," Beth promised solemnly.

Alix leaned against the wedging table, watching them rinse their hands, shaking her head. "What little pigs! Guess I'll be doing laundry tonight..."

"Don't worry," I told her. "Unlike terra-cotta, it washes right out."

"I don't even care. Good times outweigh good clothes, two to one. When can we go eat?"

"Now," I said. "I'm starving."

I pushed her toward the front door, flipping over my sign as we left. *Closed* it said, for anyone who cared. Funny contrast, I thought. Because suddenly *I* felt wide open to every possibility.

To my surprise, Alix drove past the town limits, far from any restaurant I could recall. Her attention was focused on the road, so I could get away with watching her closely. As she tracked the turns, I thought I sensed an element of daring held in careful check, a hint that daddy's good little girl might break loose one day. Every now and then when Alix shifted gears, her hand grazed my knee, searing my flesh right through my khakis. I'd have stayed in that car forever, enjoying her profile, hoping for a miracle. But I made myself ask, "Where are we going?"

"Maintain thy soul in patience," she answered with a wicked, sideways glance. "You're not the only one with secrets."

Alix slipped a cassette into the tape player—Barbra Streisand—and we rode in wordless appreciation. The girls talked quietly behind us, calmed by an energetic hour with clay and the motion of the car. Suddenly everything felt very, very good. So good I wanted to break into song. I managed to resist the impulse though. Alix is a *musician*, I reminded myself. Why torment her? Besides, no one should have the gall to sing along with Streisand. She stands alone.

At the stone gates that flank the entrance to Chinquapin State Park, Alix slowed then swung in. She followed a narrow road, passing up two parking lots before she brought the car to a halt in a third. "Less competition for the playground here," she told me in answer to my unvoiced question. "Most visitors pull in at the first opportunity." In what seemed a single motion, she climbed out, opened doors and helped the girls out. Years of practice, I supposed.

"Is it a picnic, Mommy?" Cindy asked breathlessly.

"Yes, baby."

"My kind of woman!" I announced, as Alix popped the trunk to reveal a trio of bulging grocery sacks. We carried the bags and a blanket to a level space lush with new grass. "What a great idea, Alix."

"I've been a mother for a long time, you know. I had a hunch none of you would be fit for *Chez Louis*."

"You shopped, my friend. Let me take care of the rest."

Sometimes a season telescopes and everything blooms at once. In the park, dogwood and redbud trees were ringed with jonquils. Fire bush and bridal wreath had gone wild. Under the towering oaks, lily-of-the-valley and grape hyacinth thrust through layers of crackling brown leaves. Everywhere I looked fresh violets had tinted vast swathes of lawn a rich purple. I couldn't imagine a finer dining room—or better company.

I spread the blanket, then arranged the groceries on top while Alix played tag with her children. When I straightened up, she was running in the sunshine, her hair alive on the breeze. So beautiful that I couldn't bear to watch. Looking away, heart thudding against my ribs, I whispered into my hands the thing I'd vowed not to say aloud: "I *love* you, Alix Dunnevan."

A second later she was beside me. "Hey—I thought you were hungry. When can we eat?"

"As soon as you round up the girls, my friend. I'm ready."

Despite the lavish array of food, Cindy and Beth ate indifferently. The nearby playground had much more allure than lunch. The simplicity of their approach was seductive and they won me over instantly. Nothing mattered so much as one more turn on the spiral slide, one more push on the swings. But after working with clay that morning, the spacious sandbox couldn't satisfy them.

"Clay is much better," I agreed. "The sand keeps slipping away." Nevertheless, we kept on building. By two o'clock, the children had begun to droop.

"Had enough?" Alix asked me.

"Never," I said. "Cindy and Beth look wiped out, though."

"Oh, that's easy enough." Alix returned to the blanket and snapped it briskly, scattering crumbs. Then she called her children over, gesturing for them to lie down on the soft fabric. Sitting between them, she stroked their hair with a gentle, purposeful monotony. "One song apiece," she said, "and then a short nap."

I leaned back, studying blue sky through spring-green leaves. After the little girls made their choices, Alix closed her eyes and began to sing unselfconsciously. Her voice, clear and vibrant, resonated in my bones, became the only thing in my world.

First she sang for Beth—a simple, lilting melody that I remembered from my own childhood. But Cindy's song, nominally a lullaby, was contrived from pain, despair and loss. Before it was done, depression had settled on me like a shroud. I saw I'd fallen into the pit yet again. Would I *never* learn to stay away from this woman?

I sat up suddenly and fled to a massive tree. Leaning against it, I steeled myself. I knew what I had to do.

She rose at last, easing off the blanket, and gazed at her sleeping daughters for a heartbeat. I seemed to see them through her eyes just then. Dappled with sunlight. Bright T-shirts stretched across delicate bones. Cheeks pink from exertion. Skinny little legs, pointy little elbows. Totally trusting, wholly precious beings. The center of her universe.

Alix looked around, found me, beckoned. I pried myself away from my tree and joined her on a weathered bench where we could keep an eye on the children while we talked.

"What was that song?" I asked her. Anything to delay the inevitable.

"The second one? That's a favorite of mine. It's an old slave song about separation, about having to be with someone you don't love when your own people need you."

"The heartache's really there, isn't it? The composer caught it all."

Alix touched my sleeve. "You seem down all of a sudden, Lynn. Is something wrong?"

I removed her hand from my arm, holding on for one wrenching second. Then I released her and took a deep breath. "Yeah, Alix—I've got a problem. I've decided to drop out of the women's group…because…I think we'd better stop seeing each other, even at meetings." I could barely force the words past my dry and stubborn lips, but I made myself finish. "Despite my best intentions, I'm embarrassed to confess that I've fallen in love with you."

She sat beside me, still and tense. I felt the full weight of the moment, the world whirling out of control. At last she released a shaky sigh and reached for me.

"Thank *god*, Lynn! I thought I was *alone* in this."

I held her lightly, more in sorrow than in joy. Tipping her face to mine, I said, "Darling, you don't understand. All we can get from this is grief. Better not to begin."

"Oh, really?" Alix asked. And then she kissed me.

The world is so old and tired—who will believe me if I say her kiss was like no other? That sweet, yielding readiness. The soft, spreading warmth that sparked to a heated urgency. I pulled back, trembling. Then raising her hand to my lips, I traced my tongue along her palm. Her eyelids fluttered like aspen leaves and she lay back in my arms, giving way to pure sensation. The wind died down. The trees were motionless. Every movement felt strangely buoyant, like underwater ballet. It isn't easy to stand without knees, but I managed.

"Better wake the girls, Alix. I need to go home."

CHAPTER TEN

My dreams were troubled that night—full of fear and longing and frustrated pleasures. They shattered my sleep into a dozen jagged segments. I woke with the conviction that I had to see Alix one last time. To make her understand. To say a final goodbye.

I phoned her as soon as I was sure she'd be up. It was hard to talk. My voice was rough and uneven. Sounding strange and remote herself, Alix agreed to meet at my house that evening. Throughout the day I honed the arguments, searching for flaws but finding none, hating my certainty. By sunset, I was a wreck. Couldn't decide what to wear. Braided my hair. Shook it loose. Braided it again.

Alix arrived early. She stood on my threshold, strained and nervous. More beautiful than ever, damn her. I felt calm, yet hollow. A bell once struck might have echoed forever within my center. There was an awkwardness about the situation: do you offer wine and music with farewells? At least that would forestall the agony for a few brief moments. I filled some goblets with merlot and fumbled with the stereo, trying to choose records with no significance, songs I'd never have to hear again.

Then there was nothing to do but face Alix. I had no idea what was in her mind, or what might have changed since she'd kissed me in the park. When I took her hands, she could have withdrawn. Instead, she gripped me hard and nodded. The electricity was real—we both felt it. Small, warm blossoms uncurling in our veins.

I wanted one luxury before I started the hard work of undoing this magic. I cupped her cheek in my palm, drinking in the texture of her skin, the indescribable arch of her brows, the unutterable perfection of her lips. Her eyes held mine, reflected mine—the terror and the misery.

"I love you more than I've ever loved anyone," I told her.

"Then don't say goodbye to me tonight, Lynn."

Some smoothly functioning mechanism in my brain recorded and filed the irony. For a solid year after Sarah left, I'd ached for a lover who'd beg me to stay. Now I was the one who had to break away. I picked up my wineglass and leaned back on the couch. "Listen to me, Alix. Really *hear* what I'm saying. I have just enough strength to do this."

Rolling the cool goblet between my hands, I delivered the speech I'd rehearsed all day. It was short, simple, inarguable. "You're married, Alix. You have children. There's no future for us, and that's the only way I'd want you. This isn't about a few nights in a motel room—I'm an all-or-nothing kind of woman. *Please* trust me. The price is much too high."

Angry eyes flashed at me. "Lynn, are you the only one who makes decisions around here? Don't you need to hear from me first? I think we might work this out."

I banged my glass down on the coffee table with such force that the stem snapped. The bowl clattered to the floor, where it rolled back and forth, spraying wine in a bleeding arc.

"Damn it, Alix! I told you once—you don't know how this works!"

"I know how much I love you," she said quietly. "I know how long and hard I've fought that feeling. But it doesn't go away, no matter what I do. Don't we owe it to ourselves to explore the possibilities?" Her chin came up and a steely gaze challenged my own. "I've never thought of you as a person who wouldn't give an argument a fair hearing."

"Okay," I sighed. "You talk, I'll listen."

Alix leaned toward me, hands on my knees. Her face was taut with emotion. "I've never felt about anybody the way I feel about you. I've spent a long time trying to talk myself out of it, for exactly the reasons you listed. And then I quit trying. Because I *do* love you—I *want* to love you. Of course you're right about some of this. There is a lot at stake here, and I don't know the rules of the game. That doesn't mean I can't learn. And it doesn't mean I won't pay to play."

There was a simple way to cut this short. Her knapsack was on my coffee table. Opening it, I sorted through the contents as if I had a right. Positive I'd find what I was seeking, I flipped to the photo section of her wallet. I stopped at facing snapshots of Cindy and Beth. Sliding them from protective plastic, I placed the pictures on the couch between us.

"Even if this is the price?" I asked her as kindly as possible.

Alix lowered her head in defeat. "I don't know..." she admitted. "My *daughters*..."

I made her confront me. "This is it, sweetheart. They're the reality we can't evade. Neither of us can pretend for one second that we aren't deciding something about their future tonight."

Her voice seemed to come from far away. "When they're frightened, I always ask them, 'What's the worst thing that could happen?' Tell me, Lynn."

"No," I said. "You'd make them answer. Now it's your turn."

Alix wrenched her tortured eyes from the photographs. "Scandal, publicity, pain. I could lose my children." Her shoulders sagged under the weight of it. "I don't *understand*," she whispered. "How could all that ugliness come from the love I feel for you?"

My cheeks were as tear-stained as hers. "I don't know, darling. I never have."

She looked at me defiantly. "What will I *do* with this emotion, Lynn? How do I put it to death?"

I was so tired. Why did I have to come up with all the answers? I stood and pulled Alix upright. "As quickly as you can," I told her. "No more meetings, no more postcards. We stop now before anyone else gets hurt."

Alix put her head on my shoulder, fragrant hair soft against my cheek. When she spoke again, her voice was childlike, bewildered. "I don't *want* to give this up, Lynn."

"Neither do I, love. But we'll make it. We're survivors." I kissed her forehead then wrapped my arms around her. She was small, so small in my arms, inches shorter than I was. I wanted nothing more than to cherish and protect her forever. Alix released a deep, sobbing sound and pulled me closer. A final kiss, and then a clean break.

"Goodbye," she breathed. She bent for her keys and she was gone. I stood at the window watching, my palms flat against cold glass, long after her car had disappeared around the curve.

* * *

The weather turned damp. A steady spring rain saturated the ground beyond its capacity. The gullies in my valley overflowed with rushing water, and the sky was as gray as freshly-milled clay. Everything I touched felt heavy, heavy, heavy.

I roamed my shop aimlessly. Throwing was pointless. Each shelf in the studio was already lined with pots that wouldn't dry in the high humidity. Firing bisqueware in the outdoor kiln was impossible—I couldn't expose the delicate glazes to that relentless downpour during the loading process. I'd completed an inventory and ordered new supplies. My paperwork had never been so up to date or my studio so orderly. I could think of nothing else to do. Cosmic forces seemed to have conspired, miring me in the restless workings of my mind.

On an impulse, I picked up the phone and dialed a number in Chicago. An agent there had wanted to represent my work for a long time. I'd been stalling him, uncertain about the wisdom of taking on another commitment—and most recently, if I were honest, afraid of missing a chance encounter with Alix. But suddenly I was eager for a distraction, grateful for the excuse to leave town. In less than an hour I'd made arrangements to meet with the agent, scheduled a flight for the next morning, and hired Pam to care for Solly in my absence. I'd stay away as long as I could bear it.

* * *

I hated Chicago. It was grim, dirty and depressing. On my very first visit there, back in the late sixties, millions of rotting fish had blanketed the beach where Lake Michigan laps at the heart of the city—the annual alewife die-off. An unwelcome consequence of a species outlasting its sole predator. The stench penetrated the depths of the Art Institute and hung like a toxic cloud over the famous stores on State Street. And images from the Division Street riots were still fresh in my mind. Two weeks of violence fueled by the death of a young Puerto Rican at the hands of Chicago police. There was something lasting and metaphorical about those initial impressions, the violence and decay. I could think of no more appropriate place to take my relentless grief.

I'd forgotten that winters are longer up north. There, springtime was still a distant, nebulous concept. After concluding my business, I spent three days trudging grungy urban streets, my mood a match for their wintery bleakness. Even the museums held no interest for me. Just beyond their doors, I paced a stormy shoreline while waves of emptiness and yearning crashed through me. For once the city and I were in perfect accord.

I hoped, futilely, for some lessening of intensity, some surcease from that howling anguish. But I couldn't stop obsessing about Alix, day or night—wondering what she was doing, how she felt, if she thought of me. I went to a movie and forgot to watch it. I sat in restaurants where I couldn't swallow the food set before me. I tried to sketch the towering skyline outside my hotel window, but couldn't remember why that mattered. At last, I gave up. No feeling of relief was going to overtake me there. I caught a taxi to O'Hare and made my way home.

CHAPTER ELEVEN

My capacity for self-deception is highly evolved, so I take full responsibility for what happened next. I'd been back from Chicago about a week and I was still finding the workdays dull, the evenings excruciating. One night when I felt particularly adrift, I drove to a mall on the outskirts of St. Louis. Forty-five miles there, forty-five miles back, just to kill time. Wow, you *are* a mess! I told myself. You *never* do anything like this! But I pulled into a parking slot and joined the throngs inside.

Browsing the endless, branching corridors lined with shops of every type and size, I felt a profound sense of alienation. It seemed I was the only person alone, the only one with empty hands. In that huge and varied array of offerings, there was nothing I needed, nothing I wanted. Still anything seemed preferable to entering my shadowed house again.

I ate lousy crab Rangoon in a food court, then returned to the crowded walkways. The sole bookstore was going out of business, all the good stuff long gone. I couldn't work up an interest in the clothing boutiques. Couldn't help wincing at gaudy, mass-produced ceramics in the card shops. Even spumoni ice cream failed to cheer me.

Then I saw it: a new music store, its plate glass window plastered with *Grand Opening* signs. I entered and searched the stock with fatalistic conviction. I was right. None of the feminist labels were available there. Surveying the glitzy, top-forty merchandise, I shook my head with disdain. But on my way out the door, a display of blank cassette tapes caught my eye. I chose four of the most expensive type, and handed my credit card to a bored cashier. Minutes later, I was striding briskly toward my car. I didn't understand why I felt so much lighter on the drive home.

As soon as I'd peeled off my jacket and fed Sol, I began to sort through my albums, trying to decide which cuts to record. At least it was something to do. I debated the relative merits of categorizing by artist, genre, mood or chronological order. Once I'd settled on a strategy, I inspected each vinyl disc minutely, scanning for imperfections. Then I cleaned them all with fanatical care.

Till that moment, I'd viewed cassettes as a stop-gap substitute for the real deal. My usual approach to recording had been quick-and-dirty. I filled cheap tapes with erratic duplicates to play in my car, never minding much when the volume varied from piece to piece, or a song broke abruptly at the end of a reel. If I recognized that my newfound precision betrayed an ulterior motive, I suppressed the thought.

Over the next few days, I spent every spare hour adjusting those recordings. Finally, I was satisfied that I couldn't improve on the quality without investing in a better sound system. When I was finished with the process, the tapes contained most of the women's music that had stirred my mind or body over the years. I stayed up ridiculously late on Friday night, carefully printing titles on the pasteboard insert of each little storage box. Smiling, I arranged the plastic cases in a neat stack on the coffee table, then headed for bed.

* * *

After breakfast on Saturday, I took a second cup of tea into the living room. Sol curled beside me in a bright spot on the couch and I stroked him absently, wondering what to do with my empty weekend. The world turned, the sun shifted, and suddenly that gleaming stack of cassettes caught my eye. I raised a toast to unfathomable technology. So much beauty, so much emotion, so much creativity and courage were hidden within those cases, encoded on coiled lengths of magnetic tape. A treasure trove of feminist music. And in that instant, I allowed intent to seep through me like a revelation: I was either an idiot or a liar, because those recordings had never been meant for me.

Ablaze with sudden purpose, I dashed upstairs. My desktop was littered with paperbacks, pamphlets and sketches. Clearing it hastily, I uncovered a muddy Polaroid of the Abbies in costume for our historical program. At center stage, her face shadowed by that severe black bonnet, Alix was barely distinguishable. No matter. I remembered every detail of her exquisite face. I pinned the photo to my bulletin board, before I reached for pen and paper.

Sweet, darling woman—

In my desire to protect you from further injury, I've neglected to say some important things. This past week, I've thought of nothing except those omissions. It's made me crazy that I spent so *much* time telling you why we couldn't be lovers, and so *little* time explaining why I love you.

I want you to know that from our first meeting, I've felt some tangled interweaving of possibility between us, a deep-rooted connection capable of growth and flowering. If you thought it was easy for me to turn my back on that promise, let me assure you that nothing has ever felt so counterintuitive, so wrong. I find you beautiful, both inside and out. I know I will never hear certain music without remembering and regretting this loss.

Believe me, I'll love you always—
Lynn

Folding the letter into a small rectangle, I fastened it atop one of the tape cases. Then I wrapped the stack of cassettes in brown paper and bound the package with string. Even writing Alix's name on the label gave me a rush.

Still refusing to recognize that I was violating the agreement we'd made, I drove to the post office just before closing time. I didn't know the balding, sardonic clerk behind the counter—which I suddenly realized was a good thing. He took my parcel to weigh it. As he filled out the insurance receipt, he said, "Ain't likely to get lost between here and there, lady."

"You don't know my luck," I told him. "This is important to me."

A guilty tingle raced through my body as I exited the building, yet I wouldn't admit the risk I was running. Couldn't let myself consider the harm my actions might cause.

* * *

My pulse became a time clock, ticking away the minutes. By Monday, Alix might have received the tapes, read my letter. By Tuesday she might have listened to some of the recordings. By Wednesday, she might have found favorites of her own… Until Friday, I was breathless and exhilarated. Caution seemed the hallmark of fainthearted fools.

But when the weekend rolled around with no response, that sense of anticipation waned. Though I hadn't consciously hoped to hear from Alix, her silence was devastating. I was alone with my bad behavior, feeling like an ass. Embarrassed that I'd cracked, that I'd broken my own rules. Humiliated that I'd mailed the letter. Sorry I'd sent the tapes.

I imagined a dozen variations on the theme of their arrival. Alix stricken with unwelcome emotion as she listened to those songs. Or tossing the tapes in the trash, unheard. The most dismal scenario featured Charles intercepting my package so Alix never even knew I'd made the effort. Agonizing—*unbearable*—to imagine Dunnevan reading the intimate message intended only for his wife.

There was nothing to do but resign myself to this degrading state of affairs. If all I had now was work, at least I had plenty of that. I buried my heart at the bottom of a clay barrel and wore myself out on the kick wheel. And the funny thing was that sorrow gave rise to far better art than joy ever does. Go figure. Even *I* had to acknowledge that some of my work approached masterpiece status. Each Saturday, everything I put in the front window of my shop was snatched up by day-trippers from St. Louis. I couldn't fill all the orders from galleries, and had twice as many invitations to exhibit my work as I could accept.

I began to wonder if I should hire someone to manage the showroom so I could concentrate on production alone. But who had time to advertise and interview? And would the expense of adding an employee outweigh the benefit? Business calculation was *not* my strong suit. I kept putting off the decision. Besides, the more frenetic my days, the less time I had to notice my gnawing loneliness. Get back to the kick wheel, I told myself. Work until you can't swing your leg one more time. Fall into bed too tired to think. Do it all over again.

* * *

One sunny afternoon, when I'd almost accepted a life of perpetual solitude, I saw Alix and her daughters crossing the square. She was headed for my storefront, Cindy and Beth urging her to greater speed. Without warning, that weary acquiescence to heartbreak fell away, leaving me painfully exposed.

With shaking hands, I completed a sale for a customer and swaddled his purchase in tissue paper. It was just possible to tuck that bundle into a sturdy gift box and add a glossy lid. But tying ribbon was beyond me. I could only jam the carton into a shopping bag and hasten the man on his way. As he exited, he held the door wide for Alix and the girls. When they crossed the threshold, I thought my heart might stop.

Beth came straight to me, arms up. I lifted her to my hip, touched by her trust. Tightening her short legs around my waist, she chattered like a little monkey. I tried to pay attention but I was too overcome with emotion, almost undone by this unexpected proximity to Alix. At first glance, she looked radiant and a grin crept across my face, stretching wide to match her own. But her smile masked a darker truth—there were shadows under her eyes and hollows beneath her cheekbones.

She didn't flinch from my candid inspection. Meeting my eyes directly, she said, "The girls keep reminding me that they've left something here, Lynn. They thought it might be ready by now."

I didn't trust myself to reply. I just led them into my studio and reached for the box high on a shelf. "Close your eyes, Alix," I managed to say.

I knelt and handed Beth a flat, tissue-wrapped object. "This is the one *you* made, honey." Cindy held out impatient hands. "This is yours," I said to her.

"Okay, Mama," Cindy announced, in charge as always. "You can open your eyes."

"What *is* this—Christmas?"

"It's a secret!" shouted Beth, waving her package.

"I didn't think the kids would have a chance to finish them," I told Alix, my voice husky with meaning. "And I wasn't sure what glazes they'd have chosen, so I added them to one of my salt firings. Just in case."

Beth's gift lay unwrapped in her mother's hands. A crude, square tile embossed with criss-crossings from decorative rollers I use in my work. The salt had given it a rich, brown hue and a low-gloss sheen.

"Why, baby, is it a trivet?" Alix asked.

"No. It's a *present*," Beth answered firmly.

Our laughter was interrupted by Cindy's urgent demand. "Open mine, Mama!"

Alix peeled away tissue to expose a coil bowl, only slightly lopsided. "Oh, Cindy," she exclaimed, her appreciation evident, "it's so pretty!" She balanced the small pot on her palm. "I know just where I'll put this."

"It's remarkably good," I confirmed. "Far better than the usual first effort, especially for a child her age. She seems to have a real feeling for clay. I've seen worse work from junior high students—"

"Bloody hell," groaned Alix, interrupting me. She pointed to the far end of the studio, and I saw that her daughters had wandered off as we spoke. Beth was elbow-deep in a clay barrel already, and Cindy was closing in fast.

I laughed. "It's okay with me, if it's okay with you. Or do the girls need to stay clean?"

"No. We were just on our way home from shopping. We can hang out a while, if we're not in your way."

My expression telegraphed the simple truth—Alix could never be an inconvenience. But what I said was, "Terrific. Let me get the kids settled so we can talk."

Forcing myself to break away, I scooped up a pair of empty five-gallon buckets. Then, struggling to steady my voice, I called over my shoulder. "It's wonderful to see you, Alix!"

At a low glazing table, I upended the buckets. "Pretend they're stools," I suggested as I seated the children on them. They watched with hungry eyes while I gathered rolling pins and an assortment of tools. Slicing a large ball of clay in half, I handed a piece to each girl.

"Don't touch anything else, you guys," Alix cautioned.

They set to work on the clay immediately, pounding and rolling and pinching. Fantasy quickly took over. Scraps and lumps morphed into cookies and cakes for an imaginary birthday party. Cindy was the bossy baker, and Beth her cheerful assistant. Soon the girls were so deeply engaged in make-believe that we'd ceased to exist for them.

When Alix pulled me toward an alcove at the front of my studio, I didn't resist. Hidden from her busy children, there was no other choice—we came together instantly. For a long while it was enough just to hold her.

"My *god*, my *god*," I whispered into her hair.

Alix tilted her head to study my face, tracing the contours with a smooth fingertip. When she reached my smile, she stood on tiptoe. "Kiss me, Lynn."

At first I touched down lightly, just sliding my tongue along the sweet curve of her mouth. Then I began to suck her lower lip. She moaned a little, and pulled me close. I went deeper, tasting her, loving her, wanting her as I'd never wanted another woman.

She was melting against me, opening to me, when suddenly I heard the laughter of her children, so close. I made myself pull back, lifting her hands from my hips. Leaning against a shelf for support, I exhaled raggedly.

"This is *craziness*," I sighed.

"But irresistible," Alix insisted.

"Oh, yes," I answered, honest at last.

It took a childish conflict to disrupt that timeless interlude. Beth and Cindy competing for a favored clay tool. Alix and I separated reluctantly at the sound of shrill voices, entwined hands sliding slowly apart as we stepped into the studio proper. With the ease of long practice, she resolved the argument, wiped away tears and organized a cleanup. The girls were at my sink splashing happily when she turned to me.

"I need some time with you, Lynn. Will you talk with me tonight?"

My hapless heart leaped and I nodded agreement. But I had to warn Alix, even if she already understood: "I can't promise to limit myself to conversation."

"So much the better."

CHAPTER TWELVE

The rest of that day passed in a shimmering haze. I don't remember eating or how I handled business. I was so high, I was useless. After closing the shop early, I drove home singing fragments of every love song I knew. There was just enough time to fill my living room with flowers from the garden and take a quick shower.

Standing in the steaming water, I tried to figure out how Alix and I had arrived at this moment. But I'd have been hard-pressed to offer a rational reason for the sudden shift in our behavior. Alix had made the call, of course, which was only fitting since she had the most at stake. Then somehow—virtually without discussion—we'd blown past all the barriers we'd so prudently erected. Maybe I'd said it best in my studio: we had simply lost our minds. But I couldn't care about caution anymore, couldn't hold back any longer.

I was at the door before Alix knocked. We didn't bother stepping inside, just stood on the porch hugging and kissing and laughing at ourselves. There *are* advantages to rural living.

Finally I became aware of coolness and crackling paper behind me. "It's wine—I brought wine," said Alix, releasing me.

I took the long brown bag from her hand, shouldered her knapsack and waved her through my front door. In the kitchen I filled our goblets with sunshine and moonbeams. Or maybe the wine just seemed so extraordinary because I was sharing it with Alix.

The night was chilly. I lit a fire and we sat on my couch, legs stretched out, feet on the coffee table. I slid down to rest my head on Alix's shoulder, arms circling her small waist. There was so much we needed to know, so much we'd never been able to talk about. We gave each other such gifts as lovers have to offer, our longings and remembrances.

We analyzed the intense attraction we'd felt the night we met, exclaiming at the randomness of fate. We chronicled the history of our growing affection, recounting separate details, seeking shared perceptions, finding delight in the most trivial of coincidences. Alix told me how she'd suffered in our time apart. I described my blank desolation and flight to Chicago.

"What made you come to my shop this morning?" I asked.

"The horrid emptiness. Your marvelous letter. The tapes, of course."

"Thank god!" I said fervently. "I thought they'd just sunk into a void."

"Oh, no, my love! I read your letter to tatters. And whatever you hoped the tapes would mean, they were my salvation. I played them every solitary minute, feeling so connected to you. They assured me that the caring would go on forever, even if we never saw one another again. Listening to the music, I knew I was still alive in your mind. It was almost enough."

"But not," I pointed out happily.

"But not," she agreed. Then, "In a strange way, Lynn, your tapes have opened up a lot of *other* music."

"Meaning?"

"Well, for instance, I had a funny experience in the dentist's office the other day."

"Mutually exclusive possibilities," I insisted.

"No, really. There was muzak playing in the cubicle, stupid popular stuff, and I'd mostly managed to ignore it. But suddenly, as if the volume had been turned up, I tuned in to a woman's voice. She was singing that old Captain & Tennille song—the one about longing to touch a new lover more than she'd wanted any man? Suddenly the words took on a very different meaning and I couldn't quit snickering. It was a far cry from my usual attitude in a dental chair. I'm sure my poor doctor thought I'd gone nuts."

I laughed, then turned the conversation another direction. "Is this really the first time you've loved a woman, Alix?"

"Yes, hon. I've asked myself over and over how this can feel so natural if that's true. But I honestly can't remember noticing women romantically before I met you."

"Astounding," I said. "Why *me*?"

Alix grinned and started to speak. Then she stopped herself. "I was going to make a dumb joke, but I've changed my mind. I want you to know that I fell in love with your pride and your anger. I used to watch you with the Abbies, thinking that you were the only person in the room who knew what was important and how to accomplish it. I could see that you'd wade through acres of crap to teach one woman how to use her power—even somebody who felt threatened by you, or afraid of your sexuality."

Then she bent her head to whisper in my ear: "Of course, it didn't *hurt* that you're so damned *hot*—after every meeting, I'd go home and fantasize about you for hours."

"Not really!" I said, looking up at her, surprised.

"Well, of course, dumbshit. How do you think I ended up here tonight? I'd lie in bed next to Charles and tell myself that I was being ridiculous, that you'd never notice me, that I was damned by my alleged heterosexuality. But none of that worked. I kept imagining what it would feel like to kiss you." She dimpled. "For a long time, I thought I'd die happy if I could kiss you just once."

"Oh, god," I groaned, "both of us kicking ourselves around the same block for months. Think how much time we've wasted!"

"Pathetic!" Alix confirmed.

Another record dropped on the turntable. I stood, pulling her off the couch. "All right, darling, this is a test. Dance with me."

She came into my arms, lifting her face for a kiss. We began to move, our bodies a perfect fit. The moment was mindless and tender. "Is it strange for you—being with a woman?" I asked softly.

Alix shook her head almost imperceptibly. "I feel like I belong here, like I was meant for this."

Something exultant flared within me. I held her closer, rejoicing. Whatever reality lay beyond my walls, we were content to ignore it for this evening. Swaying with Alix, immersed in the music, I could only imagine one thing more desirable. When the stereo clicked off, we returned to the couch. Wrapped around her there, I voiced the question that had occupied so many sleepless nights.

"What are you like in bed, Alix?"

Laying her cheek against mine, she said, "I could tell you that I'm noisy and that I like everything and that I never want it to end…but why don't I show you instead?"

Her hands touched down on my shoulders, sending a surge of warmth through my entire being. Turning me, she lifted the thick braid that reached halfway down my back and kissed the nape of my neck till I shivered in the heat. Then she loosened my hair and knelt on the floor in front of me. She combed her fingers through the streaky strands, lifting them in her hands, burying her face.

"Do you have any idea how long I've wanted to do this?" she whispered. "The most gorgeous color—such an amazing texture—it feels just like silk…"

Scarcely able to breathe, I watched as those hands released my hair, moved to unfasten my shirt. Her fingers were deft and certain, but she took her time. Every button was undone before she pushed the fabric aside.

"Christ," she murmured, "I've wanted you so much, but I never dreamed you'd be this *beautiful*." Her palms cupped my breasts, thumbs stroking expertly. I sat very still, every nerve tingling.

"You're *sure* you've never done this before?" I asked hoarsely.

"Never, my love. I must have been waiting for you."

The thin tank top slipped over her head without resistance. Her bra unhooked in front. When I reached for the clasp, Alix turned my hand away. "It's a bit tricky," she explained. In a second, she'd slid the straps off her shoulders. Her breasts were high and round on her delicate architecture. A few pearly stretch marks veined the rosy bisque of her skin. I pulled her to me, bent my head, circled softness with my tongue, holding back a little till she cried, "*Please!*"

Trembling, we stood to face one another. Alix drew a long, uneven breath as our naked flesh touched. Pressing her to me, nearly faint with desire, I ran my nails lightly down the sweep of her back. Her knees buckled and I had to steady her. When I led her upstairs, my own legs felt unreal, as if I were treading green seawaters along a shifting shoreline.

In my bedroom, we held each other for a long time before I said, "Stand still, sweetheart." She reached for the looping frame of my brass bed while I unzipped her jeans and turned the denim back. Suffused with emotion, I knelt to rest my cheek against the smooth skin of her stomach. Then, fingers curled around the luscious curve of her ass, I kissed the dense triangular darkness above her thighs. At last, I slid her jeans lower. Alix shuddered, her free hand clutching my hair. I held each cuff till she lifted her feet out. Then I began to undress myself.

My work is hard and physical. To do it well requires strength. I've been sculpted by clay as surely as I have sculpted it. When I stood fully nude before her, slender, firm and muscled, Alix inhaled sharply. She extended a trembling hand to brush my hair behind my shoulders, exposing me completely to her gaze. I knew what she was thinking: we looked very different, yet very much the same.

I folded back the linens. We were poised on the edge of my bed, on the brink of incalculable risk, on the rim of impossible ecstasy. Sheltering Alix in my arms, I asked, "Are you afraid, darling?"

"A little," she acknowledged. "What if I get this all wrong?"

I laughed softly. "Most of it's love, the rest is practice. We've already got the important part under control."

Alix lay back on the cool sheets, while I paused to bind my hair again. "Don't, Lynn," she said. "Leave it loose, okay?"

"You'll be sorry," I warned, releasing the long strands. "It'll be everywhere."

"I want to feel it against me," she insisted.

"All right, sweetheart," I said, kissing her gently.

But beyond that one request, I sensed that she needed me to take the lead this first time. I rolled her onto her stomach then straddled her, gasping when I made contact with the velvet skin at the small of her back. Bending forward, letting my hair drape and sway around Alix, I began to massage her neck and shoulders. She moaned and moved beneath me as I worked my way slowly downward, caressing, kissing, biting, licking, letting tension build to the outer edges of our endurance. When at last I laid the length of my body atop hers, she flexed sharply against me. Almost undone by the intensity of my response, I turned her toward me crying, "Sweet Alix!"

She found my hand then and pulled it down to a deep, wet urgency. "Love me, Lynn," she breathed.

I was desperate to see her first, this woman I'd wanted for so long. Pushing myself upright, I studied her for a long, reverent moment. "*Jesus god*," I said, "you look like a *rosebud*." Needing just one taste, I ran my tongue along pink fullness that tapered to delicate, fluted edges. Alix sighed and writhed and pulled me back to her.

I held her, lips at one breast, fingers finally tracing the path my tongue had already blazed. She felt like heaven under my hand, her body in such constant motion that I had a hard time staying with her. When she came, it was with a prolonged and noisy joy. For an eternity, I lay still in her embrace, so rigid in those languorous arms.

At last she released me and knelt on the bed. I was flat on my back, quivering, as Alix pulled the sheet slowly away, revealing me an inch at a time. After I was totally uncovered, she reached out to stroke the damp wedge of hair between my thighs, allowing her thumb to graze me ever so slightly, ever so maddeningly.

"I've been crazy curious, you know," she said in a husky voice.

I lifted a quizzical eyebrow.

She laughed. "Dark or light?" still stroking, still teasing. "With your coloring, I figured it was a coin toss."

"Disappointed?"

"I knew you'd be perfect either way," Alix answered, leaning forward to plant a kiss on those curls. She sat back on her heels again, a speculative look in her eyes. Even more than I wanted her hands on me, I wanted to know what she was thinking about just then.

"How many ways I can rock your world," she whispered. "How much I want to touch every part of *you* with every part of *me*. How long I can make this last…"

She bent my knees and spread my thighs wide, her brown eyes taking in every detail. Questing fingers opened and explored me—tentatively at first, then with increasing certainty. "You'll have to tell me, darling," Alix murmured. "Does *this* feel good? Does *this*?"

My arching body answered her questions again and again.

The next time we had the strength to speak, Alix asked, "Have all your lovers been women, Lynn?"

"Only the important ones, sweetheart," I said, drawing her closer. "It's just that the best people in my life have been female. Every relationship I had with a man seemed to hinge on my willingness to make accommodations and allowances no woman would ask for. Finally I couldn't imagine why I should put up with that shit. So I gathered my courage and found my true vocation."

Alix stirred in my embrace. "Have you slept with a *lot* of women?"

"No, baby. I'm a real serious type. This is too important for me to share with just anyone." I hugged her harder. "Will you believe me if I swear you're the best of a small, select circle?"

"Probably not. But don't let that stop you."

There were periods of cradling rest and moments of hungry awakening. In the middle of that night, I remember saying, "You're incredible, Alix. It isn't supposed to be this easy."

"Maybe all that piano practice has finally paid off," she murmured before lapsing into sleep once more.

* * *

When next I opened my eyes, stripes of late morning sun rippled across the sheets. I'd kissed Alix twice before panic set in. "My *god*, sweetheart! Charles and the children—"

Stretching, Alix grinned at my frenzy. "Relax, love. Something got lost in the shuffle last night. I don't think I explained that they're out of town—that's why I was free to be with you. They left yesterday afternoon to visit Charles's family. They won't be back till late Monday."

My eyes widened in wonder. "Are you *mine* till then? For three whole days?" I asked her.

"Only if you can keep me interested," Alix said archly.

"My dear, I'll try my damndest," I promised. And I did.

Saturday and Sunday sped by. If I'd known such happiness before, it was too remote to remember. We kept delaying the hard part, the necessary considerations, pretending we had an eternity together. There was hardly a second when our bodies weren't in contact. If we weren't busy in bed, we were cuddling on my couch, deep in conversation, trying to make up for lost time.

"Why did you become a potter?" Alix asked dreamily, kissing my ear.

"Because it rained one day."

"Where I come from, we called that a *non sequitur*."

"Oh, I bet you didn't."

"Well, all right," she admitted. "Back home, most folks would think we were discussing a shortage of glitter. But, then, they'd be one step ahead of me—I have no idea what we're talking about."

"*Thunderstorms*, Alix. Pay attention!"

She raised her arms to the heavens and rolled her eyes imploringly. The gesture had a distinctly negative impact on my comfort.

"Okay, okay, I'll behave," I promised, resettling myself against her softness. "I was an undergrad, majoring in art, but 'undecided about my area of concentration,' as my faculty advisor put it."

I shrugged a little. "I can't tell this story without sounding egocentric, Alix, but everything about art came easily to me. And whatever I tried I loved—each new experience was totally engrossing. That was almost more of a problem than a virtue. At one time or another, all my instructors had attempted to recruit me to their own disciplines but I just couldn't focus my attention on any single medium. Then one day during a ceramics workshop in my sophomore year, it rained."

Alix nodded sagely. "Of course. It all makes perfect sense now."

"Hush up," I said playfully. "So, we were all outside working on a massive wall of wet clay that had been erected between two pillars of a colonnade. In the midst of our amusement, a violent storm blew up. A lot of the students were frightened, and most went indoors. But we crazier types were having a terrific time. In the beginning, we were sheltered by the colonnade, and too… mmm…adrenalized, I guess…to be scared."

"Or too dumb?" Alix teased me.

"Well, maybe. Anyway, we just kept working through the storm, seeing what we could make of the clay. The wind grew unbelievably fierce—even under the roof, we got soaked by blowing spray. There was brilliant violet lightning against an immense bank of black clouds and the thunder that followed was deafening." I stopped for a moment, reliving it all, feeling the energy again.

"And then?" prompted Alix.

"And then some interior voice spoke quite clearly. I heard the words *Earth*, *Air*, *Fire*, *Water*—a list of the ancient elements.

It was strange, Alix, like an omen, like being told that this one discipline encompassed everything that mattered. I'm not at all mystical, but still it was an astonishing experience. At the very least it helped channel my energies. So that's why I became a potter."

I shifted my position so I could see her face. "Turnabout's fair play, you know. How come you're a musician?"

Alix looked startled by the question. She turned her palms upward, miming helplessness. "Unlike you, I never had a choice. Everything always turned to music in my head. Legend has it that I sang before I spoke. And I was that rarest of creatures, a child who wouldn't quit practicing piano till her parents threatened her."

"I really envy you that. Of all the skills I'd like to have, musical ability tops the list."

"Well, you know, it's perfectly useless."

I was shocked. "That's heresy! Music's *such* a gift. When you share it with people who lack the talent, it's priceless."

"Maybe so," she said, looking away. "I guess I was thinking of something else. So few musicians can support themselves with their art. Sometimes it seems pointless to have studied so hard. I could wish for your abilities in a concrete world."

"Stoneware, Alix. Stoneware."

"Lousy joke," she told me.

"Best I could do on short notice."

But a darker tone had seeped into our conversation and I wanted to change the mood. I lifted Alix's hand and matched it to one of mine. Hers was much smaller, of course, but the proportions were remarkably similar. We each had long, slender fingers—fingers that had been trained for the keyboard, for clay. Fingers that had developed the exquisite control demanded by those practices. Fingers that knew exactly what to do in every conceivable circumstance. Like this one. I licked each of her fingers in turn then opened my thighs to press her hand tight against me.

The rawness of my invitation ignited something primitive in Alix. Her response was faster, harder, more anonymous than anything that had gone before. Something less about romance or reverence than about tooth and claw and unmediated need. Something that left her mark on me—in every sense of the word.

When we came to rest, we were on the area rug in my living room and I couldn't even remember the transition from couch to floor. "Holy god, sweetheart," I breathed into her ear, "I won't worry about things getting dull around here!"

Her answering laugh could only be described as sultry. "I *told* you," Alix reminded me, "I like *everything*." Suddenly her hand was on me again, in me again—a powerful, possessive, persuasive hand. As I rolled helplessly in her arms, she whispered, "Were you paying attention to *me*, darling? *Were* you? Because I *also* told you that I never want this to end."

CHAPTER THIRTEEN

I woke early on Monday, feeling gloom gather in the pit of my stomach. I knew I had to seize control of my mood right away or depression would spoil our last day of freedom. I curled my body around Alix's warmth and began to nibble her neck. Half asleep, she sighed with pleasure, rolling to face me.

"Wake up, woman," I ordered. "We're going on a hike."

She blinked sleepy eyes and turned away. "Crazy person," she mumbled.

I yanked the pillow from under her head. Alix lunged for mine, stuffing it beneath her, smiling triumphantly. I just grinned back. "Now that I have your attention, I want you to visualize the woods. Birds! Trees! Sun! Sky!"

Alix hit me with my own pillow. Then, stretching slyly, she made a sweeping gesture. "Envision the bedroom: warmth, love, sex, sleep."

"Silly baby," I told her, "we can have *all that* in the woods." I grabbed her by the ankles and dragged her out of bed. She landed on the thick pile of the carpet with a muffled thump then leaped up, rubbing that sweet ass. I took off running. Alix chased me through my house till she found herself outside, naked in the light of dawn.

"Maniac!" she shouted, as I danced on dew-spangled grass.

* * *

Back in my bedroom after breakfast, Alix pulled a bra and underwear from her knapsack. I snatched those silky little nothings from her hand and tucked them back in the bag. She raised questioning eyes to me.

I smiled suggestively. "Why complicate matters, love?"

She sent a long, smoldering look in my direction before smoothing a T-shirt over her nude body. As she stepped into shorts, she said, "This hike's sounding better by the minute."

While Alix packed a simple lunch, I gathered knapsacks, blankets and binoculars. We set off hand-in-hand before the pink had faded from the sky, walking in that sensory state where the intellect seems scarcely to function and speech is an impediment to understanding. We pointed out each jay and squirrel, stopped to track the flight of every butterfly.

Summer was upon us now, all the trees in full leaf, with dense shadows beneath. Deep in the woods, we luxuriated in the cooler air. We helped each other over weathered boulders and giggled helplessly when a sapling gave way under my weight. I skidded down that steep slope, but Alix met me at the bottom and pulled me upright again. A metaphor, I hoped, for the rest of forever.

We crossed from the woods into a vast meadow on the floor of the valley. Wildflowers spangled the shade at the edge of the field then rioted in the sunlight. Of course there were waving patches of Queen Anne's lace, chicory, and brown-eyed Susans. But there were other less familiar flowers, plants that Mattie had long ago taught me to notice and appreciate. Their old-fashioned names unreeled in my mind, unbidden, unforgettable: crown vetch…heal-all…bird's foot trefoil…partridge pea… By the time we'd reached the outer edge of the meadow, I was so saturated with color and scent, light and shadow, I felt intoxicated.

On the far side of the valley, our meanderings led us to the abandoned quarry. All the workings of man had failed to defile this primal glory. Rather, the rock seemed to revel in exposure, its ancient strata inviting awe. Enchanted, Alix kicked off her boots and lay on her stomach, dropping pebbles into the clear depths of a broad reflecting pool. Supported on her elbows, bare toes waving in the air, she had a wild, elfin aspect that made my heart swell. I smoothed out a blanket and spread our spare meal. Then, collecting her cast-off boots, I beckoned my wood sprite to lunch.

Afterward, Alix rested her head in my lap while I stroked her glossy hair. She was looking beyond me through sun-struck leaves at the blue, blue sky. Completely absorbed, I examined every flickering shadow, every fleeting emotion that crossed her luminous face. When her gaze shifted to me, our eyes caught and held. Shaping my mouth to a phantom kiss, I felt her breath quicken.

I placed my index finger on her lower lip and she licked it lightly. With slow deliberation, I drew that finger downward, over her chin, along her throat, until I reached the neck of her shirt. Slipping inside, I met with unearthly softness. I flattened my hand then, rotating it until the up-thrusting firmness of her nipple traced tantalizing paths on my palm. Alix arched her back, pressing against me, moaning low in her throat. I slipped her shirt over her head and tossed it aside. The subtle modeling of her breasts overlay a prominent rib cage that sloped sharply to her waist. Awestruck, my hands came to a halt.

"Baby, baby," Alix begged, "don't stop now."

I ripped off my own clothing and rolled it into a pillow. As I tucked it under her head, Alix pulled my face to hers, sharp little bites melting into an eternal kiss. I ran both hands over her torso until I found her waist. Then I stripped off those shorts in one quick motion. Totally still, she lay like a miracle in the sunlight.

Raising her hips, I slid my knees beneath them then sat back on my heels. Alix lifted her legs to my shoulders, urging me toward the loveliness between her thighs. Those dark eyes closed as my tongue found her, and I wondered whether I could survive that onslaught of sensation.

When the ripple that began at my lips stopped radiating through Alix's surging body, I lowered her slowly to the blanket. Only dimly aware that she called my name again and again, I rested my cheek on her sleek thigh. I think I wept.

"My darling, my darling," Alix cried, "let me hold you!"

I flung myself alongside her and she took my face in her hands, kissing me with a drowsy earnestness. Then, quite suddenly, she sat and swung one leg across my waist. She was facing away from me, the perfect punctuation of her spine tempting my hand. When she leaned forward, she was completely exposed. My hips rose in response and I stretched out a thumb to caress her.

"Don't distract me, Lynn. I want to concentrate on you."

But I couldn't help myself. I pulled her down to my lips and began once more. At length, she collapsed atop me, laughing.

"I see you can't be trusted," she said. "I'll have to try a new approach."

"Oh, please, Alix—stay there. I love this so much!" Without answering, she bent her mouth to me, sketching indelible lines, promising, promising. I thrust toward her, vibrating, shaken to the core. Strong hands held me almost immobile, her tongue flickering until I felt I might go mad. Then, with a final rush, that delicious tremor began in my thighs, traveling upward with heightening intensity.

The sun traced its endless arc across the sky, and still we lay in one another's arms, too spent to stand. I wasn't sure how we'd manage the long trek home. But it was hard to care when we were so at ease right where we were. Alix trailed lazy kisses across my face then laughed softly. "Contrary to popular opinion," she pronounced, "women smell wonderful."

"Amen, sister," I affirmed, returning those kisses. "You heard it here first."

* * *

Back at my house, we showered together, soaping each other, hugging in the steamy spray. But a quality of desperation had crept into our play as dusk overtook daylight. Soon Charles and the children would return.

In my kitchen we prepared dinner, our actions interweaving in the effortless way that women have. After our day in the woods, we had reason for hunger, but neither of us ate well. Our eyes kept meeting, then glancing away. Our smiles—tremulous, half-formed things—quickly faded out of existence.

At last, we could no longer fend off reality. We were huddled on the couch when Alix murmured, "I can't believe this is almost over." The finality of her words was devastating. I'd been naïve to hope for more.

Dropping my head back against the cushions, I felt tears etch my cheeks and pool in my ears. "I love you, Alix," was all I could manage.

"Where do we go from here?" she whispered, burrowing her face into my shoulder.

"Sweetheart, only you can answer that question."

"Why me?" she asked forlornly.

I lifted her chin and made her meet my eyes. "You *know* why, Alix. You're the one with a husband and family. If it weren't for them, I'd say we'd be morons to turn our backs on this."

I sat upright, wiping away warm tears. "This weekend has meant so much to me that I don't know how I'll watch you walk out my door tonight. But how can I ask you to stay?"

"Oh, ask me, Lynn! At least ask me!" Alix breathed.

"I'm here, darling. I'm available. I won't run from you anymore. But you're the one who calls the shots."

Alix raised my hand to her lips and held it there, considering. Her eyes were focused on something long past. "You don't know very much about Charles and me," she said quietly. "There's a lot I need to explain, although that's not how I intend to use the rest of this evening. Let's just say there have been times when

I've contemplated divorce—it's not a new idea. But I'm not sure I'm ready for it."

She swallowed hard and lowered her head again. "I can't ask you this. It's right out of a trashy movie…"

"There's nothing you can't ask, Alix."

She covered her eyes with laced fingers. "Lynn, I love you. I want to be with you. But I need a chance to sort this out…My children…A job that pays our way…So many things I haven't figured out yet…"

"And in the meantime?"

"Would you still see me? Could we be together as much as possible? Can you *stand* it?"

I knew what she was asking. She was a long way from a decision. I'd be agreeing to accept whatever spare moments her family life allowed. I made myself visualize Alix in bed with Charles, and an agonizing fist clenched around my heart. I knew how it felt to wait alone while the woman I loved was with someone else.

Later, when I'd had time to analyze it, I realized that my response was both the safest and the most dangerous one possible. But just then, I had only one conscious thought—if I could be tough enough, I could keep the dream of Alix a little longer. There was caution in my voice as I answered. "For a while, Alix. We'll give it a try." I gathered her into my arms, overflowing with bittersweet yearning. "Call me tomorrow if you change your mind."

Alix pushed me back against the cushions and kissed me till I was breathless. Sliding electric hands under my shirt, she said, "I'll call you, sweetheart, but I won't change my mind."

CHAPTER FOURTEEN

Damn it all to hell, Mattie!

Why don't you have a phone? I'm desperate to talk with you, but you won't even receive this letter for days! Get in touch when you do, okay?

You've probably seen this coming in recent communiqués—or anytime now you'll learn it from some unprincipled gossipmonger. So hear my confession first: I've committed an offense against the sisterhood and only you can grant me absolution. *Mea culpa, mea culpa*—I've fallen in love with a straight woman. And not just *any* straight woman. Oh, no—*I* had to pick Alix Dunnevan, a state official's wife!

Even more remarkable, she's responded in kind. As you might guess, few of my friends are sympathetic. In fact, they think I'm downright crazy. And if I weren't so fucking happy—and so happy fucking—I might be more inclined to share their opinion. Or at least some of their well-founded alarm. But you know me, stubborn, willful woman that I am.

And I know you. You'll love Alix. If it's okay, I want to bring her to meet you sometime soon—and maybe her children as well. *Yes*. There are children. I know, I *know*. But if there's anyone who can believe in us and support us, you're that person, Mattie.

Let me tell you briefly: Alix is the musician I've mentioned from time to time. We've been lovers for almost three months and it just keeps getting better. Quit laughing—this is truth, not hyperbole! After endless agonizing, we've come to believe that we can make a go of things, but getting out with the children will be a challenge.

The husband, a pretty self-absorbed type, has traveled a lot this summer, so we've been able to really explore feelings and possibilities. We're very certain of our commitment, but we're rapidly approaching the moment when we'll have to tell Charles about the situation. Alix thinks he'll handle it fairly well. I have my doubts.

It all sounds workable on the surface, but you know married ladies. They have to suppress so much that it becomes automatic. I've gotten some conflicting information about Charles from Alix. Add that to my personal observations (pretty negative) and I conclude that this will be rough. Alix is determined to be totally upfront about our relationship. First because she's honest to a fault, and second because she's convinced that will protect us from blowback in the future. But I fear she may have miscalculated both the depth of her stored anger and the extremity of Charles's reaction. I certainly don't expect him to respond with perfect equanimity. Especially given his public position. But I've hardly ever been so willing to be wrong.

Does it sound like I regret finding myself in this place and time? When you meet Alix, you won't wonder at my foolhardy behavior. And I *do* want you to meet one another very soon.

Please let me know whether the four of us could descend on you without prior notice—we may well need an escape route.

Thank you, dear friend.

Love always,
Lynn

More than a week passed before the USPS delivered Mattie's reply. As usual, her economical script adorned the reverse of some previously-used paper. Over the years, Mattie has sent me words of warmth, wisdom and comfort on grocery store tapes, expired library cards and shoe repair tickets. I've kept them all—there's quite a collection now—and I've thought more than once that they'd form the foundation of a great collage series. Today's note was nearly indecipherable. With singular brevity, on the translucent tissue of someone else's charge card receipt, she'd offered us sanctuary: Love you no matter what and trust your judgment absolutely. The more the merrier—Mattie

I held the crackling lifeline in shaking hands and admitted my relief. For a second, my eyes blurred with grateful tears. Then, putting paranoia behind me, I flipped the receipt over to examine the original notations. God only knew how she'd come by this one. Two years earlier, someone named Agatha B. Falkenberry had charged a rotary tiller at a hardware store in the town nearest Mattie.

I held the crumpled receipt to my heart. "Oh, Agatha B.," I declared aloud, "you may yet achieve immortality through the medium of collage!" After posting the note on the mirror in the foyer where Alix would see it first thing, I went into the kitchen to chop vegetables for a chef's salad.

I was on my porch admiring the sunset when Alix pulled into the driveway. She looked splendid. I had to whistle at the white halter top against her smooth, tan skin. Patting the step, I motioned for her to sit beside me while I finished with the brilliant sky. We were comfortable just then, but soon mosquitoes would be out in full force. Before the light died away, Alix took me by the hand and heaved me to my feet.

"Come on, lazy," she said. "Feed me."

So we went through the screen door and got to work. While I mixed salad dressing, Alix put music on the stereo then set the table. My heart filled with joy as I watched her moving through my house. I cherished this everyday marvel—mundane tasks, counterpointed by casual conversation. To secure it forever, I thought, I'd walk the length and breadth of hell itself. Suddenly I realized how unlikely our luck had been this summer—how quickly it could change. Perhaps I felt a chill of premonition.

"How was your day?" I called into the dining room. "Did you get the girls off to your mom's on time?"

"It was hot and hectic," Alix answered, coming to the kitchen doorway. "It's no joke packing two kids for a visit with grandma. The girls wanted to take everything they own—including the goldfish—and my mother was willing to let them. The woman has *no* common sense!" Alix threw a challenging look in my direction. "You're sure you want to buy into this ready-made family stuff?"

I crossed the room and pulled her to me, tingling from head to toe as my hands slid over her bare back. "Are *you* part of the package?"

"Just an optional accessory for the discriminating customer."

"Can you guarantee immediate delivery?"

"Yes," she grinned wickedly, "but the salad will wilt."

I pushed her away in mock horror. "Heaven forefend!" I cried, returning to my recipe.

Alix was checking her hair in the mirror when I set a basket of hot rolls on the table. As I passed by the foyer, Mattie's message caught my eye. "Oh, yeah, Alix—did you read that note?"

She brought it to the table with her. "Am I supposed to be able to decode this?" she asked, unfolding her napkin.

"Only if you know Mattie. It's actually an invitation in response to a letter of mine. She wants to meet you and the girls."

Alix stopped buttering a roll to say, "You've mentioned Mattie before, but I don't have a very clear picture of how she fits into your life. I gather that she's extremely important to you?" A raised eyebrow accented the question.

"And she will be to you, darling. Mattie's like that. I'm almost afraid to introduce you two. Among other things, you have music in common."

"And *you*?" A whisper, really.

"Yes, Alix," I acknowledged. "And me. A very long time ago."

"And now?"

"Now she's my second favorite person on the face of the earth."

Alix looked into my eyes and caught confidence from my unwavering gaze. She relaxed and turned her attention to the salad, eating with real appetite. I put down my fork and leaned a cheek on one hand, watching her. Since we'd become lovers, Alix had lost that haunted look and gained back a little weight. She had the supple slenderness of something untamed and healthy—a gazelle, maybe. I felt giddy with pride and pleasure.

"Quit staring at me and eat, weirdo," she commanded, threatening me with a spoon.

Laughing, I picked up my fork again. Dinner was wonderful that night, but dessert would be even better.

CHAPTER FIFTEEN

Trimming the bottom of a ceramic bowl is an act of faith. When first thrown, the vessel rises from a thick mass of clay. After it dries slightly, the bowl is cut free from a thick plaster disk—the bat—and repositioned upside down. Then the excess clay can be carved away, leaving only a small base for support. To blindly duplicate the interior curve of the bowl, a potter depends on memory, intuition and experience. Miscalculation results in ruin—a gash that wrecks everything, or a graceless resolution of form.

Hunched over my wheel, I was trying to concentrate on that routine drama. The challenge was to ignore the silent telephone. Because I'd lose an entire week's work if I couldn't totally immerse myself in the process of trimming this series of bowls. At the end of the day, there'd be more than scrap dissolving in my slurry bucket.

I devoted as much time as I could to the task, purposely extending the finish work. Rather than shaping a low foot on the bowls as they spun on my wheel, I carved them all to naked domes. Then I attached a fat coil of clay to the bottom of each one, producing a new throwing surface. Revving the motor of my electric wheel, I worked that coil into a tall, sculptural column just wide enough at its base to support the extravagant flare of the bowl.

Nice work! I congratulated myself, as I made every pot more daring than the one before. But no matter how deeply involved I got, my attention reverted to Alix as soon as I completed a piece and set it aside to dry.

The night before, we'd agreed it was time for her to discuss our relationship, our plans, with Charles. Alix hoped to confine any unpleasantness to the period that her children were away. If her faith in Charles were justified, the worst would be over before Beth and Cindy returned from their visit to Belmont.

To say I found this scenario optimistic would be an understatement. Even so, I was unprepared for the fury that was about to erupt. I'd been beguiled by Alix's confidence in Charles, and dumb enough to doubt my own perceptions.

When my phone finally rang that afternoon, I was shocked by the stress in Alix's voice. She sounded drained of any faith or feeling. Charles had scraped through her shell of certainty, thinning it dangerously, ripping a gaping hole in her confidence. I knew I had to see her, hold her, hide her, or go mad. "Come here now!" I ordered.

"I can't meet you today," Alix said dully. "Things are too unstable over here."

"When then?" I asked frantically.

"As soon as I can," she told me. Then she hung up.

Devastated, infuriated, I stumbled back into my studio and stared at the long line of elaborate bowls I'd just completed. They were still upside down on those heavy plaster bats, where they'd remain until dry enough to fire. Their wholeness, their perfection, seemed to mock me.

One by one, I raised each disk above my head and hurled it to the concrete floor. The soft bowls collapsed upon themselves, shattered bats settling at mad angles atop the formless heaps of clay. They hadn't made nearly enough noise.

My sense of frenzy and entrapment was so intense I had to flee. Tearing out the door, I roared toward home in my car. Nothing mattered as much as finding a place to scream. Later I would remember that I'd left the shop unlocked. Luckily, I was the only vandal there that day.

* * *

Twenty-six agonizing hours passed before I saw Alix again. She entered my shop unannounced, flipped the *Closed* sign to the outside and pulled me into the studio. The instant we were out of sight, I swept her into my arms, noticing how frail and vulnerable she felt. She released me, dropped her knapsack on the wedging table and removed her sunglasses. There was such an aura of abuse about her that I was relieved she wasn't black and blue. A woman who'd wrestled with grief, and lost, would look like this, I thought.

"My god, Alix," I cried, kissing her swollen eyes, "is it that bad?"

"Worse," she choked out. "Thank god the girls are away."

"When did you last eat?"

She considered carefully, an obedient child pondering a difficult question. "Salad at your house," she said finally.

"And sleep?"

"What's that?" she asked, aiming for humor, and missing.

"Can you stay with me for a while?"

Alix nodded jerkily. "He's out of town overnight. Some hush-hush political meeting. It almost killed him to go—he knew I'd come straight to you."

This time I remembered to lock up the shop. Thinking fast, I decided not to leave Alix's car parked out front. I settled her in the bucket seat as carefully as if she were an invalid and found the keys in her bag. Her hand lay unresponsive in mine as I drove toward home.

My house was hot and stuffy. Alix stood motionless in the foyer while I closed every window, then turned on the AC. Appalled by her passivity, I slipped an arm around her waist to guide her upstairs. As bathwater ran, I set out fresh towels and undressed her. Alix made no move to participate. Cooperation seemed beyond her. When I helped her into the water, she reclined passively against the cold, sloping back of the tub.

"Try to relax, darling," I said, though she looked catatonic. "I'm going downstairs to warm some soup. I'll be right back."

I was climbing the steps, balancing a tray, when I heard the bathwater draining. Alix lay on my bed, a damp towel draping her nude body. I made her sit and slipped a thin caftan over her head. Then I propped pillows behind her and set the tray across her lap. Breaking open a muffin, I spread it with strawberry preserves.

"Eat something," I encouraged her, so she picked up the spoon. She managed to finish most of the soup, but swallowing the muffin was beyond her. When she pushed the bowl aside, I lowered the tray to the floor and lay down beside her. Alix rested her head on my shoulder as I rocked her a little in my arms.

"The soup was good," she told me. "I feel a lot better."

"Don't talk, baby. I want you to sleep now."

I held Alix until she was breathing slowly then tiptoed out and left her in peace. For the next four hours, I struggled to make sense of an experimental novel, but my thoughts were more fragmented than the plot. I'd set the book aside and was simply trying to endure when my bedroom door creaked open. Alix came downstairs, still shaky, but looking less like a zombie. I called her to me and she stretched out on the couch, head in my lap.

"Thanks for taking care of me, Lynn. I really needed the rest. I'm sorry I couldn't talk before."

"Talk can wait," I said, trailing my fingers across her forehead.

"No," she insisted. "There's so much to tell, and you must have been out of your mind with worry."

"I've had some hard moments," I admitted.

Alix looked troubled. "Poor baby—I'm not sure I'm worth all the pain I've caused you."

"I'm the final authority on that," I said. "Tell me what happened after you left here Saturday."

She pressed her temples as she organized her thoughts. "I went to bed early, but I couldn't sleep that night. I lay awake for hours trying to compose myself for the next day. Sunday morning, I told Charles I needed to talk about something important. He looked annoyed, but he agreed in that very patient voice of his—maybe you haven't been around him enough to know what I mean."

No, but I'd lived with Sarah for seven years. I said, "I know exactly what you mean."

"Well, anyway, he had some preparation to do for the meeting he's attending tonight. He granted me an audience, *provided* we could conclude the conversation in time for his golf date."

First-class control freak, I thought to myself.

Alix sighed wearily and licked dry lips. "Waiting made me pretty nervous, but I figured I could handle the situation. A couple hours later, Charles came into the living room and sat down. I could see him checking his watch, hoping he could wrap things up quickly and still make it to his club." She laughed weakly. "Maybe I should be grateful that he didn't bash my head in with a nine iron."

"Not funny, Alix."

"Oh, but quite possibly preferable, my dear. I'd tried to structure the discussion so Charles would be prepared when I got to the real news. I began by reminding him that I'd been unhappy for years, that I'd asked him to make some changes and that he'd been unwilling to respond to my needs. He did a fair imitation of listening judiciously, but I knew that behind the mask he was thinking, 'Same old, same old.' And then I told him I wanted a divorce. He just kept nodding in that distracted fashion for a minute, until the word caught up with him. There must have been something determined in my tone, because his face went white and his voice turned icy."

"What did he say?"

"One word—no."

I was exasperated. "What was *that* supposed to mean?"

"I don't know, Lynn. Some gut reaction, I guess. He was so tense that I knew I was in trouble, but I thought it would be better to tell him everything all at once, so I went on."

Alix closed her eyes. Her voice fell into a low, monotonous pattern. "I told him that I expected custody of the children and a fair division of our property. I knew he wasn't keeping pace with me—he was all bound up in wounded pride. So naturally the first question he asked was the one I'd been dreading."

"'Is there someone else?'" I anticipated, rolling my eyes.

"Yes. So I told him about us." Tears welled from under her closed lids, highlighting the curve of her cheeks. "At first he just laughed, Lynn. Then it got ugly. He yelled that he'd see me dead before I exposed the girls to 'this kind of perversion.' He said he'd use every legal technicality, and all the political clout he has, to keep me away from the children."

"He *can't*, sweetheart, he *can't*," I promised her through gritted teeth.

Alix waved a dismissive hand. "Finally, he seemed to calm down a bit. He put his arms around me and started to stroke my hair—I could hardly believe it. He told me we had a 'wonderful marriage,' and said that I was just 'momentarily confused.'"

"And then?"

Alix gulped. "Then he suggested that I should be hospitalized for a while. He said I needed help, but might be too 'disturbed' for outpatient care."

"He *what*?" I shouted.

Alix covered her face with both hands. "He told me I needed professional help as soon as possible—said he'd ask my father to arrange treatment at BelMed right away."

"My god, what's he got in mind? A little electroshock, followed by a light lobotomy?"

"Just a series of shots," she joked feebly. "I told Charles I wasn't sick, except sick and tired of the marriage. He was like a broken record. He kept telling me how special our relationship had been until a few months ago."

"When I cast an evil spell on you, I presume."

"Probably. I told him that he hadn't been paying attention. But he just kept hammering away. I had to bite back everything

I wanted to say, had to keep my cool so I didn't look as deranged as he said I was. Ultimately, Charles said he wouldn't insist on immediate hospitalization, if I'd agree to 'therapeutic intervention' before beginning divorce proceedings."

My face was frozen, immobilized by shock and horror. Alix pressed my hand to her cheek. "I was *so scared*, Lynn, I said yes. Otherwise, he really would have had me committed."

"Scared" didn't do the situation justice. She was terrified. Genuinely frightened of her husband and father in a way that I'd never feared anyone. "When you get right down to it, baby," I said soothingly, "your dad's *got* to back you, doesn't he?"

"Like your dad's there for you, Lynn?" she said pointedly.

I thought about the man who was nothing but a fading photo in a family album, the father I hadn't seen since my toddler days. "But *your* dad raised you. He knows you. He *has* to put you first."

Alix shook her head vehemently. "You haven't met him. You haven't seen my father and Charles in action. It's weird the way they reinforce and amplify one another—the whole is greater than the sum of its parts."

"Hold me, honey," I said. Alix sat and we clung together, seeking elusive comforts. At the same time I was trying to reassure her, part of me was hysterical with self-loathing. In the whole range of reactions I'd tried to anticipate, this brisk, efficient disposal of Alix had never occurred to me. Through selfishness and stupidity, I'd jeopardized the safety of a woman I claimed to love. I'd courted this danger as surely as I'd courted Alix, knowing—as she couldn't—how vicious the game might become.

"We've got to talk with a lawyer tomorrow morning."

"I can't do that, Lynn. I promised to see a therapist first, and I will."

"Jesus Christ, Alix! You don't have to honor an agreement made under duress."

"Oh, yes I do! Don't you understand? If I'm not a good little girl, Charles and my father will find some nice legal way to punish me. Meeting with a counselor will give me space to plan my next move. And in the meantime, Charles may relax a little."

"Better he should die of apoplexy!" I spat out. "Damn it, Alix! Going for therapy is like admitting you're unsure about our relationship!"

She looked trapped. "What choice do I have?" she asked. "Besides, as long as you and I are secure about this, Lynn, we can cope with the farce."

I backed off. "Okay. You're undoubtedly right, sweetheart. Now…where's this counselor going to come from?"

"Charles knows a man—" began Alix.

I held up a hand to interrupt her. "Oh, no! Charles is *not* going to feed you to some hand picked Freudian who'll tell you how infantile you are, then jack off thinking about us in bed."

Nodding thoughtfully, Alix said, "Seems only fair that I should get to choose my own headshrinker. For 'good rapport,' and all that."

"Right," I agreed. After a moment of reflection, I made up my mind about something. "When will Mr. Wonderful return?"

"Late tomorrow night, he said."

"Hallelujah! A *fait accompli*! By the time Charles gets home, you'll have scheduled an appointment with a feminist counselor. I think that's one thing we can ram down his throat."

"Do you know someone?" Alix asked.

"I know someone who knows someone—I'll check it out tomorrow morning," was all I'd say. "Come on, darling. Let's go to bed."

We'd hardly settled between the sheets before Alix fell asleep again. I didn't know whether she was still exhausted, or simply needed to escape. Maybe both. But I couldn't relax. Hour after hour, I watched moonlight cycle slowly through shuttered windows. At last the room was dark and my frenzied thoughts had lost some momentum. I drifted in and out of fitful slumber. Every time I woke, I checked on Alix, but she slept soundly, undisturbed by my restlessness.

After breakfast she drove me to town and said goodbye in a quavery voice. Then she merged into traffic and disappeared from sight. I hovered on the sidewalk outside my shop, vacillating.

I could phone in advance, or just drop in unannounced on an old friend.

"Better to ask forgiveness than permission," I said aloud. Unlocking the car door, I braced myself to face yesterday's stale heat.

CHAPTER SIXTEEN

The general public has a misguided notion about the gentility of academic life. All those British movies have brainwashed us, I suppose. Arcross University, a St. Louis institution, boasted none of the cinematic amenities. No marble staircases or leaded glass windows or carved wooden wainscoting. Despite the school's national reputation, a staggering endowment and daunting tuition, the faculty offices were a labyrinth of flimsy drywall partitions. Overlapping waves of sound—telephones, typewriters, ponderous male voices—provided the only real privacy.

I'd never been to this high-rise campus, so the Arts and Sciences building held no memories for me. On the tenth floor, I followed the complicated directions provided by a secretary in the dean's office. At last I made the final turn and found myself confronting a hollow-core door sporting a black plastic nameplate:

Sarah J. Forrester
Associate Professor

If I'd been able to inhale, I'd have taken a deep breath before knocking. The answering voice was still the same—low, intriguing and slightly imperious. It was worth the trip just to see Sarah's face when I crossed her threshold.

She was seated, slender ankles propped on the open drawer of a file cabinet. Though the posture wasn't conducive to swift upward movement, Sarah shot out of her seat. Papers spilled from her lap and tepid coffee sloshed over the rim of the mug she was holding. A mug *I'd* made for her.

She didn't even curse at the dark stain spreading over light blue linen, which told me a lot. Her dress was trashed, and Sarah would hate having to teach in it. Still, she pretended indifference to the damage—a gesture as precious as a well-chosen gift.

"Hi," I said brightly.

"Lynn!" she cried. "How are you? It's been too long!"

"Just long *enough*," I countered.

We still had some shorthand between us—she understood what I meant. "I'm glad to hear that," Sarah said warmly.

Despite her friendly greeting, I could tell she intended to wait me out. She didn't know why I'd come, and was determined that I'd make the first move. I took advantage of the pause to sort out my emotions.

I knew everything about this woman. I knew the kind of restaurant she enjoyed, the wines she'd order there. I could predict who she'd vote for, and why. I knew there was no label at the neck of that dress—Sarah's skin was hypersensitive and she'd have cut it out first thing. I knew she despised country music and looked down on those who didn't. Knew she was a natural blonde. Knew she'd once been a smoker and would yearn for a cigarette until she died. I knew she was fearsomely competitive. In a tennis match, her second serve was deadly and I'd seen her hurl a racquet in rare moments of defeat. I remembered—would *always* remember—what she liked in bed. I knew every single thing about Sarah Jane Forrester, except why she'd left me.

But insulated by the passage of time—not to mention my infatuation with Alix—I could see her almost objectively. Sarah's designer haircut and country club clothes sent a shock wave of wonderment through me. What in *hell* had we been doing with each other? How had such an unlikely pair lasted seven years? What outrageous compromises had we each made to keep our relationship intact for so long?

For the first time, I understood that she'd never belonged at the small community college where she'd taught until we broke up. She fit in at this urban school, with its high profile and rigorous admission standards. Suddenly, I felt good for her, the way you can when luck strikes someone very dear.

I looked around her workspace. "So this is the real deal."

"Yes," she confirmed. "It's worked out well."

"Got a brand-new crop of DFs, I'll bet." Devoted Fans—those hungry, big-eyed undergrads who recorded her witticisms in their journals and slid maudlin poetry under her office door.

"More than ever," Sarah groaned. "It's the one drawback to a larger student body." Gesturing at a chair buried under stacks of student papers and publishers' brochures, she said, "I'll clear this if you can stay a while."

I could see the wheels turning, could feel her trying to figure out why I'd reentered her life without warning. Time to show a little mercy. "Actually, Sarah, I need a favor, so I came to invite you and Greer to lunch." I said it as casually as I could, though it wasn't casual at all.

Her eyes widened and a slow smile lit that familiar face. "Greer won't be free for forty-five minutes, but I'll call her as soon as her seminar ends."

"That's doable."

Sarah touched my arm tentatively. "She's wanted to get to know you, Lynn…Somehow she's gotten the idea that you're pretty special."

I cocked my head at the tribute, then said, "I've missed you, Sarah." And while I meant it sincerely, it didn't hurt anymore. I waved in the direction of her desk, thinking we could each use some time to regroup. "Look, you're working and I want to check out the campus bookstore. I'll be back in an hour, okay?"

Sarah nodded and I sensed her relief. Whatever was coming, she'd have backup when we met for lunch. As I let myself out of her office, she was blotting vainly at the stain on her dress, aware that it was already much too late.

In the bookstore, I browsed the fiction racks, picking up several novels I thought Alix might enjoy. Checking my watch, I saw I still had time to kill. A perky cashier gave me directions to the nearest snack bar where I drank a cup of chamomile tea, hoping to settle my nerves. Because I was tired to the bone after a night of broken sleep—hardly ideal, given the stressful encounter that lay ahead. Just before rejoining Sarah, I stopped in a restroom to assess the damage.

Something primal rose up in me as I studied myself in the mirror, a feeling I couldn't label. It might have been insecurity. Or a profound sense of inadequacy—after all, *I* was the person who hadn't measured up for Sarah. And very soon I'd be face-to-face with the woman who'd bested me in a contest that once had seemed a matter of life and death. Setting my bags on the Formica counter, I ran cool water over my wrists.

Then I called up a hazy memory of Greer's austere appearance and compared it to my own reflection—wounded green eyes under dark, level brows. Tense mouth, no slightest trace of a smile. That fringe of red-gold bangs. I reached back, found my braid and worked an elastic band off the end. After I shook out the plaiting, I began to brush. I didn't stop till my hair hung around me like a shield of burnished bronze. *For contrast*, I told myself. But maybe what I really meant was *for courage*.

When I returned to Sarah's office, her eyes flickered over me, noting the change. She made no comment, but she didn't need to. She knew me as well as I knew her, knew every quirk and nervous habit, could deduce my state of mind with a single glance. I might as well have stripped naked in front of her. Again.

After she locked up, we cut across a broad quadrangle on our way to join her lover. I'd be lying if I said that wasn't an awkward, self-conscious trek. Neither of us spoke until we entered the Social Sciences building. In the elevator, Sarah pushed a button, but all she could say was, "Fifth floor."

My heart was thumping as we walked through Greer's doorway. She was talking on the phone, so she motioned us toward a pair of chairs. Her office, somewhat larger than

Sarah's, was considerably less cluttered. Calm and order had been imposed on this space—and no one, I thought, would dare disrupt it. The only break in its calculated neutrality was a bold, framed serigraph on one wall. I veered away from Sarah to check it out: an abstract design, all saturated color and twisted geometry. Fine work. I moved close enough to read the title: *A Good Defense Mechanism is Hard to Find*. Amen! I thought, and finally felt a smile break through. Best of all, I'd avoided rubbing elbows with my former partner.

"I love the print," I said as soon as Greer greeted us.

"Isn't it great? A gift from one of my former students. She thought it was perfect for a psychologist's office—and she was right. It's provided some comic relief over the years."

We'd been examining one another as we spoke. I couldn't deny that I found Greer's colorless, cultivated masculinity off-putting, couldn't understand why circumspect Sarah had been attracted to her. For my own part, I'd always loved being female, had always been drawn to an earthy femininity that Greer not only lacked, but appeared to reject.

Now, though, I could see something beyond her choice of clothing and haircut. There was that phenomenal intellect, of course. But there was also vitality in Greer's aging face, a hint that those crows' feet had been acquired through a lot of laughter. And the eyes themselves were disarming—they seemed to understand and accept me at the deepest levels of my being. Maybe I'd never fully relax with this woman, but I might come to value her uncompromising spirit.

"I can't thank you guys enough for letting me barge in on you," I said. My smile was broader, genuine, and included them both. "Lunch is on me, but you'll have to pick the place. I don't know this part of the city very well."

The restaurant they chose was small and friendly, the sandwiches there excellent. As we ate, I explained enough about Alix to allay any fears regarding my unexpected intrusion into their lives. Once Sarah and Greer knew that I was otherwise engaged, they could afford to sympathize with my appeal. But I waited until we'd finished lunch and achieved a degree of ease before I asked my favor.

"What I really need, Greer, is a referral to a feminist therapist. And—knowing Sarah—I was sure your recommendation would be right on target."

Greer actually grinned. "I'm happy to help and so glad you took the risk. This afternoon's been beneficial for *us* too." Reaching for Sarah's hand, she said, "I think we might be able to put certain guilty feelings to rest at last."

I met Greer's eyes directly and nodded. "Do that."

* * *

The station wagon was sweltering when I unlocked it to leave for home. I turned on the AC, but drove the first mile with my windows down, trying to clear hot air from the car. The inrushing breeze blew hair about my face, sparking a sudden thought: for Alix, loose hair signified romance and seduction. When I told her about visiting Sarah, I didn't want to arouse a single fear about my intentions. Pulling off the road, I fumbled in my bag for my hairbrush. In a matter of moments, I'd woven a new braid and steered back onto the highway.

As I drove, I thought about my adventures since we'd parted that morning. It was a relief to have broken the ice with Sarah and Greer—but infuriating to have been forced into the interaction by Dunnevan's power play. I patted my pocket and heard a reassuring crackle. I'd secured a list of feminist counselors for Alix, so the benefits of my excursion definitely outweighed the stresses.

Every mile that brought me closer to home lightened my mood. Because surely any expert worth her salt would see at first glance that Alix didn't need therapy. And once she'd satisfied her husband's absurd demand, we'd finally be able to move forward. Together.

Alix was sitting on the porch swing when I got home. She looked a little better, not quite so pale, but still seemed listless.

"Did you get more sleep, darling?"

"Hours and hours," she assured me.

"Eat anything?"

"Some leftover soup. An apple."

"Great," I said, wishing she'd had more. Charles certainly wasn't going to worry about her diet. I handed over the weighty sack from the university bookstore. "Brought you some presents."

Alix considered the Arcross logo on that slick plastic bag, obviously mystified. Then she examined the spines of the books, and thanked me warmly. But her attention was plainly elsewhere. Stacking the novels beside her, she said, "First, an update."

I tapped the sack from the bookstore and began. "I went to see Sarah today, Alix."

Her head jerked slightly and she stiffened under my hand. "Why *Sarah*?" she whispered.

"Because her lover heads the psychology department at their university. I was pretty sure Greer could give me the name of a reputable therapist. So I dropped in on Sarah this morning then took the two of them to lunch."

Alix could guess what that might have cost me. She made a rapid emotional adjustment, setting aside her own vulnerabilities to inquire about mine. "Are you okay, Lynn?"

I pressed her hand to my lips. "Better than ever, baby, but thanks for asking. Seeing Sarah just made me realize how much I love *you*."

Alix closed her eyes for an instant, then shot me a grateful smile. "So tell me," she said.

I sketched in the background lightly, but I knew she needed information about the therapist more than anything. "Greer wouldn't give me just one name, hon. She said she didn't want that kind of responsibility. So she made a list of women with good reputations. She was positive one of them would be right for you."

We pored over Greer's notations. She'd indicated which counselor was most expensive, whose approach was more confrontational, who was qualified to administer medication, and so on.

"Not that one," Alix said definitively, crossing out a name. "I don't need any drugs."

We talked on, circling the problem warily. Finally Alix sighed, "I feel like I'm flying blind."

"I know, love. It's pretty scary."

"After all," she pointed out, "I don't even *want* to see a counselor."

How do you make a decision like that anyway? Especially when you're so pressed for time that you can't interview the therapists, compare their answers, debate the pros and cons? In the end, we just dialed some of the phone numbers. One psychologist was on vacation. Another wasn't accepting new patients. Emilie Harrold, the last on the list, had two openings late in the week. Alix scheduled an appointment for Friday. Then she had to leave me.

At home, Charles would be waiting.

CHAPTER SEVENTEEN

I didn't know how I'd get through the rest of that week. My only goal was to pass time until Alix met with the therapist. I was counting on a miracle from the woman, some brilliant solution to Charles's trap no layperson could imagine or devise. Failing that, I believed we were dead in the water.

Dunnevan had rearranged his packed schedule to spend a few days with Alix. She was virtually under house arrest. I had almost no contact with her. My stomach was continuously in knots, and anytime I came up for air in the studio, my heart raced wildly.

I passed time by replenishing my supply of mugs and small planters. Those I could throw on automatic pilot. Once I got started, the work claimed me, as it nearly always does. I challenged myself to invent new glaze combinations—near misses wouldn't be so costly on the little items I was cranking out. But I was just messing around, and I knew it. The sustained concentration necessary for more inventive, more satisfying pieces was utterly beyond my reach.

On Wednesday, taking advantage of a moment when her husband had dashed to the supermarket, Alix phoned me. But our conversation was frustratingly disjointed. I learned only that Dunnevan was still behaving erratically. One moment, he'd threaten and ridicule her, the next he'd grow nostalgic about their shared past. I began to think that *Charles*, not *Alix*, should keep the therapy date on Friday.

Late Thursday night, the telephone woke me from a troubled sleep. Alix was on the line, whispering, yet clearly frantic. "Can you hear me, Lynn? I'm afraid to talk louder."

"I can hear you, baby. What's wrong—are you okay?"

"I'm all right physically, but something's happened. Oh, Lynn, I need to be with you so much."

"Come over, darling. Or meet me somewhere. *Please*. I can't keep dealing with this long distance."

There was a heavy silence before Alix said, "I'll try to come, but I'm scared. If I'm not at your house in half an hour, you'll know that Charles woke up and stopped me."

"Just hurry, love—but be careful."

I grabbed a robe and pulled it on, then shuffled into flip-flops. Splashing cold water on my face made me feel more alert. But bright light would be an unbearable assault on my aching eyes. I felt my way through the shadowed house, down the creaking stairs. In the living room, I lit several candles and sank onto the couch, wondering what the hell Charles was up to now.

Almost before her car screeched to a halt in my driveway, Alix was in my arms. I couldn't let go of her—nothing else was real. We made it into the house at last, but talk seemed secondary. After so much time apart, some vital physical link had to be restored first. I was kissing her forehead when Alix said, "Will you make love to me, Lynn?"

"Are you sure you want that right now, sweetheart?"

"More than anything," she assured me.

She seemed to need comfort, rather than passion. Drawing her down beside me on the couch, I began to undress her, carefully reining in my own emotions. When I slipped my arms around her, she nestled closer. We rocked together without urgency until at last my fingers found a melting wetness. Still I refused to rush. I caressed her slowly, gently, stopping for a heartbeat, starting again. After a long, languid time, Alix quickened under my hand, then finished, sobbing. But she was relaxed against me now, calmer, almost as if she'd absorbed strength from my touch. I wanted to hold her forever in that dim, flickering quiet.

Soon she stirred, reaching for me. "No, sweetheart," I told her. "I'm content. Just tell me what's going on." I slipped off the couch and tucked an afghan around her, then sat on the floor nearby. Our heads rested on the same pillow. We held hands as we talked.

"Things are so weird at home," Alix began. "I never know what to expect next. Thank heaven the girls are still visiting my parents! Charles has always been so cool and rational—or I believed he was. Now he's just…peculiar. Tonight, I think he told my mother that I'm insane."

"My god, Alix," I shouted, "I'll *kill* the prick!" Then I realized she couldn't tolerate much more tension. "I'm sorry, honey," I said soothingly. "I'll try to behave. Tell me what happened."

"Well, I guess the girls had started to miss me, so Mom said they could call home. But Charles answered the phone. Apparently he had quite a conversation with my mother before I knew she was holding for me."

Alix was crying and needed a tissue, but I couldn't make myself break away. She pushed herself upright. "Jesus, I'm drowning." Knotting the afghan around her like a sarong, she said, "I'll be back in a flash." When she returned to the living room, she was carrying a box of tissues in one hand and two beers in the other.

"Wonderful woman," I approved, rolling the icy bottle against my hot cheek. "Continue."

Alix sat facing me and took a swallow of beer as she gathered her thoughts. "Okay, to recap: Charles and my mom had a long talk before I got on the phone. You don't know my mother, so you won't really get the picture. Let me just say that despite her southern belle tendency to be indirect, she's exceedingly transparent. Well-meaning, but transparent. The minute I started talking with her, I could tell something was up. She kept asking how I'm feeling. Finally, I told her that I've been awfully tired—that I'm not sleeping well. Mom leaped on the opening and said, 'Is that *all*, sugar?' By that time, I'd begun to get the picture. I told her I was fine, really—why did she ask?"

"And?"

Alix's index fingers sketched quotation marks in the candlelight as she continued her narrative. "Mom said that Charles was 'terribly concerned' about me. That he seemed to feel I hadn't 'been myself' lately. He implied that I was overextended, had been under a lot of pressure. He said he was 'certain' it was nothing serious…but could Mom please make sure that no one in the family 'upsets' me right now."

"He's a busy fellow," I said bitterly. "Is that all?"

"*Oh*, no. He offered to drive to Mom's this weekend to pick up the girls. To make it 'easier' on my parents. God knows what he'll do once he's in Belmont. Mom and Dad think the world of Charles."

Rubbing the bridge of her nose, Alix said, "I hate to admit it, but I helped convince them that he's a minor deity. I thought he was once, you know. My parents have never really believed that I deserved him."

"You didn't, baby, you didn't."

"Well, anyway, once he's down there, Charles will put on his sincere suit and talk to them for hours. They'll never question a single thing he says."

"Can you dash to Belmont and beat him at his own game?"

Alix shook her head impatiently. "You forget we're dealing with an accomplished strategist. That was his main claim to fame in the courtroom. I can't go to Belmont tomorrow—that's my therapy date. If I miss it, he'll have me hospitalized."

To my raised eyebrows, she said, "He really *will*, Lynn—you have to believe me!" She leaned forward, fists clenched, her face grim in the low light. "Once Charles starts something, he never backs down. We're talking no-holds-barred combat. I've seen the pattern a dozen times during his political career. But I never dreamed that *I'd* be on his enemies list one day. It's a pretty creepy feeling."

Looking into her frantic eyes, I saw she meant every word. "Sorry, sweetheart. It's just hard to imagine that anyone could be so malicious."

Alix acknowledged my apology with a cursory nod. "And, as always, Charles is way ahead of me. He knows perfectly well that I'm tied up on Saturday too."

I slapped my forehead. "The piano recital!" I cried, feeling like a fool. Her students had been preparing for the event all summer.

"Yes. Miss *that* and I'll be lynched by throngs of irate parents."

Outflanked again, I thought. Aloud, I asked, "What's the bastard hope to accomplish with your parents?"

"I can't tell, Lynn. It looks like something ugly, though." Her face clouded over. "Do you know how hard this is for me? I'm learning not to trust Charles, but what's worse is that I can't *anticipate* him. I feel like I'm playing some dangerous game with a total stranger." Alix raised her chin and tried a joke. "Pretty soon those filthy rumors about my nervous breakdown may be true."

"Not a chance," I insisted. "You're tougher than you know."

Alix just smiled wanly. I wanted to brighten the mood, to promise her that things would break our way. Unfortunately, I was no longer convinced of that myself.

We psychoanalyzed Charles for another hour or so until Alix felt she had to go home. She agreed to meet me for a late lunch the next day before her first therapy session. Then I pulled her to her feet for one last, lingering kiss. When she slipped out my door, disappearing into the darkness, I tracked down Solly and held onto him for dear life.

CHAPTER EIGHTEEN

The fun and games were over—at least for the predictable future. Alix and I seemed to have said everything that could be said about our present, and neither of us dared to project ahead. Charles was pulling the strings. Puppets that we were, we could only dance to whatever tune he played.

Lunch in a crowded restaurant that Friday was an eerily isolating experience. Alix sat silent, just across the table from me, behind thick, impenetrable glass. Despite my best efforts, I couldn't rouse her, couldn't find words to shatter the barrier between us. Come back, Alix! my mind wailed. I *miss* you! I *need* you!

But a close look at her face told me she might fall apart if I applied any pressure. Her hands were trembling, and tears were only a nudge away. Quit pushing, you jerk! Quit pushing! I ordered myself. Give her some space, for god's sake. *Her* whole world is hanging in the balance, and *your* pathetic ego needs attention?

I gestured for the waitress, signed the charge slip, led Alix onto the sidewalk. As we headed for the therapy appointment, I shoved a cassette in the tape player. We scarcely spoke until we reached our destination.

The address we were seeking was on the edge of University City in a building that had once housed a prosperous family. Renovations had long since chopped the gracious old place into rental spaces for a handful of service-oriented businesses. In the lobby, a brass plaque on a walnut door informed us that we'd arrived at the offices of Harrold & Lane, Counselors.

I found Alix's fingers and squeezed for good luck. She tried to respond, but her smile looked more like a grimace. I turned the doorknob and we entered uncertainly. The waiting room held only a vinyl sofa, coffee table, stiff chairs and a few potted plants. Not a receptionist in sight. Sign-in somewhere? Knock on a door? We simply didn't know.

Before we could make a move, a tall, skeletal woman appeared, seemingly from nowhere. Too young to be the counselor, I was sure—a graduate student, interning, most likely. She had a clipboard full of forms and a cool, no-nonsense demeanor. After establishing Alix's identity, she separated us, dispatching me to the seating area.

Then she steered Alix into a tiny cubicle. Intake paperwork should be completed there, I heard the intern explain. The doctor would meet with her afterward. Backing out of the minuscule room, she pulled the door tight, severing the link between Alix and me. Ninety never-ending minutes would pass before I saw her again.

I was alone in the waiting room, where the thermostat was set so low I couldn't understand how the plants had survived. I sank onto the sofa and tried to adjust to the chill. But I was tense—and much too cold to relax. I found myself speculating about the doctor's motives. Would freezing one's clients suggest latent hostility? It was certainly food for thought.

In that environment, every action, every object, seemed to take on new significance. I was stupidly self-conscious, almost immobilized. Even selecting a magazine from the rack might be a diagnostic activity: Are you shallow?—intellectual?—extroverted?—eager to impress?

And what posture is appropriate in a therapist's office? Casual? Erect? *No*, for god's sake—not *erect*! Pacing the floor? Probably not a good move. Curling into a fetal position? Contraindicated, I was quite sure.

Unable to take any more of this nonsense, I checked the time. Still the better part of an hour before Alix should reappear. Extracting myself from the sofa's chilly embrace, I strode from the waiting room.

At the end of the block, a park beckoned under late August sun. Even at a distance I could hear the splash of a fountain and high, childish laughter. Strolling that direction, I found my way into a refreshing oasis. Under a canopy of old trees the air was softer, almost spring-like. A small pond boasted darting goldfish and an extravagance of water lilies. Gingerbread pavilions created a charming tableau. It was magic hour—the time of day that I loved best. Golden light slanted through the trees, intensifying every color. The shadows stretched long and thin. I chose a bench beside the pond and sat down to watch a pair of mallards feeding on that spangled surface.

After a while, a small man in a piratical bandana caught my attention. He was working his way around the perimeter of the pond, using a long, gnarled branch to drag litter from the water. Park crew, I thought automatically. As he approached, I saw that he was younger than I'd assumed. He had a distinctly hippie vibe, and there was something of the poet or the prophet about him. Despite his impressively broad shoulders, I felt no sense of threat, no need to uproot myself from this pleasant spot.

When he was quite near, a smile gleamed through his cropped beard and he called a pleasant greeting. Waving, I watched his struggle to capture a bobbing plastic cup. At last he succeeded. Tossing it into a trash can, he settled himself on the closest bench and let out an audible sigh.

"Satisfaction or despair?" I inquired.

"Maybe a little of both," he answered, slipping a knapsack from his back.

"Can you believe that people are such pigs?"

"I have no choice," he told me, "but I guess I've never gotten used to the idea."

His knapsack was open now. He made a little still life of Chinese food cartons, fresh fruit and tofu on his bench. Stretching to offer me a glistening crescent of pineapple, he said, "I've concluded that certain people can't resist wrecking something wonderful after they've enjoyed it themselves."

"So true," I said fervently. But I wasn't thinking about trash in a pond just then—I was cursing Dunnevan's cruelty, remembering Alix's troubled eyes.

"It never ceases to amaze me," the man continued, shaking his head in dismay. "I come here almost every day after work and it's always the same. I spend the first half hour just cleaning up the view."

So much for my powers of observation. Of course, he was a civilian. Park employees wore uniforms and badges, not earrings and bandanas… Just to make conversation, I said, "When I saw you picking up trash, I figured you worked here."

"I *wish*," my companion answered, as he crumbled his fortune cookie for a suspicious pigeon. "They keep me cooped up in a studio most of the time."

"Studio?"

He looked like he regretted exposing himself, but he was too courteous not to explain. "I'm an artist, or so they tell me."

And I understood. We shared a reluctance to confess ourselves as creative types to strangers who'd never understand our passions.

"It's okay," I whispered conspiratorially. "*I'm* a potter."

"No kidding?" He smiled, offering more pineapple.

I made a show of my biceps. "Really."

"That's cool! We won't have to deal with any bullshit."

I glanced down at my watch. "We couldn't anyway," I told him, licking juice from my fingers. "I have to leave now."

"It's been nice talking," he said. "I'm Sven Jarlsberg, by the way. Metalsmith. I work in the Capeheart District near the Central West End." He dug a card out of his wallet and passed it to me.

"Lynn Westfall," I replied, sorry I wasn't carrying my own card just then. "Stoneware and porcelain. Quillan's Crossing."

"Really?" he said. "My friends tell me that's a happenin' kind of place these days."

"Getting to be, yeah. Two years ago, I was the only starving artist on the square. Now there're a half-dozen of us. Come take a look before they raise our rents and squeeze us out."

"Sounds like a plan," he said, flashing that grin again.

Our eyes met, and I winked. Sven and I shared more than our vocation. The man was gay. I knew it about him as surely as he'd guessed it about me—in that instantaneous, intuitive way you can never explain to a straight person.

I rose from my bench, and nodded goodbye, thinking we might meet again, *hoping* we would.

Rather than retracing hot sidewalks, I struck across the grassy lawn in the direction of the therapist's office. The sound of youthful voices drew me to a playground busy with exuberant children. I couldn't help thinking about Cindy and Beth, remembering the day that we'd picnicked in the park. I wondered what would happen when they returned from visiting their grandparents. Once they were home, Charles would have to dial back the craziness a little... Wouldn't he?

Making my way through a birch grove, I emerged very close to the building where Alix was meeting with the counselor. Well before her time was up, I was shivering on that sofa again, but the appointment ran over schedule. When Alix finally entered the waiting room, tired and shaky, she wasn't alone. "Dr. Harrold wanted to meet you, Lynn."

A little frisson of panic zinged through me as I rose to my feet and extended one hand. The woman was about my age, prettier than I'd imagined. She said, "I've been hearing a lot of nice things about you, Ms. Westfall."

How do you respond to something like that? "Alix is very generous with her praise," I answered formally.

"Or perhaps you're just modest?"

"No doubt with good cause," I replied, feeling that we were jousting with one another for some inexplicable reason.

The psychologist considered me a second longer, as if I were an interesting specimen, then turned back to Alix. "I'll see you next week," she said. Opening the door to the lobby, she showed us out.

The asphalt parking lot was still steaming under the dying sun. Watching Alix fumble ineffectually in her purse, I offered to drive back. She leaned against hot steel and handed over her bag. "Oh, would you, Lynn? The keys are in there somewhere."

We made the trip homeward in rush-hour traffic, caught in the weekend exodus. I didn't really mind. The later we were, the more certain we'd be that Charles had left for Belmont. But glancing at Alix's slumped shoulders, I was worried. She didn't begin to speak until we were on the highway.

"I'm trying to sort things out," she told me at last. "I'm afraid I didn't do a very good job of explaining the situation to Dr. Harrold. It was awfully hard to get started, and then I couldn't seem to make her see how bad things are. She kept concluding that I should work to save my marriage."

"Well, goddamn her!" I exploded, slapping the wheel.

"No, it was really my fault," Alix insisted. "For one thing, I had trouble being completely honest about Charles. It's hard to accept that I've been so wrong about him." She rubbed her eyes wearily. "Dr. Harrold said there are ways to save the relationship—that Charles and I have enough emotion left to make it work. She told me that it's only hopeless when people are indifferent to one another. But at the very end, I think I made her understand a little."

"How?" I wanted to know.

"She asked what adjustments I'd have to make before the marriage could stabilize. When I told her that I'd have to accept depression as a daily reality, she started to catch on."

"Smart woman," I observed dryly.

"I didn't get around to telling her that Charles had wanted to hospitalize me until the very end of the session. *That* seemed to shock her."

"Good!"

"But when I said that all I want is a divorce so the girls and I can live with you, Dr. Harrold was pretty tough on me. She said I shouldn't count on you for rescue—that I have to learn to solve my own problems without relying on someone else."

"Let me get this straight," I said, changing lanes with a vicious jerk of the wheel. "If you and *Charles* can work things out, that's a satisfactory conclusion. But any solution involving the *two of us* is unwholesomely dependent?"

"Sounds that way, I suppose," sighed Alix.

"This is hardly what I expected," I ranted, feeling all hope for a speedy resolution evaporate. "In the first place, Alix, she's treating you like you're actually disturbed. What about the fact that you've been fine, that you were literally forced into her office?"

"I don't know, Lynn. Maybe psychologists operate on the assumption that everybody needs counseling. Or at least a little fine-tuning now and then."

"I'm not sure I buy that theory," I said sourly. I spent several bitter moments in silent contemplation: if a counselor's income depended on a steady stream of patients, wouldn't everyone she met seem like a candidate for her services?

"Just remember, Alix," I said at last, "she's not the only therapist in town."

"Well, I liked her all right. It was just so confusing. This really *was* my fault, love—I couldn't seem to communicate very clearly."

I made soothing noises, but internally I was fuming. I didn't like Alix's report about the counseling session—didn't like any part of it. Didn't like knowing that every card was stacked against us.

When we exited the highway and turned onto the secondary road that leads to Quillan's Crossing, Alix put her hand on my arm. "Lynn, if we swing by my house for a minute, I'll grab a change of clothes and spend the night with you."

"Wonderful!" I exclaimed, feeling good for the first time that day. "Pack everything you need for the recital too—then you can stay at my house all weekend."

"Oh, perfect!" Alix exulted. "What took us so long to think of this?"

The million distractions we've had, I thought. The fact that your fucking husband's *blackmailing* you. But all I said was, "I don't know, sweetheart. We're just a little slow, I guess."

I was relieved to see that Dunnevan's car was gone from their driveway. Too awful to imagine coming face-to-face with the bastard. We entered the house from the rear and I wandered toward the front while Alix ran upstairs to pack. I had no desire to follow her into the bedroom she shared with Charles.

But the first floor was nearly as hard to bear. Everywhere I looked I saw emblems of their life together. Alix and Charles beamed at one another in a family portrait atop her piano. One of his pipes scattered ashy litter across a stack of her sheet music. In the foyer, two coats hung side by side, sleeves touching. Dunnevan's tweed jacket with leather patches on the elbows, the down parka Alix had worn the night we met. Worst of all were the yellow rosebuds in a florist's vase that weighed down a note from Charles. Even his handwriting struck me as egocentric and coercive:

My darling,

I know your recital will be a great success. Sorry that I can't be with you. I expect to return with the girls late Sunday afternoon. I'll give your love to the folks.

Always,
Charles

Standing there, rereading that message, my spine prickled. The note implied that nothing had actually changed. Obviously the man was yielding no ground, had no intention of taking Alix seriously. That was consistent, I saw, with his claim that her derangement was temporary. The scope of the battle began to overwhelm me. I felt despair making dangerous inroads on my spirits.

Stop it! I lectured myself. Stay angry! That's the only chance you'll have against this asshole.

I heard Alix on the stairs and called her to me. She came through the archway swinging a miniature duffel bag, looking somewhat more cheerful. I hated to disrupt her mood, but I could see no good way around it.

"Look at this," I said, pointing to the flowers.

"How *dare* he?" Alix cried. Wadding Charles's note into a ball, she flung it the length of the room. "He has no *right*! He has no right to tell my family *anything*!"

I picked up her bag and took her by the hand, backtracking through the kitchen. She locked the door, and we bolted for my car, leaving a dozen long-stemmed roses to unfurl in an empty house.

CHAPTER NINETEEN

I tried to persuade Alix to go to bed early that evening. She was pale as porcelain and clearly exhausted. But she shook her head with stubborn determination.

"I'm too wound up to sleep. I'd just lie there worrying about Charles," she told me. "And it's so good to be here with you, Lynn. Let's enjoy tonight. We can sleep in tomorrow."

So we stir-fried some vegetables and made sandwiches. After eating, we stayed at the kitchen table folding programs for Alix's recital the next day. Since I'd never been to a children's concert, I said, "What will it be like?"

"Mass hysteria. Twelve kids in various stages of panic. The littlest ones sometimes vomit or wet themselves—I always have their parents bring a change of clothing, just in case. The older ones get stage fright, or swear they can't perform because of some pimple that appeared overnight."

"Sounds like a lot of fun, babe. I can hardly wait."

"Oh, in the long run, it's okay. The kids usually pull themselves together. The babies are so cute nobody cares how they sound. The teenagers are so earnest you wouldn't dare notice their mistakes. And there's enough applause from all those doting grandparents to satisfy everybody."

Gesturing at the stack of stiff blue paper we'd been folding, I said, "Why so many programs? Surely a dozen kids can't generate a crowd this large."

"Of course not. But most of the other instructors around here will encourage their students to attend, which is a good learning experience for the kids. It's also great a way for teachers to support one another and to generate audiences for their own recitals."

"Will you conduct?"

"No, silly. I'll just welcome the guests and introduce each performer."

"Darn," I teased her, "I was hoping to see you in tails—or a tux, at the very least."

Alix giggled. "Well, I *have* conducted, but never in tails."

"You've conducted? What's that like?"

"It's a rush!" she said, her eyes sparkling.

I was surprised. "So, I'm confused…I've always assumed that the real work would be done in rehearsal—that conducting was just a formality."

She shook her head vigorously. "Oh, no! It's not like that at all. You're really in charge of what happens in the performance. When everything's working right, you feel like you drew it out of the musicians. There's a wonderful sense of connection and control."

"Why, Alix," I drawled, "I'd never have guessed that you were into power games."

"Just behave yourself," she warned with a wink.

"But, sweetheart, that's no fun at all."

* * *

We lay in bed talking deep into the night. I'd needed this time with Alix. Lately the spaces between us had seemed frighteningly large and Charles's ability to expand them had unnerved me. Drifting in summer darkness, we slipped into mute appreciation of cricket song. Left to our own devices, I thought, we could make this comfort our constant reality, creating it for one another world without end, amen.

* * *

The shrill, insistent ring of my telephone woke me. Stretching across Alix to answer it, I squinted at the clock. It wasn't even eight. My voice was still blurred with sleep when I answered.

There was a momentary hesitation before a tight, male voice replied. "This is Charles Dunnevan. Is my wife there?"

My heart began to race and I couldn't seem to breathe. It hadn't occurred to me that he might call my home. I wondered fleetingly whether to lie—but what if something was wrong with the girls?

"Could you hold on for a minute?" Pressing the receiver into a pillow, I shook Alix lightly. "It's Charles," I mouthed.

She sat up, sleepy-eyed, running one hand through thick hair. Taking the phone, she answered calmly. "Yes, Charles?"

I rolled out of bed and pulled a loose T-shirt over my head. Alix might prefer privacy for this conversation, I thought. Padding barefoot to my kitchen, I put water in the kettle, turned on the broiler and buttered English muffins. By the time I had breakfast assembled on a tray, my hands were steadier. But a sense of intrusion still clung to me—I felt shaken inside. There was no doubt Charles knew we'd been in bed when I answered the phone.

The call was over before I returned to the bedroom. Alix looked undaunted, exuberant, happier than I'd seen her in weeks.

"What's up?" I asked.

"Just Charles checking up on me. Confirming his worst suspicions. All under the guise of reporting that he'd arrived safely, of course."

"Too bad," I growled. Then, "What's so funny?"

Alix extended both arms over her head and arched her back luxuriantly. "Nothing—everything! I love it that *he's* in Belmont and *I'm* here and there's not a damned thing he can do about it. Best of all," she said with a grin, "he knows he made this weekend possible."

I could imagine a bleaker perspective. Charles was a formidable opponent and I hated to give him any more ammunition. Still, if Alix could focus on this day, on her recital, on our time together, I'd keep my concerns to myself. She deserved a break from all the doom and gloom.

I set the teapot on the nightstand and popped the tray over her lap as I climbed onto the bed. When I reached for a muffin, Alix slapped my hand away playfully. "Not until we even things up, Lynn."

I raised questioning eyebrows.

"Take off your shirt," she commanded. "I like to look at you."

Peeling off the cotton knit, I dropped it to the floor. "Voyeur," I accused.

"It's actually kind of embarrassing—I've always ridiculed men for being obsessed with breasts, and now I find myself in a similar state."

"Understandable." I grinned. "Women do have fabulous bodies."

"*Oh*, yes," Alix murmured, her mouth full.

* * *

We had very little of that day to ourselves. There were so many last-minute details to take care of that Alix designated me her unofficial assistant. At a flower shop, we picked up two large baskets of chrysanthemums, then drove to the performance space. Once part of the school system, this building was slowly being refurbished by newcomers hell-bent on making Quillan's Crossing a cultural center.

Alix unlocked double glass doors then turned on the cooling system. "It might help a little at first, but don't get your hopes up," she warned me. "The committee's made lots of improvements here, but they're still raising money for new AC units. The old stuff's not very effective against three hundred bodies in this kind of heat."

In the auditorium, we moved a piano downstage, then drew ancient velvet curtains behind it. Alix sat on the bench and opened the keyboard. "Hope we didn't screw up the tuning," she said to herself. Fingers agile on the ivory keys, she ran through a bit of Pachelbel's "Canon."

I'd never heard her play. Leaning against a wall, listening with my eyes closed, I could scarcely believe that I was hearing a solo instrument. Some trick of overlapping resonances, of layered vibrations, produced impossible richness. The brief, occasional silence became an entity in itself—a shockingly appropriate contrast to that dense complexity. And *this* was just a quick-and-dirty sound check on a tired old piano. I could only imagine what Alix was capable of when she was actually performing.

Lost in the music, I jumped when she stopped in mid-passage. "Not too bad, considering," she said matter-of-factly. "One of the pedals sticks a bit, though."

I pushed myself away from the wall and joined her. "My god, Alix—that was fabulous! We've *got* to get a piano for the house!"

"Goof," she said, "I already have a piano."

"Yeah, but you can't play that one for me…and now that I know what I've been missing, we have to remedy the situation!"

I could see Alix was touched by my urgency, but she had other things on her mind. "Let's talk about it later," she suggested, pulling a list of tasks from her pocket. "Right now I need to stay focused on preparation."

She picked up a flower arrangement and placed it alongside the piano, studying its position critically. Then she said, "Come upstairs with me. I have to check the sound board and the lights."

I followed her up rickety steps to a small booth crowded by banks of electrical panels. "I'm not the mechanical type," Alix confessed. "Tech work terrifies me. I was promised that the lights would be set so I wouldn't have to worry about them."

She frowned at the controls and muttered, "Pray that he came through—otherwise I'm dead." When she slid several rheostats, the stage took on a pleasant glow. "Bless Robbie's heart," Alix sighed with relief. "Now for the lobby."

We positioned a battered folding table between the two entrances, camouflaging it with a navy blue cloth and the second basket of mums. I arranged pale blue programs in neat stacks, while Alix sorted through a folder, nodding with satisfaction. "It's all here." Then she explained for my benefit: "Somebody usually forgets sheet music, so I ask everyone for duplicates of their recital pieces, just in case."

"They don't work from memory?"

"They could. This is really a backup system, kind of a security blanket. There's no point in making the kids crazier than necessary."

"What else has to be done?"

Alix consulted her list again. "The parents are in charge of cookies and punch for the reception afterward, so we don't have to worry about that. There's only one thing left—check the restrooms for toilet paper and paper towels. Then I'll change clothes."

"You don't leave anything to chance, do you?"

"You laugh," she said, "but this is the voice of harsh experience speaking. Will you direct any early performers backstage?"

No one had arrived before Alix rejoined me. As she approached from the far end of the long, narrow lobby, I was able to watch unselfconsciously. She was wearing tailored black slacks, a silky gray shirt that draped beautifully at the wrists and killer heels. Antique silver circled her throat, gleaming in late afternoon light. Her smile was shy as I took both hands.

"Well," I told her, "it's not a tux, but you look lovely just the same."

Alix kissed me quickly, all too conscious of an expanse of plate glass behind me. "From here on out, I'll be a bit stressed, Lynn. Why don't you find a seat in the auditorium? I'll see you after the recital."

I slouched on lumpy upholstery in the cooling hall, hearing an occasional footstep or muffled voice. Alix's pupils were arriving. Soon the building would fill with their families and friends. I tried to imagine how it would feel to be very young and very frightened in the center of that broad stage. Just the thought made me twitch. My own art can be performed in solitude, my errors made in private. That suited me in a way this high-tension world never could. Yet I loved its product—the live, immediate music cutting to my core.

An impressively large crowd had begun to assemble. There was a constant stir, a hum of recognition and greeting. But when Alix finally appeared from the wings, the sound died instantly. She had that elusive thing called stage presence and it was impossible to look away from her. Haloed in warm light, she seemed taller, regal, possessed of an almost otherworldly grace. Suddenly I saw that her clothing was a *costume*, every element chosen to enhance that impression. I could feel the audience falling under her spell—I wasn't the only one enthralled by Alix Dunnevan just then. And her timing was superb. After a brief, charming welcome, she led the first child to the piano. The recital was underway.

As I've matured, something inside me has shifted toward irrational sentiment. For reasons I can't explain, witnessing youthful effort always floods me with emotion. I snuffled and choked back tears throughout the recital, embarrassed by my disproportionate response, hoping to escape detection. And, yet, there was reason to be proud of these children.

Alix had arranged her students in order of age and relative expertise. The youngest ones were endearing, casting simple strains into the air, so proud of themselves. The grade-schoolers were mostly methodical, striving mightily to coordinate the separate demands of the process. But the program built toward real promise, concluding with an exhilarating concerto played by a delightfully coltish teenage girl. A baby dyke, unless I missed my guess.

At the reception afterward, watching Alix move among her students, I couldn't help wondering what she felt. While she conferred and congratulated, did she also mourn? Was it painful to teach when she'd been trained to perform? Had that been part of the high cost of her marriage, or didn't she miss the stage at all? But curious as I was, I knew I wouldn't ask her until much later. If sorrow or anger lay beneath her smiles, any other time would be better for talking about it.

For Alix was blazingly alive that evening. I took her to dinner fifty miles away. There was something too vibrant about her to be contained by our prosaic surroundings. Besides, there were places in St. Louis where we could hold hands across the table without causing comment, and where dancing was more than possible.

CHAPTER TWENTY

I was glad that we'd made the most of that celebration—it was our last pleasant experience for quite a while. Dunnevan had used his weekend in Belmont with ruthless efficiency. Alix's parents were convinced that she was on the verge of mental collapse. And when Charles returned, he brought her favorite college roommate for a visit. He had, of course, enlisted Stephanie Thornton's sympathies during their long drive home.

I could picture it clearly: handsome, charismatic Charles talking endlessly in soft, measured tones, while his children dozed behind him. Charles painting Alix the unwitting victim of a predatory dyke. Playing the brokenhearted husband, desperate to reclaim his beloved wife. Portraying himself as a devoted father, determined to protect his impressionable daughters from my malevolent influence. By the time they arrived at the Dunnevan residence, Alix's old friend would have been primed to represent Charles in the struggle.

Throughout her visit, I was totally isolated from Alix. Charles and Stephanie devoted their combined energies to deprogramming her. They worked her over individually. They browbeat her together. They didn't hear a word she said.

At first, Alix had welcomed Stephanie. She'd tried to enjoy spending time with her old friend, had even hoped she might have an ally. But intent on her mission, Steph Thornton had diverted every conversation. She was relentless in her reminiscences of Alix and Charles, dazzling in young love. She asserted that their marriage was an ongoing inspiration to everyone who knew them, the benchmark against which all others were measured. And she predicted nothing but heartache should Alix persist on her present course. Life with me was a path to certain ruin.

On the second day of Stephanie's visit, Alix went on the offensive, doing her best to explain, to illustrate, to persuade, to lobby. But by the final day, her strength had been sapped. As nearly as she could tell, everyone she might have counted on for support was backing Charles.

I saw Alix at last on that third afternoon. She'd driven Stephanie to the bus station then shopped at the supermarket. On her way home, she detoured to my house. We exchanged urgent kisses and telegraphic news. I was alarmed by Alix's appearance—could scarcely believe this wounded, defenseless person was the same woman who'd kicked off her heels and danced so tirelessly at *Femme Seule* a few nights earlier. We'd only been together for fifteen minutes when Alix said, "I have to leave, darling. My frozen food's melting."

I held her to me. "What profiteth it a woman if she saveth her spinach, yet loseth her lover?"

Her smile was brief and forced. She twisted uneasily in my embrace. "If I'm not home soon, Lynn, Charles will come here looking for me."

I released her angrily. "So let him! What could he do once he got here—besides make an ass of himself?"

"I don't know, honey. Something bad. He's so bizarre these days that I hate to leave the kids alone with him." Alix was agitated, shredding a tissue as she spoke. "I really have to go now."

"All right," I sighed. "Will Charles be away any evening this week?"

"Tomorrow night, I think…yes, I'm sure of it."

I opened the car door for her. "You and the girls come for dinner then. We need to talk."

Staring straight ahead, she nodded agreement. "I love you, Alix," I told her.

She lurched forward, head drooping till it rested on the arc of the steering wheel. "I don't know why!" she cried.

"Oh, my god! You're *such* a marvelous person, Alix!" I leaned through the open window, trying to make her face me. "Please, please don't let Charles do this to you. I can't stand it if you feel bad about yourself!"

She straightened, then patted my cheek dispiritedly. "I'd better go, Lynn. The girls and I will be here tomorrow a little after six." Then she rolled up the window and blew a sad kiss in my direction. Backing her car around, she drove slowly away. Even at a distance, I could tell she was crying.

* * *

I was out back, arranging charcoal in my grill, when I heard tires on gravel. Running toward the drive, I met Cindy and Beth halfway. Beth leaped for my arms.

"Oh, honey," I warned, "my hands are dirty."

Alix caught up to us. "It doesn't matter, Lynn. They've been so excited about seeing you again."

Beth had a strand of my hair in her fist, running her fingers down its length. Maybe it was the first time she'd seen me without a braid. "Are you *Wapunzel*?" she asked, her eyes round with wonder.

I laughed, thinking maybe it was past time to whack off a few inches. "No, sweetie. I climbed down from the tower all by myself. No handsome princes were involved."

Alix snickered, but Beth looked bored. She tapped me impatiently on the shoulder. "We brought you a 'prize," she announced.

"A surprise?" Then I noticed that Cindy was carefully balancing a small object tented in newspaper.

"Our grandma helped us make it," she said, holding it out.

I set Beth down and dropped to my knees beside the children, glancing at Alix. She winked at me and my heart turned over. I made a ceremony of unwrapping the gift. Inside the folds of newsprint, I found a tiny plastic pot that held a little slip of wandering Jew—green and violet leaves curling above dark, rich soil.

"Oh, wow! This will look so good in my house! And when it gets bigger, you guys can help me make a special planter for it." I hugged both girls at once. "Why don't we take it inside?"

I placed the cutting on a bright windowsill in my living room. "This is the perfect place for it," I told Beth and Cindy. "The sun will make it grow fast."

Satisfied with my reaction, the children broke away, running outdoors to find Solly. Alix came into my arms as soon as the screen door banged behind them.

"Your *mother* sent the plant?" My voice was high with disbelief. She nodded, her hair tickling my neck. "Is this significant?" I asked.

"Maybe. Mom wouldn't dare defy my dad openly, but this might be her idea of subtlety." Alix laughed deep in her throat. "Charles was *so* pissed. First he tried to tell the girls that the plant couldn't survive the journey home. Then he tried to 'forget' it. I gather that Mom ran after him and shoved it into his hands at the last minute."

"Good for her!" I said, as hope and fear vied for ascendancy in my heart. Aggravating the man would hardly do us good. Still, I couldn't deny my delight at the thought of Charles as unwilling messenger. And if Alix could set aside her terror temporarily, I'd match the effort. I took her face between my hands and kissed her, then we joined her children in the backyard.

Cindy and Beth were funny and spontaneous that night, helping maintain our buoyant mood. They darted back and forth, seeking attention first from their mother, then from me. Something easy and natural was developing between us, strengthening throughout that long summer evening. It took me a while to identify the sensation. At last I had it: we'd begun to feel like a family.

By moonrise we'd done our best to deplete the local hot dog supply and the girls had roasted a dozen marshmallows. They were sticky, tired and happy. When Alix brought a guitar from her car, we sat on the patio singing all the childhood tunes we could recall till Beth grew heavy on my lap. We carried both girls inside then and spread a soft quilt on my couch. Alix dimmed the lights and kissed each child goodnight. After a brief turf war over throw pillows, they settled down. Alix and I held hands in the dark, waiting for their breathing to slow. Then she signaled me and we went to the porch to talk, sitting close enough to hear any sound of distress from the children.

Suddenly Cindy was at the screen door. "I have a question, Mama."

I was learning that Cindy would always have a question at bedtime—and often it would be so interesting that we couldn't resist responding. It was her favorite strategy to forestall sleep. Alix called her outside so she wouldn't disturb Beth. "What do you need, baby?"

Cindy peered at me through the dark. "How did you do it, Lynn?"

"Do what, sweetie?" I said, completely confused.

"Get down from the tower."

I almost choked on my lemonade. I'd had no idea I'd be taken literally—and hadn't guessed that Cindy was paying attention when I made my offhand joke.

Buying time, I said, "I'll tell you another day, when you're not supposed to be in bed." Then I picked her up and carried her back to the couch.

"*Promise*, Lynn?" she said, as I tucked her in again. "'Cause I really, really want to know."

"I promise," I told her, wondering what the hell I was going to cook up by way of an explanation. "Sleep tight, squirt."

Returning to the porch, I sat cross-legged on rough wooden floorboards facing Alix. She clung to my hands as she described Stephanie's recent visit in fuller detail. "When Charles brought Steph back with him, of course I was wary," she began. "But we've always been good for each other. I was sure she'd want this for me, if she knew how I felt about you—how much happier I am now. But I think I only succeeded in scaring her."

"What do you mean, love?"

Alix sighed with frustration. "This is going to take so long to communicate. I wish you and I could just have a total mind meld." She sorted through her thoughts in silence, then said, "Let me try to set this up: Stephanie and I are extremely comfortable with one another physically. We've always touched a lot—hugs, back rubs, you know. In college, there was even a rumor about us...plenty of people thought we were lovers. It amused me because I knew I didn't feel anything sexual for her."

I tipped her chin to look her in the eye. "Maybe you just weren't paying attention?"

Alix rejected the idea immediately. "Nope. For what it's worth, when I reach back in time, I can't find anything like what I feel about you, Lynn. It simply wasn't there."

"Just a thought, baby. Sorry I interrupted you."

Alix made a *no problemo* gesture then continued. "Okay, so here's Stephanie fifteen years later and she's married to a real horse's ass. No kidding, Lynn—Doug is such a jerk! From the beginning, I couldn't see why Stephanie was attracted to him, and I don't know how she stands living with him. But she obviously intends to keep on coping with a bad situation. So what does it mean to *her* if *I* love a woman—if my 'perfect' marriage wasn't enough?"

"Remember, Alix—I told you that nobody can think about homosexuality without evaluating themselves. That's why most people can't think about it at all."

"Yeah. I kept hearing what you said after the Holly Near concert. Which was certainly true for *me*. And I could see that Stephanie was refusing to deal with that, with the implications for her own life. So the only thing she could talk about was my 'cure.' How with time and patience, I'll be willing to relinquish this fairy tale."

I hooted and Alix groaned. "Excuse me—no pun intended."

"Watch your step," I teased. Then I said, "But seriously, folks, I am *never* going to understand why so many great women stay with second-rate men. And what's worse, they pressure their friends to stick it out too. Sometimes it just makes me sick."

"Well, as a person who's considered divorce for years," Alix told me, "I *do* understand that. Maybe in a way you can't, Lynn. If you're a housewife—meaning you spend most of your time at home—you hardly ever have the chance to compare notes with other women. Not really. And if you did, how could you admit dissatisfaction to friends who insist they're completely content? The guy in your life tells you you're nuts, nobody else has these problems—like *he* would know! And over time, you begin to *feel* crazy. Maybe you think about leaving occasionally, but you worry about money, about how you'd support your kids."

My eyebrows lifted at that, and Alix said, "I know, I know. That's the lament of the privileged middle-class mommy. But that doesn't mean it's not true—I *don't* have any real-world skills. Not a lot of openings for concert pianists around here, right? And, even if I *found* work, you know that most women are paid too poorly to survive alone."

Yes. I did. Fifty-nine cents on the dollar compared to men doing the same job. That disparity had complicated every second of my mother's adult life. It was a large part of the reason I'd gotten involved in the effort to pass the Equal Rights Amendment.

But Alix didn't stop there. "Then you think about the kids. Sometimes you're afraid of what divorce would do to them. Or you wonder whether you'd have enough time to give your children while you juggled all the other responsibilities too. It's just a fact that most women can't afford to divorce unless a new man promises a better life." Alix raised her head defiantly. "And maybe the only difference between me and those other ladies is that I've found a *woman* instead."

"But that's a big difference, Alix. You probably don't know how huge, yet. It's a real act of courage to give up society's blessing. This isn't a decision for the faint of heart."

I swiveled around so I was sitting beside Alix and put my arm around her shoulders, punctuating our conversation with kisses. "Of course, there are advantages too. There's a special kind of freedom in loving women—you only stay because you want to. And every day you can measure the degree of your commitment against all that social disapproval. You'd be stupid to stay if you weren't happy. You'll find a lot of good in my world. I promise."

"I'm ready for it, Lynn. I'm pretty tired of all the bullshit. The worst thing about Steph was the way she stuck up for Charles. That really sucked—she's supposed to be *my* friend. But she was so fucking 'unbiased' that I could have screamed. If she'd told me one more time that she loved us equally, I think I'd have strangled her. Why couldn't she see how badly I needed her support?"

Alix looked so vulnerable. I hugged harder. "Ever consider this, darling? Maybe Stephanie has feelings about you that you've never reciprocated. If she's too sympathetic, she might have to reexamine her situation. It's so much safer to act dispassionate, to score points for neutrality."

Alix had the kind of face that displayed every emotion. I could practically read her memories as she sifted through them. "You may be right, Lynn. At least, I can make the theory fit the facts. But a huge, whiny part of me still wants to wail, 'It's not fair!' Pretty immature, I suppose."

"What's maturity got to do with this, babe? You're hurt and you have reason to be—Steph let you down in the crunch. Unfortunately, that's typical. We can't count on getting much aid and comfort from the straight world."

"Sometimes I'm afraid I don't have what it takes to make it through this," Alix whispered.

I tipped her chin up again and kissed her nose. "Of course you do. Look at the crap you've handled in your marriage. We'll make it because we're tough enough and because we care enough. Trust me, love."

"With my life," she said, smiling up at me.

CHAPTER TWENTY-ONE

Bent over my electric wheel, I was centering clay. Exerting pressure against centrifugal force, my hands forming and reforming the heavy gray mass. Over and over, I shaped it into a cone then flattened it, striving to eliminate every irregularity. When I was finished, the clay would be evenly distributed on the bat, totally balanced, ready for throwing. But until the centering was perfect, I could produce nothing stable or beautiful.

The motion was soothing—a sensuous, rocking rhythm that belied the strength necessary to control twenty pounds of clay spinning at high speed. When I'm centering, a trance-like state claims me and my mind is almost blank. As I worked that day, one word kept floating to the calm surface of my consciousness—Mattie's name, repeating itself like a mantra. Suddenly I realized how badly I wanted to see her. And it was long past time to introduce Alix. Cheered by the thought, I worked on until noon.

Then I closed the shop and drove home to shower and change. Alix had another appointment with her therapist, so we planned to eat dinner in the city. I drove through town and found her outside her house, waiting for me on a huge cedar deck. She looked even more distraught than was customary on counseling days. I'd learned not to press her on these occasions. Anything of importance would have to wait till later. As we headed toward the city, I worked hard to keep our conversation light and minimal.

Neither of us had settled on a firm opinion about Dr. Harrold. My judgment—formed exclusively from Alix's reports—fluctuated almost weekly. Sometimes the therapist's comments could be interpreted as purposely confrontational. More than once I'd suggested that she might be trying to provoke outrage and resistance in Alix, whose anger was buried so deep it was hard to tap.

But too frequently, the psychologist had made statements that seemed inconsistent with feminist practice. Then I'd question Greer Barclay's regard for this woman. Periodically, when we could find no way to cast a favorable light on one of Harrold's observations, Alix had debated seeking a new counselor. But that would mean beginning at the beginning, telling her story to another expert she might find just as frustrating. And increasingly, as much as sessions with Harrold exhausted her, she seemed to depend on them.

Seated again in that chilly waiting room, I listened for Alix's footfall. At last I heard her quiet voice just beyond the door. She sounded controlled and steady as she confirmed her next appointment with the therapist. But when she walked through the doorway, I saw that was a façade. Her hands shook as she tried to cram her checkbook into her shoulder bag and she was already wearing dark glasses. I got her to the car as quickly as possible. Once we were on the road, I asked, "Do you want to go straight to my house, Alix?"

"Yes, please. This was a bad session—I don't think I could keep up a front in a restaurant. And I couldn't tell you anything about the appointment without making a fool of myself."

I pushed a cassette into the tape player and fiddled with the volume. "Why don't you just recover while we're on the way?" I said.

Alix angled her body so that she could curl up slightly on the car seat. "Thanks, Lynn. We'll talk over dinner," she promised.

Within moments, she was asleep. Mary Watkins sang her heart out while I maneuvered my car through heavy afternoon traffic, but I was scarcely aware of the music. I was too preoccupied by my fear that therapy was transforming a perfectly healthy woman into a psychiatric patient.

* * *

Maybe *I'd* lost track of my promise to explain how someone could make a solo escape from a sealed tower, but *Cindy* hadn't. The next time the girls stayed overnight at my house, she seized upon my commitment, using it as one more excuse to extend the bedtime ritual. She had, I thought, her father's gift for strategizing.

I checked my watch, then looked at Alix, hoping she'd veto Cindy's request. Instead, she winked at me. "Might as well get it over with, Lynn. The girl never forgets a thing. I'll be in the kitchen loading the dishwasher."

Great. I hadn't a clue how to start this—or how to end it. I was missing a middle too, for that matter.

"Let's start with Rapunzel," I said, deploying my own tactical skills. "Remind me how the story begins." I wasn't only delaying the inevitable. I wanted to make sure that whatever nonsense I invented meshed with Cindy's version of the tale.

She, of course, loved nothing better than being the center of attention. Plopping down on my couch, she faced Beth and me, instantly transforming us into an audience. Then, in her best fairy tale voice, she began: "Once upon a time, a lady wanted some special food from a witch's garden. The witch caught her husband stealing the food and made him give her their baby. Then she locked the baby in a tall, tall tower."

"The baby's name was Wapunzel," Beth confided.

"*Ra*punzel," Cindy pointed out with six-year-old superiority. "She couldn't get out because there wasn't a door."

"The witch climbed up her hair!" Beth crowed.

"But that comes later, Beth—hush!" Cindy ordered.

And so the girls told the story, arguing the fine points as they went along. When they got to the part about Rapunzel wanting to explore the world, I took over.

"Now Rapunzel was a very, very smart girl. She didn't think it was fair that she was stuck in the tower while the witch could come and go as she pleased. And she wasn't willing to wait for someone to rescue her. So she thought and thought and thought about how she could get down from that tall tower by herself. Then she realized that the answer was right in front of her. Or, rather, *behind* her," I said, stroking my own braid to provide a clue.

"Her hair!" Beth cried.

"Yes. Her hair. Every day when Rapunzel brushed her long, golden hair, some strands got caught in her hairbrush. Always before, she had let the birds make nests with that hair. But now Rapunzel had a clever idea. She began to collect every single strand she found in her brush and hide it in a box under her bed. It didn't take long before she had enough to weave into a nice, thick braid."

"Like yours!"

"Right. Only much, much longer. And hair is very strong—that's why the witch could climb up the tower. Rapunzel waited till the witch went to town one day. Then she tied the braid to her bedpost and put the other end out the window. She looked down, down, down to the ground, and saw the very, very, very end of the long braid curled on the earth below. Rapunzel remembered how the witch had climbed from the tower and she was sure she could do the same thing. Still, she was pretty scared when she crawled out that window. The ground seemed awfully far away."

"But she didn't fall," Beth guessed.

"Course not," Cindy said authoritatively.

"She didn't fall. She worked her way carefully down the tall, stone tower. It took all morning, but finally she reached the bottom. For the first time, sunlight kissed her skin. For the first time, she felt cool grass under her feet. She picked her very first flowers and wove them into a crown for her beautiful hair. And for the very first time, Rapunzel was perfectly happy. She set off to see the whole wide-open, wonderful world. She walked and looked, and walked and looked, and for all we know, she is wandering still."

"Is that the *end*?" Cindy asked dubiously.

"It is," I affirmed solemnly, hoping I'd fulfilled my obligation.

"Where's the prince?" Beth wanted to know.

"I think he must be in the stable still, feeding carrots to his favorite horse. It turns out that Rapunzel didn't need his help, after all."

"What about the witch?" Cindy again. Wrapping up every loose end.

"The witch? Well, when she found out that Rapunzel had escaped, the witch was so mad her hair burst into flames. She jumped in a lake to put out the fire, and was never seen again."

"But," Cindy complained, "Rapunzel didn't get to be the queen."

"True. But she found out that being a queen is almost exactly like being stuck in a tower for your whole life. *Her* happily-ever-after ending was to be free in the world."

Maybe I was sounding a little desperate by then, because suddenly Alix reappeared, rescuing me from my fairy tale.

"Time to sleep, girls. *Really* time to sleep," she said, turning out the light.

* * *

Mattie, my friend—

The invasion is imminent. Unless you contact me to the contrary, four females of varying descriptions will descend on you next Friday. Estimated time of arrival: five o'clock. We'll bring sleeping bags and plenty of food. Don't do one damned thing except greet us with your famous smile. Life's been tough around here lately and I need you.

As I've indicated in recent letters, Charles's behavior gives new meaning to the word vicious. Apparently he's willing to drag all of us through a full-scale custody battle. Alix is pretty strung out and depressed. The worst part of this is how little support she's gotten from those near and dear. As a matter of fact, her father wants nothing so much as to check her into BelMed and take control of her "cure." What a nightmare!

Moreover, her therapist doesn't seem to understand the strain she's under. Charles has been applying a lot of pressure on the sexual front. When Alix explained the problem, her counselor was completely unsympathetic. She seemed to feel that his demands were only what one should expect under the circumstances. She went so far as to imply that Alix could buy herself a little peace that way! I wanted to suggest that Charles should buy *himself* a little *piece*, but politics prevented me—hookers are sisters too!

At any rate, it's a horrendous tangle right now. For the first time, I begin to comprehend—*really* comprehend—what you went through with Diana, and I need your advice about all of this. Besides, I can hardly wait for you to meet Alix. You're going to be impressed. And so is she.

Love you,
Lynn

CHAPTER TWENTY-TWO

My ponderous old station wagon, bought cheap from an aging aunt, has always provided amusement for certain friends. They consider it deliciously ironic that I own such a classic symbol of suburban maternity. No matter how I've protested that I need it for business—for hauling seventy-five-pound bags of powdered clay, crates of pots, stacks of bats, and so on—they jokingly insist that the vehicle's actually a deep-seated symbol of repressed desires. A pickup truck with a camper shell would work just as well, they point out. "Yeah," I counter, "but the station wagon's paid for."

Now my car seemed to be fulfilling its destiny. Stacked to the dome light with toys and suitcases, pillows and sleeping bags, not to mention crackling cellophane sacks of junk food, it took on a distinctly domestic air. On the road to Mattie's place, I felt like Alix and I were incognito—indistinguishable from all those thirty-something women who travel in pairs transporting children to one location or another. And I had to admit that I didn't mind the sensation at all.

Alix was on the bench seat next to me, with Beth on her lap. Cindy was beside her, pointing out the window, bouncing with excitement. We might have arranged the rear better and settled the girls back there, but in truth, we wanted this closeness. We were trying hard to pretend our trip was purely recreational, not a flight from escalating fear and tension. All in all, we weren't doing too badly.

Alix kept leaking little phrases of song and I couldn't be depressed while her thigh moved rhythmically against mine. Sunlight through glass blanketed us in great, irregular patches of warmth. There was a kind of healing in that and I couldn't help myself—I was happy. Suddenly *I* was singing too. Alix switched to harmony, trusting me to keep the melody intact. We drove that way for hours, deep into the Ozarks, the children nodding in and out of sleep.

When we arrived late that afternoon, Mattie was rocking on her porch. She waved, but stayed put while we eased the girls into wakefulness. I wanted to see with her eyes as Alix and I walked up the path, two women carrying love between them like a dangerous treasure. How did we look to my old friend?

Coming from behind, joyous in their freedom, Cindy and Beth circled us. Kicking up bright crisp leaves, they raced for the wooden stairs and ran directly to Mattie's chair. Without hesitation, Beth clambered onto her narrow lap. Cindy balanced on one rocker behind them, catching a ride. At the bottom step, Alix halted, surprise arching her brows.

"You *are* magic!" she exclaimed. "Those are ordinarily two very shy children."

Mattie just hugged them, grinning.

"I told you, Alix—there's nothing alive that Mattie can't charm. She's kind of the Auntie Mame of the wilderness."

Snorting, my old friend stood. She hoisted Beth and took Cindy by the hand. "You all unload," she directed us. "I have a job for the girls indoors." And they vanished, leaving us alone for the first time that day.

Alix threw her arms around me. "Better hang on tight, Lynn," she teased. "That's an *extremely* magnetic woman."

I kissed her for a long time—slowly, thoughtfully, deeply—before responding. "I won't worry about my best friends liking one another, baby. Consider the alternative." Then I gave her sweet ass a playful swat. "Let's get to work, lazybones. Someone seems to have packed everything we own."

Our growing pile of gear substantially reduced the floor space in Mattie's cabin. At last we finished unloading my car. We collected the trash and brushed out most of the crumbs. After a final, hasty hug, Alix and I went indoors to join the others. The girls were standing on stools at the kitchen counter busily arranging feathers, leaves and seedpods in a round raku pot. I set Alix's guitar case on the floor and went to watch.

"Look, Lynn!" Beth said. "We're using one of your bases for the table!"

"*Vases*," Cindy corrected her.

"Pretty neat, punkin," I said, ruffling Beth's hair. "It already looks beautiful."

Over the girls' heads, I sent Mattie a bittersweet smile. That pot had a history. I'd hand-built it on her porch from clay I'd quarried right here on her land. We'd fired it out back in a little temporary kiln I'd set up on one heartbreak afternoon when she needed all the distraction I could provide. The simple vessel contained more emotion than anyone else could ever deduce.

Cindy jumped down from her stool, took my hand and pulled me to the dinner table. It was set with enameled tinware and there were bandanas in place of napkins. But Cindy was pointing beyond the table, chattering about a crazy quilt that hung on the wall.

"Mattie told me all about it, Lynn! She knows where every little piece came from." The child's eyes were brilliant. She concentrated hard, remembering the quilt's history. "Her grandma made it and every scrap tells something about Mattie's mama." Touching white brocade with a careful fingertip, Cindy said, "This was her mother's wedding dress, and this is what she wore on her first day of school. This is from her crispening gown—"

"Christening, sweetie."

"That's what I *said*," insisted Cindy, who hated to be wrong. "Mattie, is the yellow one from graduation?"

Mattie squinted in our direction. "No, honey. It was a party dress for her sixteenth birthday."

We studied the patchwork, its seams overlaid with silk embroidery. I said, "It's lovely, isn't it, Cindy?"

She nodded vigorously. "When I grow up, I'm gonna make one too."

Not for the first time, it occurred to me that Cindy had an instinctive attraction to all things esthetic. On the spot, I vowed to share everything I knew about the arts with her as she grew. That could be a special connecting point between the two of us—and I could begin right away.

"Before we leave," I promised her, "I'll ask Mattie to show you the back of the quilt. It's pretty too, but in a different way."

Just then, my old friend appeared at the table holding Beth whose small hands clasped the rustic centerpiece. With careless grace Mattie tipped the child forward. "Now put it right down in the middle, Beth," she directed. The pot was positioned there and we all exclaimed over it. When we'd run out of compliments, Mattie said, "Let's eat, folks."

Her bread alone qualified Mattie for sainthood, but the vegetable soup was a miracle of textures and seasoning. The peanut butter cookies and vanilla ice cream she offered for dessert were homemade wonders. All five of us ate in worshipful silence until we finally had to confess ourselves too full to do more damage. When we pushed our chairs away from the table, Alix waved everyone outdoors.

"I'll clean up the kitchen," she said to Mattie. "Lynn drove, and you cooked. I haven't done a damned thing all day."

So Mattie and I sat on the porch talking sporadically while the children chased squirrels under a vanishing sun. The twilight air was thick with the scent of autumn and deeply soothing. I yawned then stretched with satisfaction.

"Somewhere inside all that weariness, there's an ecstatic woman," Mattie observed.

"Won't argue with that," I said.

"Well, she *is* pretty neat, but can she sing?"

"Just wait till you hear her. I mostly came so you two could jam."

"Then get her out of the kitchen and behind her guitar where she belongs."

Alix was wiping the counter-top when we tried to kidnap her. "I have a better idea," she protested. "Why don't we bathe the girls first then sing them to sleep?"

"Okay," I agreed. "You guys get the kids in the tub. I'll make up their beds."

I dug through duffel bags until I found pajamas and toothbrushes. After unearthing all the other things that added up to a successful bedtime—an assortment of soft toys, pillows and special blankets—I cleared a space large enough to spread our sleeping bags. As I worked, I could hear the mingled sounds of splashing water, infectious giggling and adult voices in quiet counterpoint.

Mattie had laid a fire on the stone hearth, so I lit it. The kindling had just begun to catch when she and Alix returned, each cradling a wiggly terrycloth bundle. We popped the girls into pajamas and tucked them into their sleeping bags, with plenty of kisses all around. Then I sat between them rubbing their backs while Alix and Mattie gathered guitars, glasses and a bottle of Chablis.

Heads together, they conferred over tuning until they'd satisfied some standard that would forever remain mysterious to me. They kept the music simple and familiar while the girls were awake. But then the night was ours. Mattie began to strum softly and I recognized her introduction to "House Carpenter," which she knew I loved. She'd learned the ancient ballad from a recording, but Mattie had always sung it much slower than Joan Baez, like the dirge that it was.

"Do you know this?" she asked Alix.

"Yes, but I call it 'The Demon Lover' and play it a little differently. Let me sit out for a minute." Closing her eyes, Alix listened intently, nodding every so often. Then she straightened and picked up her guitar again. When her clear voice chimed in on the third stanza, Mattie's eyes narrowed appreciatively. On the next verse, she found a throaty, mournful harmonic line and held it against Alix's plaintive melody until the hairs on my arms lifted. As the last notes died away, we sat without speaking. "House Carpenter" is so laden with sorrow and remorse that it deserves a respectful silence.

Coming out of the spell first, Alix threw her capo at me. "Hey, you creep! Why aren't you joining in?"

"Ruined my throat singing in the car today," I answered. But, truthfully, I didn't want to participate. I wanted to listen—*really* listen—to be engulfed in sound, to hear the separate currents of their music merging.

The fire leaped higher and then burned low. Still Alix and Mattie sang on, matching each other, teaching each other. I lay a bit apart, a spectator to their pleasure, enjoying them both. Finally even they had to acknowledge fatigue. Sliding the guitars into their cases, they grinned at me. I poured more wine and we talked a bit longer near the dying fire.

Just before she headed for bed, Mattie kissed me on both cheeks. "You know whereof you speak," she murmured in my ear.

When I heard her door close, I took Alix by the shoulders and held her to me. I could read exhilaration as well as exhaustion in those dark eyes. We lay together on top of her sleeping bag, wound around in mine. Glowing embers snapped and flared in the darkness as Alix began to breathe deeply, at peace in my arms. I closed my eyes at last and let go of consciousness, feeling it slip slowly from my grasp like a helium balloon on a long, long string.

* * *

I awoke at dawn to the sounds children make when they're trying their best to be quiet. Rolling off the sleeping bag, I crept to the door. Cindy and Beth were barefoot on the front porch, undeterred by the morning chill. "Hey, you guys, it's early," I whispered through the screen. "Come back to bed."

Beth turned reproachful eyes on me. "You made the bunny go away, Lynn!"

I stepped onto the porch, careful to close the door softly. Crouching, I wrapped an afghan around the girls' thin shoulders. "Bunnies, huh? You guys want to see bunnies?"

Brightening, Beth nodded. "Well, come in then. We have to get dressed. But you've got to be as quiet as mice, or you'll wake your mom."

They tiptoed into the cabin. As quickly as I could, I got the children into warm clothes. While they sat on the porch wrestling with their shoes, I stuck a hasty note on the handle of the coffeepot, Mattie's first stop every morning. As nearly as I could tell, we hadn't disturbed Alix. She appeared to be sound asleep, totally relaxed against the jade green liner of her sleeping bag. Maybe she'd actually get some rest if we stayed out an hour or two. God knows, she needed time to recover from all the stress Charles had inflicted.

At the last moment, I remembered breakfast for the girls, so I slipped back into the kitchen. I filled a cotton flour sack with raisins, bananas and graham crackers. Then, on impulse, I grabbed two more bags from Mattie's stash. Outdoors again, I knotted a sack to each child's belt.

"Ready?" I asked unnecessarily. Because they were practically jumping out of their skins at the thought of adventure.

So we set off for the woods, Cindy and Beth running ahead, feet churning through fallen leaves. I had a particular destination in mind, but it didn't matter if we never reached it. There was glory in every direction. All I'd need to make them happy was a bit of luck in the form of a random rabbit. And I was pretty sure we'd find one.

* * *

It was after ten when we returned, tired and covered with burrs. I left the girls on the porch, picking away at their jeans and socks. Mattie and Alix were in the kitchen, deep in conversation, up to their elbows in apple slices.

"Applesauce," Mattie said, in response to my cocked head.

"Oh, god! How wonderful! I'm supposed to tear you two away for a few minutes, but on second thought—"

"What did you need?"

"The kids just want to show you what they've been up to this morning. Can you come to the porch and see?"

My friends kicked back their chairs and rinsed their hands at the sink. Watching them, so at ease together, sharing a linen towel, I was almost overcome with affection. I wondered what had passed between them in my absence. But Cindy was in the kitchen now, pulling on Alix's hands, urging her outdoors.

The contents of her flour sack were already spread on the rough pine planks. Poor Beth was still working on the knotted drawstring at her belt. Mattie dropped to her knees, stretching out capable hands to loosen that tight tangle. Then Beth upended her bag, dumping out a jumble of glittering rocks, acorns and weathered wood. We sat in the sunshine exclaiming over their finds.

Voices overlapping, the children told their tale—explaining, describing, correcting one another. We'd seen some wild geese and two bunnies, no *three*, counting the one in the front yard! There was a waterfall, mostly dried up, and a place where hunters could hide to shoot squirrels! The snakes were all sleeping, and did Mama know that some animals stayed asleep all winter?

"Well…most of the winter," Mattie interjected.

"Okay, okay," I said, defending myself. "I was going for the basics, not absolute accuracy." I turned back to the girls. "Mattie's really the one who should take you exploring. Nobody knows the woods better—she even writes stories about them."

Cindy and Beth didn't look impressed. Suddenly they were done with the conversation and off the porch, playing some new game under the trees. But Alix was still beside me, a baffled look on her face. Somewhat belatedly, I realized that I might never have mentioned this aspect of my old friend's life. I explained sheepishly: "In her spare time, when she's not too busy taking care of me, Mattie writes a column for *Natural Gifts*. Not to mention, the occasional book."

Alix shook her head, raising slender arms skyward in a gesture of incredulity. "Sometimes you are *such* a goof, Lynn Westfall!"

Then she addressed Mattie. "Maybe you'll tell me about your work, since I can't count on dumbshit over there to fill me in?"

"Oh, most of my books are just collections of the essays I write for the magazine. But I got lucky—after the first one achieved a bit of success, a bigger publishing house bought the rights and promoted it. Since then, they've kept me on."

"A *bit* of success?" I laughed then began to recite: "'A modern classic…A major philosophical triumph…A unique journey through nature…Mathilde Reynolds is a poetic visionary of the new ecology…'" I paused to take a breath. "I'm quoting, of course."

Mattie glared at me, while Alix stood frozen in astonishment. "Not *the* Mathilde Reynolds?" she gasped at last. "The author of *Windflaw and Other Weathers*?"

"Yep," I said proudly.

"Jesus, you asshole, get out of my way! I want to kiss her hem!"

So I had to apologize to them both—to Mattie because I'd embarrassed her, and to Alix for inadequate briefing.

Feigning irritation, Alix ignored me. "Are you working on a new anthology now?"

Mattie groaned and shot me a look. "No, I'm in the midst of a truly frightening process—I'm writing my first novel."

"That's got to be exciting," Alix said. "Can I ask what it's about?"

"Women loving women," Mattie answered tersely, "and it's all Lynn's fault."

"I protest! All I said was that it was high time you stopped waiting for Harper Lee."

"What?" asked Alix, more confused than enlightened.

"Nearly every time Mattie reads a gay novel, she bitches about it, insisting that lesbians need a book like *To Kill a Mockingbird*. So finally I told her that if she wanted a great story about the integrity and pain and beauty in our lives, she'd better write it."

"Well, I'm not sure that's what I'm doing," Mattie said, "but I get so annoyed with a lot of the characters in lesbian fiction—all those protagonists hating themselves for loving women, and all the grotesques and freaks. I just can't relate to most of them. The women I've loved are certainly unique—" she cast another pointed glance at me "—but they're all pretty healthy types. So I guess I'm trying to describe the *daily*ness of our lives—to write something I'd like to read, about women I'd like to know."

"I've seen the first draft," I told Alix. "It's remarkable stuff."

"I don't know," said Mattie, in a worried tone. "It's so different from what I usually do that I'm a little insecure about it."

Alix was looking for a graceful way to extricate Mattie from an awkward situation. She said, "I'd think it would be hard to work for a magazine that's published in New York when you live way out here."

"Oh, no! That was the best part about becoming a 'legitimate' author. I could finally justify moving to the cabin permanently. Now I just mail in the columns. When I abandoned Manhattan for the Ozarks, it made my work much easier."

A shadow crossed her strong face and something twisted inside me. "In a lot of other ways, though," Mattie murmured, "that wasn't a very good time." She shook herself lightly. "Best not to bother you with all that—I'll get back to my applesauce now."

Alix watched her retreating back with distress. "What just happened? Was it something I said?"

"Nothing you could have avoided, sweetheart. Mattie suffered an authentic tragedy back then—she lost the love of her life."

"I thought you were the love of her life."

"Far from it, sweetheart. Not everyone finds me as captivating as you do. I just helped her through a rough patch."

"Will you tell me about it someday, Lynn?"

"I can't, but Mattie may. She hardly ever refers to that period. If she's mentioned it at all in your presence, it's a sign that she's really comfortable with you."

Leaning forward, I kissed the bridge of her elegant nose. "Let's go back to the kitchen, Alix. It looked like you guys could use some help with those bushels of apples."

CHAPTER TWENTY-THREE

The three of us spent that afternoon in the kitchen working companionably amid the spicy aroma of simmering fruit. The children ran in and out, snatching bits of apple or reaching for a quick kiss. We cored and sliced, stirred and sampled, poured and sealed until we'd emptied two bushel baskets. And all the while there was music—either Mattie or Alix spilling notes, comparisons, harmonies into the steamy air. Finally, they dragged a guitar into the kitchen. One or the other kept sitting down to pick out something just remembered, or something just learned.

By the time we were finishing up, late light angled through the window, striking amber depths in the ranks of gleaming jars. I scraped the final remnants of applesauce into a container and capped it off with melted paraffin. When Alix tapped my shoulder, I realized I'd been standing motionless holding hot glass for a long time.

"Why the faraway look, Lynn?"

"I guess I was thinking about this place. Somehow it's always felt protected, enchanted—like it exists *elsewhere* and no evil can intrude."

Alix nodded soberly. "I've felt that too. There's such serenity here. Returning to the real world's going to be almost unbearable."

Mattie was lounging against the counter, her face taut with an old pain. "This place can uplift you," she said. "When I lost Diana, that sense of peace pulled me through—that and the help of a few good friends."

Alix slipped her hand into mine. I caressed her fingers as I said, "I haven't told Alix anything about you and Diana."

Mattie looked as though she wanted to speak, as though she needed to speak, but Beth broke into the room just then.

"Mommy, Mommy! I had it first and Cindy took it away!"

"Took what away, baby?" Alix inquired as Beth drew her outdoors.

"Guess we'll never know…" I said into the air. Then I turned to Mattie. Underneath her composure, there was a stricken look. Crossing the kitchen, I enveloped her. She relaxed against me, resting her forehead on my shoulder.

"Thanks, Lynn. Seems you're always there when I need you."

"The feeling's mutual," I told her.

Mattie flashed me a small grin and disengaged herself. She was labeling jars when Alix returned. The somber mood had lifted. We cleaned up our mess and made PBJs for dinner. After a day at the stove, we'd lost all interest in cooking.

* * *

That evening began as a repeat of the one before. Freshly-bathed children were sung to sleep, and we outlasted a dwindling fire. Very late, Mattie rose stiffly and rubbed her knees. She rustled around in a closet for a moment. When she came back, she was carrying an old, highly polished fiddle. Without preamble, she began to play a sensuous, melancholy version of "Old Joe Clark," almost more improvisation than melody. Alix was spellbound.

"That's wonderful!" she breathed. "I've never heard an interpretation like that."

"Diana taught it to me—it was her arrangement. I used to play a guitar accompaniment. I wish you could have heard us, Alix! You're the first person I've ever wanted to teach it to."

"I'd love to learn it." Then, recognizing the opening, Alix said, "Will you tell me about her?"

Mattie's storm-colored eyes focused off in the distance. When she found her voice, it was hushed and halting, the drawl more pronounced than usual. "Diana Kingston was a photographer. We used to work together at the magazine. At first I hardly noticed her. She was so quiet and of course she was married. But we were assigned to some of the same stories. Once or twice we were even sent on location together. I got to know her better, to like her more and more. And when we began to share music, she took me over completely. I couldn't believe I'd ever been oblivious to her."

Mattie's head went down on her knees, elbows locking around her shins. "I was afraid to tell her about me, that I was gay. Afraid I'd lose her friendship…I'd been in love with Diana for almost a year, trying hard to remember that she was straight. Then one day we were in the darkroom looking at her contact prints for a story we'd covered. We were laughing about one of the shots, our heads close over the proof sheet, when she said in this very wistful way, 'Mattie Reynolds, aren't you *ever* going to kiss me?'"

A glowing log shifted on the hearth, flinging brilliant pinpoints upward. Mattie managed a laugh. "Appropriate enough—we did strike sparks together. I thought I could bear anything to be with her, including the fact of her marriage. But pretty soon things got so intense that she moved in with me."

My dear friend drew a long, staggering breath. I handed her a glass of wine, but she shook her head and set it on the hearth beside her. Alix stretched to pat Mattie's hand. "You don't have to tell me this," she said earnestly. "I'm a stranger. I should never have asked."

Mattie raised those wise eyes and fixed them on Alix. "Do you *feel* like a stranger?"

"No," she admitted.

"There's a reason for that. You and I—we're a little short on the fine details, but we understand each other all right."

Alix met her gaze, nodding acknowledgment, and Mattie continued. "There was a lot of good between Diana and me. We fought like fury to hold on to it. But in the end, she left me. Her husband had pressured her night and day, refused to let her see their daughter, you know…all the standard tricks. He swore he'd love her forever if she returned, but destroy her if she didn't. When she went back to him, I actually thought I'd die. Eating and sleeping were no longer part of my life. Seeing her at the office was torture."

Mattie ran rawboned fingers through her graying hair. "One day when we were in the restroom together at work, I noticed a bad bruise on Diana's arm. She explained it away, but I began to watch her closely. She wouldn't talk about it, but there was no doubt she was being abused. I was going crazy—I knew it was because of me.

"It seemed that if I put some distance between us, it might help…in more ways than one. So I asked my editor for a leave of absence to organize that first book. He gave it to me. I think it was pretty obvious I needed it. I came here and began putting myself back together, piece by piece. I'd made a little progress when the letter arrived."

Now Mattie's face took on a ghostly pallor. I reached for her hand as she struggled for control. "A secretary at the magazine who'd always been kind to us wrote to inform me of Diana's death. It seemed she'd taken a nasty spill down her basement steps on the way to do laundry. There were more bruises than might have been expected, but falls are funny like that—or so the police said." Mattie sought and found a detached tone, but it was shaky. "Of course, there was not one goddamned thing I could do but grieve and wail and wallow in guilt."

I knew she needed help lightening things up, so I cut in. "And that's what she was doing when I met her, folks—howling in the wilderness."

Swallowing the last of my wine, I leaned against Alix to reassure her. "It was the summer before my junior year in college and I'd just decided to become a potter. So I'd come down here to dig my own clay—it wasn't just a great learning experience, I could get the stuff for free. Which tells you exactly how poor I was, because nothing's cheaper than clay. Anyway, I was tramping up and down creek beds, looking for a workable site to dig. And that's when I met Mattie. Imagine my surprise when I looked up to see her teetering on the edge of a bluff, railing at the skies."

I winked at Alix. "She was really something. I couldn't decide whether to console her or seduce her, so I did both."

Raising her palm in protest, Mattie said, "Now, Alix, don't you take her seriously. I invited Lynn to have lunch with me here. We got on, so I told her she could bed down on the cabin floor for a few days."

"Yeah," I said. "It took me two whole weeks to work my way into her heart—and points south."

"*Lynn*!" Mattie reprimanded me. "You're making Alix uncomfortable!" She stretched strong hands toward Alix and looked her in the eye.

"What Lynn's trying to avoid telling you with all this zaniness is that she saved my sanity. Literally. I was pretty far gone when she found me, hysterical a lot of the time, and considering suicide. Lynn made me talk and laugh and remember and feel better about myself. And finally she took me to bed. I'd needed that really badly—needed to know that something *good* could come from my loving." Mattie's voice was foggy with emotion. "Lynn brought me back to life, and that's the simple truth."

"Actually, I had an ulterior motive: I was afraid she'd quit baking bread if she got any more depressed."

"*Enough*, Lynn, *enough*!" shushed Mattie.

I looked carefully at Alix. Mattie was right. There was a hint of something unsettled in her eyes. But she made a face and ruffled my hair.

"So much for your tough-dyke act, Westfall," she said. "Thanks, Mattie. I can use this as evidence—every now and then she needs her nose rubbed in her own sensitivity."

"Maybe we should keep records," Mattie suggested with a grin.

Alix's eyes grew huge. "Jesus Christ, Lynn! There's something I keep meaning to tell you, but every time it's crossed my mind the girls were underfoot. Charles is making notes about us!"

A grave look washed over Mattie's face and she nodded knowingly. But I was still three steps behind.

"He's what?"

"It's the first thing Charles's lawyer would have told him to do," Mattie said, "if Charles weren't a lawyer himself."

I felt a chill rush of reality. The protective ring of remoteness dissolved, leaving us defenseless again. "How do you know?" I asked Alix.

"Charles has a phone in his office at home. I answered a call there while he was out of town, and I needed to leave a message for him. So I grabbed a legal pad from his desk drawer. I was flipping through it, trying to find a blank page, but it turned out there weren't any. He's done a pretty thorough job of documenting my life."

Maybe it was the late hour—or the wine. I still didn't understand. "What kind of notes is he making?"

"Dates. Times. Places. How often I'm with you, how much I'm away from the girls—all kinds of stuff."

"Whether you two are together overnight, or go to places frequented by lesbians," Mattie added. "It's standard operating procedure. Diana's husband did the same thing."

Alix chuckled bleakly. "Charles has even encouraged me to spend time with you lately. I guess he wants to incriminate me so thoroughly I won't stand a rat's chance of getting Beth and Cindy after the divorce." She blinked back tears. "God knows, I scarcely do now."

Silhouetted against a window, with a rising moon behind, Alix's fragile frame was overshadowed by Mattie's rugged angularity. My chest began to ache. If Mathilde Reynolds had barely survived, where would Alix find the stamina to see this through?

"My friends," I said, "it's time to talk strategy."

Mattie nodded emphatically, but Alix wasn't on the same page. "What a cold way to deal with so much emotion," she murmured.

"The only way, Alix—we're fighting for everything you hold dear," Mattie reminded her. Still, Alix sat silent as we began to plot a campaign.

"She has to see a lawyer now, Mattie."

"Absolutely. She needed one weeks ago. And you should probably arrange a meeting with Barbara Chase."

"What a great idea!" I said. "I think you'd like her, Alix. She was an instructor of mine in grad school, and she's a success story. She has custody of her twins even though she was living openly with a lover at the time of her divorce. She could probably give us a lot of ideas about how to work this thing."

Alix stood abruptly. Turning away, she said, "I need to get some sleep before the girls wake up." Then, in a careful tone, she added, "I know you both mean well, but I may have to do this my own way. It *is* my life, you know."

There was a ring of finality in her voice. The pain in my chest got worse. "Alix," I said urgently, "you can do it *your* way. Or you can *win*. This is no time for naïveté or high-minded idealism. That's certainly not the deck that Charles is playing with."

I could see I'd only made her angrier. Her sleeping bag unrolled with a vigorous snap and she strode briskly into the bathroom, toothbrush in hand. Mattie patted my shoulder sympathetically.

"It's late, Lynn. We're all dog-tired."

I hugged her hard and we exchanged a doleful glance before parting for the night.

* * *

Six hours later, Alix and I were on the road again, deeply immersed in our first real argument, trying to speak in code while the children jabbered behind us. I was incredulous—how could we be fighting when I was only trying to take care of her?

"All my life, people have been trying to protect me, Lynn. Give me some room to be myself."

"But, Alix, this is so important! We can't afford to make mistakes about it. We need advice from someone who knows the ropes. Think how bitter you'll be, think how much you'll *lose* if you're wrong." I was pleading with her. "Nobility can wait—we've got to be practical now."

Alix's hands were white on the wheel. "There's an old movie about politics," she told me. "I can never remember what it's called. At a critical moment in the plot, an elder statesman asks a ruthless newcomer if he believes the end justifies the means. The younger man says he does. Then the old guy delivers the film's pivotal speech. *Ends*, he insists, are an illusion. *Means* are all we have."

Alix threw me a serious look. "I believe that, Lynn. Of all the things I learned while watching my father in action, this is the most important: No matter how many miles you walk on a low road, you never reach high ground." Turning her attention to the highway, she said, "I have to come out of this mess liking myself. If I don't, it won't matter *what* I win in the end."

I looked over my shoulder. Beth and Cindy were stretched out on the backseat, sound asleep. "Not even if it's your children?" I asked in a low voice.

Alix bit her lip. "I have to accept that I may lose them. I have to come to terms with that."

"You don't have to lose them, baby! You just have to be smart enough about the system, and you can keep them. You just have to use everything you know about Charles, and you can keep them. What's so *fucking wrong* with that?"

I was sure I could make her see my point of view if only I could summon enough eloquence. "Let's fight this with everything we've got, Alix. Then if we lose, we can never blame one another for the failure."

And there was something else I needed to say. I rested my tired head on the upholstery and closed my eyes against scalding tears. "I'm afraid if we don't wage an all-out battle for the girls now, one day you'll decide you paid *much* too high a price for the pleasure of my company."

Alix's cool fingers wrapped around my hot ones. She squeezed softly and sighed. "Not possible, honey. Let's not quarrel anymore, okay? We'll find a way to work this out."

It was a relief to pretend she was right, so comforting to slip back into a friendlier frame. We were subdued, but at peace with each other, for the rest of the long drive home.

CHAPTER TWENTY-FOUR

When I awoke I was all jazzed up, so full of plans and possibilities that I could only manage routine tasks at work. I decided I'd power up my pug mill to make a fresh batch of clay—a satisfying process, though tiring. There's something ritualistic about mixing old clay with new, wet with dry, making a softness that turns to stone. By lunchtime, I'd filled four huge trash cans with heavy slabs of extruded clay and swept my mess off the concrete floor. The day was so warm that I rolled up the garage door at the back of my studio. Fresh air circulated through the room, and my mind was still as active as clay dust spiraling in October sunshine.

I cleared a space on my desk and sat there with a limp ham sandwich. Two thoughts had gained ascendancy as I'd worked. I wanted Alix to move in with me as soon as possible. And I wanted her to see a lawyer. I knew she couldn't do the first until she'd done the second.

Clenching the sandwich between my teeth, I thumbed through the thick metropolitan phone book. But the name

I remembered wasn't listed. Frustrated, I munched on my indifferent meal until an idea struck me. I picked up the phone and dialed an old friend.

"Deb!" I said enthusiastically. "Where the hell are you hanging out these days? I haven't seen you in ages!"

She laughed. "Listen, you shit, you're not going to get away with that act. *We're* all still here—*you're* the one who's gone into seclusion. And with good reason, or so I hear. Next time we get together, Susan's going to give you a hard time about it."

"Let's make that sooner rather than later," I suggested. "I'm coming to St. Louis for your opening. I'd like to take the two of you to dinner then."

"You're on. Now, what's the real purpose of this call?"

"Creep! You know me too well."

On the other end of the line, Deb laughed again. I could almost see her eyes crinkle. I said, "At one of your barbecues, I met a lawyer. I want to talk with her now, but I can't find her name in the phone book. Does she still work in the city?"

"Aha! The plot thickens! You must mean Andrea Fasteau. She's the only lawyer I know."

"Right first name, Deb, wrong surname."

"Same person, hon. She changed her last name."

"Not married?" I asked, surprised.

"God, no. She's one of ours. Thomas was her foster family's name. She finally decided to reclaim her own. You'll find her listed under Castelli, Fasteau, McManess and Morgenstern."

"What is it—the fucking UN?"

"Don't knock it, Lynn. I understand they're topnotch. You and I should make so much money."

"Well, anybody dumb enough to be an artist deserves to live in poverty."

"Tell me about it," Deb groaned. "I made the mistake of hiring someone to build my stretchers for this show and the bill just arrived. All I can say is *some* of those damned paintings better sell."

Since our conversation had veered in the direction of work, I tried to describe a series of collaborative pieces I was making with Sven Jarlsberg, the metalsmith I'd stumbled across back in the summer. I'd gone to check out his work shortly after we'd met in that park during Alix's very first therapy appointment. His stuff had knocked me out, so we'd decided to see whether we could blend our disciplines. It was almost a game, each of us trying to outdo the other. I'd present Sven with half-a-dozen fired pieces, the zanier, the better. Then he'd surprise me with hand-forged metal embellishments. Handles, cages, stands, hangers—whatever wildness my pots suggested to him. These were experimental pieces, like nothing either of us had ever seen before, much less produced. And they were selling. Sven thought we were almost ready for a show.

After I said goodbye to Deb, I sat at my desk wondering whether Alix and I should move back to St. Louis after her divorce. Much as I loved the relaxed pace of rural life, the energy of urban areas had always had a hold on me. My work was known in the metro area. With higher prices there and a larger volume of sales, I might be able to afford a small shop near the studio where Sven worked. And that would put me in a stronghold of the gay community. Our people. All at once, I knew how much I'd missed them.

But then I remembered how determined Alix was to raise Cindy and Beth in a setting where outdoor play wasn't confined to public parks and there were no concerns about safety. The children would have to be our top priority if we actually made it through this thing together. Which meant staying in Quillan's Crossing—or someplace like it…

Slow down, I told myself. It's way too early in the game to worry about residency. You have to get *custody* first.

I left work early that day. There were errands I wanted to run before the stores closed. I was full of nervous energy, and luck was with me—I accomplished amazing feats in record time. Driving toward Alix's house, I felt absurdly young and lighthearted. Charles was away on another of his protracted trips and the girls were spending the night with a friend. Best of all, yesterday's tension had evaporated. The evening stretched ahead full of promise.

When I steered my car down that steeply-pitched driveway, I saw Alix waiting outside on the deck. Her smile reflected my mood perfectly. She ran and flung her arms around my neck, kissing me enthusiastically. "Let's do something special, Lynn! I feel like being outrageous!"

"Terrific!" I said. "Let's go."

We stopped at my house so I could shower, but there was no time to wash clay dust from my heavy hair. I twisted it into a loose knot at the nape of my neck and pulled on my favorite jeans. The air was still so warm I dropped an India gauze smock over my shoulders, then dashed downstairs.

My workday had been uneventful, but exhausting, so Alix drove into the city. Just for grins, I directed her to MoonChild—a vegetarian café where she'd never eaten—pointing out Sven's studio along the way. This is a test, I told myself, only a test. There's not a straight person for blocks. Let's see how Alix responds to my old stomping grounds.

Gays and lesbians had not only claimed the Capeheart District, they'd revitalized it. But the venerable restaurant had retained its earthy menu and funky clientele. In truth, I'd always found the diners at MoonChild more appealing than the dinners. I had a hunch, though, that Alix would love the place. What I *hadn't* anticipated was the commotion my arrival created. I hadn't been there for over a year. Who'd have guessed that I'd be greeted so warmly?

When we were finally seated, Alix cocked her dark head at me. "You must be losing your touch."

"What do you mean?"

"I count three women who haven't kissed you," she observed dryly. "I thought you said you didn't particularly enjoy eating here."

"I was talking about the *food*, sweetheart."

Under the batik tablecloth, Alix kicked my shin, but I just smiled serenely. She grinned back, displaying the dimple that I found more enchanting every day. Just then Jamal arrived at her side with a miniature loaf of whole-grain bread and two menus. We settled down to the serious business of selecting dinner.

To my everlasting embarrassment, I'm still a carnivore. A meal without meat seems scarcely worth eating. More highly-evolved types are praying for my enlightenment, but that does me little good when contemplating the menu at MoonChild. I struggled to find an option I could appreciate. Alix had the opposite problem—everything sounded delicious to her. I was able to identify some of the most popular dishes, but after that, she was on her own. As she tried to narrow her choices, I had to remind her that she really didn't eat very much.

When we'd finished our salads, I could wait no longer. Reaching into my pocket, I withdrew a velvet case and placed it on the table in front of Alix.

She ran an oval nail across the domed lid. "Why, darling, are we engaged?"

"I *wish*," I sighed. "Stuff of my dreams."

She blew me a kiss and opened the box. On dark satin lining, a brass ring linked ornate keys. "To your heart?" Alix guessed.

"*And* to my home. I want you to live with me, darling. It's ridiculous to spend so much time apart. Please say yes."

"It's all I want, Lynn—you know that. But it might send Charles completely over the edge. And I don't know how it would affect my legal position." Alix lifted the ring and looped it over a finger, clasping her hand around the keys. Her eyes glittered with tears as she repeated herself. "I *do* want this *so much*."

"Then let's see a lawyer, Alix. Let's get some information. I've met a woman who might be good and I tracked her down today. If we talk with her, at least we'll know where we stand."

Alix uncurled her fingers and looked at the keys to my house. The front door, the back door. She took a deep breath. "Yes," she said. "All right."

* * *

The full moon was high overhead when we pulled up into my driveway. On the porch I hung back until it occurred to Alix to use her key. We entered holding hands and found the living room flooded with pale, cool light. Suddenly, I needed to celebrate. I grabbed a favorite album and dropped it on the turntable. It was old and scratchy, one of the rare mainstream recordings I'd worn out through obsessive use. In that silvery space, I pulled Alix to me and we danced to a soft, smoky voice crooning "The Shadow of Your Smile."

"Oh, I know that singer," Alix said. "Why can't I place her?"

"Bet you never will," I challenged.

She drew back to stare at me. "You would bet a musician that she can't identify a singer?" Alix asked in ascending tones of horror.

"Yep."

"What's the bet?"

"If you guess her, I'll fix cashew chicken tomorrow night."

"Fool," Alix chortled, "you're doubly doomed! You've made the stakes too high!"

I tightened my arms around her and we swayed together without speaking. Then, halfway through "Manhã de Carnaval," Alix leaped with excitement. "I've got her! I've got her! I can't remember her name yet, but it *has* to be the 'Girl from Ipanema.'"

"Close enough," I said. "We'll eat Chinese tomorrow."

"We'll also get a new copy of that album—it's an affront to my delicate sensibilities."

"That's an impossible mission, my dear. Believe me. I've tried. Today, no one seems to have heard of Astrud Gilberto. She's not even in the catalogs anymore."

Alix sighed. "What a shame! Some of the arrangements are a bit corny, but she has *such* a fascinating voice." Putting her head on my shoulder, she relaxed into my embrace. We floated on that airy sound for a long time.

There's a period of exquisite balance in any love affair—a moment when all uncertainty has fallen away, yet passion can still be ignited by a glance. Alix and I had been riding the crest of this perfect wave for months, but that night our lovemaking was touched by a special intensity. Maybe the discord of the previous day had shaken us more deeply than we realized. Whatever the reason, we sought and found reassurance in our heightening excitement. There was a sense of connection between us that I'd never known with anyone else. Alix always seemed to understand what I wanted before I recognized the desire myself.

We lay on my bed, awash in the moon's radiance, her fingers moving over me in an unbroken pattern. First inside, where they answered an ancient longing. Next sliding slowly upward to the source of ecstasy, then slipping deep within me again. Her soft mouth was never still. Her tongue traced lines of fire on my throat. She kissed me and called me to her by a dozen endearments. At last she held my trembling body hard against her fine-lined length.

I rested for a while in another reality, aware only of soft breathing and stroking hands. Finally I whispered, "Roll over, love." Alix turned her back to me and I pulled her close, the curves of my body seeking correspondences with her own. Easing one arm beneath her, I cupped my hand around a yearning breast and caressed her. Moaning low, she pressed herself against me and entwined one leg with mine. My other hand made its way down her rib cage, over a subtle rounding of hip, then lower still. Parting the flesh in that glorious tangle of hair, I encountered sweet, familiar moisture. Alix twisted in my arms, telegraphing her need, demanding more. At first I matched the lazy rhythm I'd established at her breast, playing it out, teasing her a little. But soon our bodies were rocking to a staccato tempo. And when my noisy darling came, I was not far behind. Waking beside her just before dawn, I felt like I'd been blessed.

* * *

"Alix? Can you come up here?"

"On my way."

I heard her running up the stairs. She arrived seconds later, a paperback still in hand. "What's up, Lynn?"

I opened the door to a spare bedroom on my second floor. It was empty except for a stack of suitcases, a few cartons of college textbooks and my ironing board. Sun spilled into the room, highlighting every defect. Peeling wallpaper. Grimy woodwork. A dinged-up floor. But Alix instantly saw the potential. "This could really be adorable! Those charming windows…the angles of the eaves…that bead board wainscot. And the light is marvelous."

"Have you ever stripped wallpaper or painted?" A fair question, I thought. Because, after all, she was a rich girl.

"No, but I'm a quick learner. I'd *love* to help bring this room up to speed."

"It would be a lot of work, but I figure it's worth it."

"Do you have a plan in mind?"

"Yep. I'm thinking white enamel for the floor. A sparkly, whimsical chandelier. A feminine paint scheme. Froufy curtains—or louvered shutters." I pointed to the far end of the room. "Twin beds flanking those windows. Maybe a fairyland mural on the ceiling. Or whatever the girls would like."

Alix was staring at me, wide-eyed and glowing. "Lynn! Do you *mean* it?"

"They can't keep sleeping on the couch, sweetheart. They need their own space here."

"And you're that sure we're going to get them?"

I put my arm around her and hedged a bit. "I'm that sure we *deserve* them, Alix. I'm that committed to fighting for them. I'm that excited about having them in my life."

She turned to nestle into me. "You're the *best*, Lynn Westfall."

"Right back at you, baby. I think Cindy and Beth should pick the wall color, but we can start refinishing the floor right away. Want to shop for supplies after lunch?"

"Who needs lunch?"

If Alix was surprised by that turn of events, I could go her one better. Because until the girls began to spend days at a time with us, I hadn't guessed how much I'd missed having a family to call my own. In their company, I realized I'd never even allowed myself to consider parenthood. The very idea would have seemed off-limits, unimaginable—as improbable as becoming an astronaut. As unlikely as choosing to strap myself into a small, constricting space for a voyage to an alien destination.

Now I'd found that something deep inside me—a hard

little kernel of denial—was softening, expanding, stretching toward the light. More and more I'd warmed to the laughter and unconditional affection that Beth and Cindy brought into my home. The question of custody had become personal. To my amazement, I'd been overtaken by a desperation that echoed Alix's own.

CHAPTER TWENTY-FIVE

A few nights later, the telephone rang after dinner, shattering my concentration. I slapped my sketchbook shut and raced to interrupt the shrill sound. Only Alix's voice would be welcome just then. "Yes," I answered irritably.

"Lynn," said Alix, sounding strained and unnatural, "are you busy?"

"Never too busy for you, sweetheart. Is something wrong?"

"Well, actually, I'm calling because Charles wants to speak with you."

"He *what*?" I couldn't get a handle on this. "Charles isn't on the extension, is he, Alix?"

"Oh, no," she assured me. "But he has this unshakable notion that the two of you need to meet and talk."

"I don't share the conviction," I said coldly. Then I had to wonder whether Alix did. Otherwise, why had she agreed to ask me? "I don't know what good it would do to meet with Charles, hon, but if you want me to, I guess I could."

"No. I told him it seemed pointless to me, but he insisted that I call you."

She sounded exhausted beyond recovery. I could have killed Charles. *Why* will men swear they love women when they grind us down so callously? "Put old Chuck on the line for a minute."

Alix choked. "Boy, he'd hate being called *that*!"

"And his feelings *are* my first priority. Give him the phone."

I hoped to make short work of this intrusion. But cheated of the opportunity to berate me in person, Charles used every conceivable strategy to prolong the dialogue. I was quickly entangled in a sticky web of insinuation and crisscrossing allegations. Reminding myself that Dunnevan was a lawyer—not to mention the lieutenant governor's main man—I chose every word with care. Even so, my fledgling paranoia unfurled wings and took flight. Charles was surely making notes as we talked, might even be recording our interaction.

It was amazing, I thought, how much his appeal depended on visuals and proximity. If you couldn't see that handsome face, couldn't be drawn in by the practiced charisma, you noticed that his voice was a bit thin and nasal, with just a hint of a southern accent. He had the kind of good looks that would have worked well on TV, but he'd never have made it in radio.

Each time I tried to shut Charles down, he overruled me. "I think whenever you close lines of communication, it's a dangerous thing."

Dangerous? Was that a veiled threat? With effort, I kept my cool. "Mr. Dunnevan, you and I have nothing to talk about."

"Now, Lynn," he replied in that grating voice, "it seems to me that we have quite a lot in common. After all, we're both in love with the same woman. And you must see as well as I do how unstable Alix is just now."

Trying to avoid all the traps at once, I said, "I don't agree with your assessment of her mental health. And at your insistence, Alix is already seeing a therapist. That seems like an appropriate way to deal with any stress she might be experiencing."

"Well, I guess I don't put all that much stock in your handpicked psychologist. I don't need another *feminist* opinion of my wife's condition. I have concrete evidence of her confusion. Just a few weeks before you seduced her, Alix wrote a letter to her college roommate. Stephanie shared it with me on a recent visit. It describes Alix's satisfaction with our relationship in considerable detail."

I didn't care whether that was true or not. It no longer applied. And I was tired of the whole stupid exchange. "Look, Mr. Dunnevan, the person you need to discuss this with is Alix."

"You know, I'd very much like to do that, Lynn. But it seems my wife is rarely home these days. Don't you think it's rather unfair of you to isolate her from her family?"

"Are you implying that Alix has no free will? That I've bewitched her?"

"All I'm suggesting is that you have a powerful hold on the mind of an extremely disturbed woman. No one else can convince her of anything. And I love her very much, you see. We have a long history together."

"Exactly, Mr. Dunnevan. You've had years to convince Alix that you care. If you've failed, that's not my problem."

There was a silence at the other end. When he spoke again, Charles had changed his tack. His voice took on a menacing edge. "I'd strongly advise you not to play with me, Ms. Westfall."

A chill ran down my spine—I'd been right about the threat. When I didn't bite, Charles dropped the hammer. "Since you and my wife seem determined to pursue this repugnant lifestyle, Alix may have her freedom. But she'll have to manage without my daughters. I'm quite capable of raising them, and I intend to do so."

Oh, god! I wanted to strangle the bastard! It took every bit of self-control to answer calmly. "Alix wants freedom from marriage, not motherhood. You know that, Mr. Dunnevan. And *she* has as great a claim on those children as you do."

Now Charles was chuckling cozily, a dizzying change of tone. "I don't think there's a judge in this county who'll agree with you. Not when he knows what goes on over there."

"Just a minute," I exploded, "*you* don't know what goes on over here! There's not a minute when we're not focused on your daughters' well-being. We read to them and we rock them, we draw together and we sing them to sleep—"

"I've heard the kind of music you people listen to!" Charles yelled. "You may have corrupted my wife with your filthy tapes, but maybe it's not too late to save my girls!"

A great wave of nausea rolled through me and I thought I might faint. "Mr. Dunnevan," I said vehemently, "I *will not* discuss *any of this* with you *ever again*!"

Slamming down the receiver, I flung myself out of the house. Solly skittered through the door behind me. We walked together under the waning moon for more than an hour, but I still felt sickened and twitchy when we turned homeward. In the shuddering silence of my living room, I built a small fire and put Cris Williamson on the stereo. Sprawled on the couch, with Sol draped across my midriff, I finally fell asleep.

* * *

Good gracious, Mattie!

So much has happened since we left your enchanted forest! After all your hospitality, you deserve an update, but this letter may run to book-length! Life here seems to go from bizarre to worse.

You know, I think of myself as a pretty ordinary person. But I seem to have gotten more than my fair share of both the weird and the wonderful in life. It's the former that occupies me at present. This particular phase of insanity began with a disturbing phone call from Alix's husband. Suffice it to say that I don't think he accomplished whatever he had in mind when he talked with (*at!*) me. So he shifted into a higher gear.

Suddenly good ole Chuck became so distraught at the failure of their marriage that he was contemplating suicide. Constantly. *I* was all for letting him follow through, but Alix is a much nicer person than I am. She's spent the last two weeks dragging him out of the woods behind their house, wresting the pills (or the knife or *whatever*) away from him. I tell you, Matt, I'm too old for all this high drama!

The prick has an uncanny knack for manipulating Alix. She's convinced that she's obligated to stabilize him before getting on with her own life. You can imagine how attractive I've found that prospect—Charles could milk it for years. I'd like to lock him up and be done with it, but I've tried to restrain my bitchier impulses...Alix has that effect on me.

Besides, I've been marking time until we have our first legal consultation, hoping for some good news there. Shortly after we left your place, Alix conceded that she'd better get advice about her life from a lawyer she *isn't* divorcing. We've arranged to see an attorney (lesbian/feminist) next week. Her name is Andrea (Thomas) Fasteau. Do you know her? I met her at Deb's a year ago and liked her immensely. She spent a long time explaining a lesbian custody case she'd argued, so she came to mind immediately.

But then I was caught off guard by another exciting development. Get ready: Charles kicked Alix out of their house! Do you believe that? He swears he's still committed to saving the marriage, but claims that seeing Alix is just too painful. So, of course, he shoved her straight (all right! all right!) into my arms. Does this make any sense?

I didn't think so at first, but now I'm not so sure. There's undoubtedly a legal angle here—some way of prejudicing Alix's custody and/or property rights. I argued against her leaving before we saw the attorney, even though I've longed to have her (and the girls) here. But, through whatever psychological means, Charles succeeded in forcing her out. It's been horrific for her to be separated from the children so much. (Not totally separated though—Charles, self-serving as ever, will actually deliver Beth and Cindy to my doorstep when it suits *his* purposes!)

Still, this has been a relief in some ways. Being apart through so many crises has undeniably strained our relationship. We've got to weather the tough times together. Just often enough now, we're like two kids who've robbed a candy store—delirious with pleasure and hoping like hell nobody catches up with us.

A really special thing happened to us recently, Matt. Once Alix moved in with me, we decided we could save the Abbies a lot of grief if I resigned. We figured the situation must be pretty apparent to anyone with half a brain. And we didn't want to give the hostile natives a foolproof way to discredit everyone else's hard work. So when the executive committee met last week, I announced that I was withdrawing from the organization for "personal reasons." The other officers hemmed and hawed and pussyfooted around the obvious. Finally dear Jenny, formerly so timid, said, "For heaven's sake, Lynn! Did you think we could only accept you as a lesbian as long as you didn't have a lover?"

Yes. I guess I did. I felt ashamed and proud and humbled and exhilarated all at once. I was so touched that I cried on my damned report. We agreed unanimously that it was too blurred to read, so we adjourned and went out for a few beers instead.

I may still leave the group. Alix and I need a lot of private time right now. We're feeling awfully exposed and vulnerable. And those beautiful women on the committee don't know how brutal this may get before it ends. But oh, Mattie! Their support meant *so much* to me! I can live on that for a long time.

Meanwhile, I've been looking for a piano to rent as a surprise for Alix. Not only does she need the emotional outlet, but her own income depends on the instrument that Charles is holding hostage. At the moment, she's had to suspend lessons with all her students, and she's afraid she'll lose them to other teachers. Wish I had your expertise in the quest—I don't really know what to look for or how to judge quality.

I suppose that's really all the news from around here.

Ah, yes—I keep forgetting that you have a life too. What's the latest word from all your animal friends, Snow White? How's the novel coming? And when will *you* visit *us*?

Write to me sometime, woman! If that magazine of yours ever folds, I won't know whether you're dead or alive.

A frenetic farewell from
Lynn

P.S. The column on wildcrafting was wonderful.

CHAPTER TWENTY-SIX

Despite my attempt to sound lighthearted, to gloss over some of our distress, I knew Mattie could read between the lines. She wouldn't need specifics to understand how frustrated I'd be by now, how weary of melodrama—she'd lived through it herself. I hated to worry her, but I realized that silence would make her anxious too. And, once again, I needed her. I was afraid to confide in many people, unwilling to accept criticism or dismissal: "Well, Lynn, *straight women*—I mean, what did you *expect?*"

What *had* I expected? I suppose I'd anticipated a more complete severing of ties between Alix and Charles. That she loved me I did not doubt, but her responsiveness to Dunnevan's ploys had injected real friction into our relationship. The man had an unnerving ability to detonate nasty little explosions all over our emotional landscape. He'd quickly become the driving force in our daily lives. And just when we thought we knew which direction he was headed, he'd reverse gears, jolting us badly. The suicide interval had taken us by surprise. Alix was devastated. I was bitter and cynical.

It started one night when she'd arrived home after meeting with the Eagle Committee. Her daughters were asleep in their beds, but Charles was nowhere in sight. He'd tacked an unsettling note to Cindy's bedroom door. Alix telephoned me immediately, anger about the abandoned children tempered by guilt and concern.

She wouldn't let me go to her, so I kept her on the line until Charles skulked in forty minutes later. As we hung up, I tried to imagine how he'd play out the inevitable scene. Every option I could envision was repugnant. I'd never known a night so long.

* * *

Alix looked bad when she met me for lunch two days later. She had the bruised and wilted look she always wore when Charles was working on her. In a restaurant that neither of us frequented, we ordered salads. I hated that I couldn't touch her.

"Well," I asked, not really caring, "how is he today?"

"All right, I suppose. He seemed fairly normal when he left for Jeff City this morning."

"What about the girls?"

"They're okay, thank god. Cindy and Beth never knew anything was going on the other night. He makes sure I'm the only one who witnesses the crazy stuff—which would make it my word against his, I suppose."

And, I thought, it *certainly* suggests he can control his behavior if he chooses. But I knew Alix needed to talk, needed me to listen. "Tell me what happened after he came in."

She took a deep breath. "Christ, it was just awful! He was caked with mud and leaves. It looked like he'd been crashing through the woods for a week. He wouldn't speak at all—just stared at me with burning eyes. He really seemed insane."

Ice cubes clattered as Alix tried to raise a glass to her lips. Embarrassed, she set it down without drinking. "I wanted to calm him, to make him connect with reality. I knelt in front of him and tried to explain that I'll always care about him at some level—that his happiness truly matters to me. He laughed horribly—I can still hear that sound. I was trying to think what to do next when something fell from his hand…a bottle of tranquilizers…enough to *kill* him, Lynn!"

"A person who loved you wouldn't put you through this, Alix."

She bit her lip in exasperation. "Don't you see? He can't help himself! He's confused and hurt—I've turned his whole world upside down."

Even to me, my voice sounded harsh. "Nobody makes it through life without major pain, Alix. Most people learn to cope with it. After all, divorce isn't the worst of human experiences."

"But what if Charles *can't* cope?"

"That's his tragedy, then. Are you supposed to sacrifice your own happiness because he can't make the adjustment?"

"I don't know," Alix snapped, "but I feel like I've destroyed him and I can't figure out how to handle that!"

Propriety be damned…I reached across the table for her hands and spoke carefully. "Look, sweetheart, one of two things is true. Charles is *either* a Machiavellian asshole who's yanking your chain for his own selfish purposes. *Or* he's a fucked-up mess. I don't even care which it is. He has no business raising your children."

The waitress was looking at us strangely. I released Alix, saying, "The man clearly needs professional help."

"He won't see anybody, Lynn. I suggested it the other night and he just laughed like a lunatic."

"Listen, you've got to get Beth and Cindy out of there right away. I'm convinced that Charles is just manipulating you, but we can't risk being wrong about this. Bring the girls to my house this evening, okay?"

Alix shoved her salad aside, untouched. "I tried that last night. He let me get everything packed before he said he'd call the sheriff if I took them through the door."

"So what could the sheriff have done? They're *your* children too."

"I asked Charles the same question. He just stood there smiling, with the phone in his hand. 'Wait and see,' was all he'd say."

"God, I wish that *you'd* come to me, at least."

"I couldn't, love. Charles was too weird, and he'd already left the kids by themselves the night before. I didn't dare go anywhere without them—as he well realized. And you have to remember something else, Lynn."

"What's that?"

"There are advantages to working for the lieutenant governor. Charles and the sheriff have all sorts of political friends in common. Anything could happen if the Old Boys' Network gets into the act."

I crumpled my napkin in furious impotence. "He's really trapped you, hasn't he? You're a goddamned prisoner!"

Too emotional to speak, Alix could only nod. I paid our bill and ushered her out of the restaurant, my mind working furiously. I bitterly resented Dunnevan's creepy behavior, which was consuming so much of our time. And I didn't believe he was a helpless victim of domestic conflict. Some underlying strategy governed all his actions. But I couldn't penetrate his logic, couldn't figure out the game he was playing.

* * *

I was no closer to cracking the code when Charles evicted Alix from their home. Right then though it was enough that we were together again. We desperately needed some time to relax and recover. Storm winds had left their marks on us. If this momentary calm was merely the eye of the hurricane, I wanted to remain within it for as long as possible. I tried to forget that a tempest raged around us. Driving home at night, I'd focus my attention as narrowly as possible. Only the next few hours with Alix mattered.

In this mood one evening, I entered the front door to find our house silent and empty. A note in Alix's dashing script was tucked into the frame of the foyer mirror.

Lynn, darling—

I know how much you'll hate this, but I've gone to meet with Charles. He's drafted some kind of custody/property agreement that he wants me to read. Don't panic, love…I won't sign *anything* tonight. That dumb I'm not.

If this looks like one more instance when Charles has manipulated me, I regard it mostly as an opportunity to spend time with Cindy and Beth. You'll understand why I couldn't pass that up. But even Charles won't be able to keep me past their bedtime. I'll be home by nine. Trust me, Lynn.

I love you entirely—

A.

I'm not always as flexible as I should be. Having expected a quiet dinner with Alix, I couldn't settle on a single reaction to her message. Waves of emotion churned through me. I wanted to be a child again, nurtured by some omnipotent entity, guaranteed safe passage through troubled waters. I wanted to smash something, to wail in pain and terror. And I wanted to take Alix by the shoulders and shake her till she rattled. Two weeks of unremitting crisis intervention had sapped my patience. For the first time in our relationship, I was angry at her.

Why was Alix putting me through this agony when Charles could have mailed the document or met her in his office? As easily as she was swayed by his histrionics, she had no business seeing him alone. Especially not at night in that secluded house where he'd acted out so many frightening scenes. Why didn't she see that she kept playing into his hands?

I could think of no good way to pass time until Alix returned. I roamed from room to room, aimless, unable to focus. I looked in the refrigerator and discovered I wasn't hungry. Reading was out of the question and sketching was a farce. At last, I forced myself to work on an antique chair that I'd been recaning. The monotonous project would demand very little concentration or energy.

Two hours later I heard tires crunching on gravel in my driveway. I leaped up, toppling the chair, anger and relief as thoroughly enmeshed as the reed I'd been weaving. I yanked open the front door and stood at the threshold peering into exceptional darkness.

A heavy cloud cover lay over the valley, obscuring Alix's approach. But her footfall had a dragging, defeated quality. When the porch light finally illuminated her face, all my fury fell away. She was drawn and pale, in need of nurturing. I gathered her to me and we clung together under that leaden sky.

She'd eaten nothing. I warmed a can of soup and cut some cheddar, but neither of us could swallow. The soup congealed and the cheese turned translucent while Alix recounted the meeting with her husband. She hadn't been given a copy of the agreement that he'd prepared. Still, enough of it had been imprinted on her brain to fuel my fury for a lifetime.

The document implied that Alix had voluntarily ceded custody to Charles for the "welfare" of their children and provided her with minimal visitation rights. Additionally, the agreement stripped her of nearly every claim to real estate, property or support. Charles had issued an ultimatum: Alix could sign the paperwork, taking what he'd offered, or she could fight for more in court. If she chose that route, he was determined to disclose what he called the "sordid nature" of our relationship.

"Fucking bastard!" I fumed. "What did you say?"

Alix looked at the floor. "I said I needed some time to think about it." Then she raised her eyes and confronted me. "But I want you to know right now, Lynn, that I'll probably sign the bloody thing."

I was reduced to stammering. "You can't mean that! You'd be *giving* the girls away!"

She wouldn't answer. I fought for control, trying to remember what Alix had already been through on this dismal night. I wanted to calm myself, to find a way of discussing this that would keep us united. When Alix spoke at last, I listened quietly.

"I'm not sure I even *deserve* custody," she whispered, heartbreak in her voice. "Is it fair to upend everything in the girls' lives because I've fallen in love with you? Why should they forgive me for taking them away from a father they adore—and from everything they've ever known?"

Hoping to cut to the chase, I said, "Who's the better parent?"

"That's not a question I'd ever asked myself before. I didn't need to. Now I'd say that I *have* been—like most mothers. I'm just not certain that's still true."

There was no point in disagreeing with her. She'd have to come to terms with this herself. And that, I could see, would be a long, agonizing process.

Alix gripped my hand, as desperate to communicate her reasoning as I was. "Lynn, someday my girls will be grown and gone. But I have to live with myself forever. There's no way for me to get custody of the children without lying. And I *won't* lie about this—not about who I am, or what I feel for you. I can't do that—not even to keep my children. I *will not* give Charles the power to blackmail me for the rest of my life. So I may as well get this over with."

I was crazy with frustration. How could we be so far apart on something so crucial? "Baby, can't you see that you fight half the battle for him? You accept his version of reality instead of looking for an alternative. Don't defeat yourself, for god's sake—you've *got* to resist Charles every step of the way!"

"For what, Lynn? He's holding all the cards. Jesus Christ could appear in court as my character witness, and they'd still take my daughters away from me. And imagine if Charles asks the lieutenant governor to get involved behind the scenes—there's not a judge in Missouri who wouldn't bend over backward to earn his support in future elections! Why should I put the girls through a messy scandal? Why go through all that pain?" Then Alix buried her face in her hands and said something too softly to be heard.

"What, sweetheart?"

She raised her tear-streaked face. "I said, sooner or later we all lose our children."

I reached for her chair and dragged it closer to mine. Alix leaned forward, resting her forehead on my shoulder. As I stroked her hair, I couldn't help wondering what she'd be doing at that exact moment if I'd never moved to Quillan's Crossing.

I thought I could afford to leave a lot unspoken that night. Our legal consultation was only two days away. If we were lucky, that would change everything. I led Alix upstairs and started a shower for her. She disappeared into the bathroom, then stayed so long I began to worry. When I stuck my head through the doorway to make sure she was okay, I heard her voice, mingled with the sound of the water. She was singing in the shower—something low and slow, but *singing!* My heart lifted with joy… until I recognized the tune. Just then, she turned off the faucet and a phrase from "House Carpenter" leaped out at me: *I do weep for my own wee babe, who never I shall see anymore…*

Her anguish hit me with the force of a sledgehammer. I backed into the hallway and dashed past the girls' room—half-finished, still vacant—then stumbled downstairs. When I bolted onto the front porch, I saw the rain had begun, a hard, steady downpour, punctuated by brutal lightning. And the wind was rising. With my back against the wall, I let myself open up like the skies. In the midst of the gale, I howled and raged. For Alix. For her children. For myself.

* * *

There was no respite in sight. A sudden plague of phone calls from Alix's parents heightened the tension in our lives. Charles had been in contact with her mother and father again, playing the aggrieved husband to good effect. I was incredulous that her family found him a sympathetic character. It seemed traitorous that they gave his complaints so much credence and Alix's so little. But, as she reminded me, her family was southern-born and Charles was a *man*, after all. That automatically made him more credible.

Three distinct themes began to emerge in those telephone calls. Alix should reconcile with Charles—their marriage was a sacred contract. Or Alix should accept Charles's custody and property demands—her sin was a punishable offense. Or Alix should move out of my house—she was only a pervert because she was living with one.

No one had tried to control *my* life for so long that I couldn't adapt to this invasion of our privacy. I wanted to go head-to-head with her parents myself. Failing that, I wanted to bash the phone to pieces so they couldn't get through to Alix. Yet she absorbed hours of criticism, advice, intimidation and long-distance prayer with scarcely a complaint. Sometimes she'd turn the phone toward me so I could hear, but her father's peremptory orders and her mother's ineffectual pleading made me wild, claustrophobic. Worse, the calls ate up enormous amounts of our time together. Sometimes I wondered if that was the point.

What Alix hoped to accomplish through this display of submission, I couldn't imagine. I asked how she endured the diatribes. She said her mother was motivated by love, however confused or misguided. She said Caldecott Edwards was a force of nature—better to lie low until the storm passed. She said that a breach with her parents would devastate her mom, and deprive Cindy and Beth of their only grandparents.

Still I argued that it might be more appropriate if she hollered or hung up. Nobody was listening to her, nobody cared what she had to say. But, clearly, Alix felt obligated to persevere, even when there was no obvious way to bridge the gap. Which didn't mean she relished those telephone interventions.

"Bloody hell," she moaned after a particularly grueling session, "I'm pretty tired of being prayed over. If I'm not saved by now, it probably ain't gonna happen."

"What was it this time?"

"Just the usual—I need to flee this godless household and restore myself to decent, Christian heterosexuality."

Words failed me. I was reduced to snarling.

"You'll love this part, Lynn—Charles told Dad that he couldn't stand idly by while the girls were corrupted by your 'rabid, man-hating philosophy.'"

"Ah," I fumed, "the ultimate tactic! The chauvinist's last resort! If you can't defeat a woman any other way, accuse her of despising men. It's a sure-fire winner!"

"Calm down, love. I thought you'd laugh this off."

"Goddamn it, Alix, I *do* hate most men! They want to be able to grind their boots in our faces, but still be told that we love them. They expect us to keep coming back for more, no matter how badly they've abused us. Yet the unforgivable sin is to admit to hating them!"

Although I knew Alix found my intensity as hard to comprehend as her forbearance was for me, I was too wound up to stop. When she said, "Lynn, aren't you overstating the case?" I blew up.

"*Overstating*! Alix, think about everything that good old Chuck *has* done or is *willing* to do to you." I began to enumerate affronts, ticking them off on my fingers. "He's destroyed your credibility with your family and friends. He's terrorized you with violent outbursts, threatened to commit you to a mental hospital and vowed to ruin you in court. He'll deprive you of your children and deny you any property, all the while insisting he loves you. Why shouldn't you hate him? But if every woman who'd had a similar experience could admit the truth, there'd be a hell of a lot more lesbians! *That's* why hating men had to be made the unthinkable thought!"

I could see I'd pushed this far enough. Already overloaded, Alix wanted to disengage. She needed peace, and I was only compounding her misery. I quit stomping around and made myself sit quietly beside her.

"I'm sorry, baby. I can see this isn't helping."

She smiled sadly. "You're probably right about everything, Lynn. I'm just too overwhelmed by the personal to deal with the political right now."

With effort, I refrained from reminding her that the two are inseparable. We spent the rest of the night in uneventful domesticity, carefully confining our conversation to trivial matters. I loaded the dishwasher, scrubbed the sink and brushed Solly within an inch of his life. All the while, my head was teeming with unspoken thoughts. Alix clipped coupons and made a grocery list, then retrieved a load of laundry from the dryer and folded it at the kitchen table. Watching her smooth out every wrinkle with quick, practiced motions, I wished that some cosmic hand could do the same for our troubled lives.

CHAPTER TWENTY-SEVEN

Alix was nervous and uncommunicative as we made the long drive to Castelli, Fasteau, McManess and Morgenstern in Clayton. She was superstitiously afraid that Charles would learn of our consultation and institute immediate legal action. There was an air of withdrawal about her that worried me. With luck, the attorney would be able to put her at ease, open her up, offer at least a morsel of hope. Still, I prepared myself to do a lot of the talking during our meeting.

We'd hardly been seated in a tasteful anteroom before Andrea Fasteau appeared and ushered us into her office. At first glance, I was amused by the contrast between her appearance when we'd first met and the way she looked at the law firm. Then I realized that she'd simply changed uniforms. For Deb's barbecue, she'd worn her dyke suit—painter's pants and a thin, ribbed tank top. For work, she'd dressed in the requisite costume of the serious young professional—silk shirt, tailored skirt, leather pumps. I shrugged. Maybe observance of protocols was characteristic of the legal personality. That sounded logical, anyway.

Fasteau seated herself in the swivel chair behind her desk and adjusted stylish eyeglasses. She plucked a pen from a pewter container and centered a legal pad on her desk. Then she looked at us with anticipation. Suddenly, she seemed to find me familiar. A quizzical expression crossed her intelligent face. "Do I *know* you, Ms. Westfall?"

"We've met. Do you remember a party at Deb Ransom's last autumn?"

"Of course! You're the potter I bored all evening! I actually own one of your pieces now. I came across it in a gallery downtown shortly afterward and I thought it was really fine—it's a stunning porcelain bowl with a torn edge?"

I remembered how proud I'd been of that series. "Thanks. Now I've brought *you* some business."

The lawyer addressed Alix. "You need information about a divorce action, is that correct, Ms. Dunnevan?"

"If only it were that simple," Alix replied. "I'm a lesbian mother—I need a *miracle*."

Maybe they discourage easy laughter in law school. Andrea Fasteau continued to wear her look of professional interest. "Tell me a little about your situation."

Alix had pulled herself out of her funk. She outlined the deterioration of her marriage and the circumstances of our meeting. I was able to sit back, only contributing an occasional observation. The attorney made lengthy notes, interrupting now and then to clarify a point. She nodded as she wrote, eyebrows rising in response to some of our statements. She exuded confidence and I found that I liked her even more than I'd remembered.

We'd been at it for over an hour when Fasteau set the pen aside and tapped her fingertips together. She smiled encouragingly. "It's true your position is not a good one, Ms. Dunnevan. But it's not nearly as bleak as you've been led to believe. There are many options open to you. The most important thing is to understand that Missouri law affords you considerable protection, especially with regard to your property rights—and I'll make certain those rights are honored. Once you analyze your circumstances from a more positive perspective, we can decide on an approach to the problem."

"*Is* there a more positive perspective?"

"Of course. You're obviously well-versed in the weaknesses of your position and the strengths of your husband's. But you haven't explored his vulnerabilities. Believe me, you'll find some. For instance, the most cursory review of your finances suggests that Mr. Dunnevan would have to pay *your* legal fees, as well as his own, in a custody action." There was just a hint of a smile when Fasteau said, "Naturally, I'd make it clear to his attorney that I intended to fully explore every option on your behalf." Her smile broadened noticeably. "And I can assure you that the cost would be quite substantial by the time the proceedings concluded."

After flipping through her notes for a moment, the lawyer said, "Next, you must settle on the question of style."

"What does that mean?" Alix asked.

"It means selecting an approach that dictates every action from here on out. For example, you could choose to be a pushover—to take your husband's threats at face value and acquiesce to them. Frankly, I wouldn't do that. The terms he's suggested are preposterous. A court of law would provide much more equitably for you. I want to caution you strenuously against signing such an agreement."

"I may not have a choice."

"Pardon my bluntness," Fasteau said, "but that's nonsense. Another alternative is to negotiate. To demand more than you expect and to settle for a happy medium. *I* would actually do the negotiating, you realize."

The lawyer leaned back in her chair, that smile tweaking the corners of her mouth again. "A third option is to tell your husband that you'll meet him in that all-out custody battle he keeps proposing."

Alix interrupted, but Fasteau raised a hand to forestall her objection. "You're correct—you'd almost surely lose if you actually went to trial, especially in Missouri. But you could turn the tables with that maneuver, threatening to embarrass Mr. Dunnevan, as *he* has threatened *you*. Because he's a public figure—and quite an ambitious one, if I've understood you correctly—that ploy would give you considerable leverage."

After glancing at her watch, Fasteau shot Alix a direct look. "There's a final possibility that involves a certain amount of dissemblance. I'm not advising you to lie, but circumstances and relationships can always be described in the most favorable light. Of course, this approach would require you to vacate Ms. Westfall's residence immediately."

Involved in consulting her appointment book, the attorney missed the pained expression that flitted across Alix's face. "I'm sorry," Fasteau said, "but I'm due in court very soon. There's still a great deal of material that we need to discuss. Can we meet again later in the week?"

We agreed to a date and time. The attorney made a rapid notation on her calendar, saying, "Excellent. That gives you the opportunity to list any questions that occur to you between now and then. And I'll have time to digest the information you've shared today." Fasteau showed us out of her office and we rode the elevator down to the busy metropolitan morning.

I was elated by her evaluation of our plight—we had much more leeway than I'd imagined. My mind raced with tactical calculations. It took me several minutes to realize that Alix didn't share my excitement.

"What's wrong, love?" I asked as we walked to the parking garage. "I took that for good news."

"You guys make me *so mad*!" she snapped. "You act like this is some kind of game—an exercise to see who can think faster or run a better bluff. That isn't how it feels to me! And I'm tired of people implying that I'd be stupid to accept Charles's terms, when that seems like the only realistic option I have."

Her steps were jerky, her tone defiant. "Everybody knows how to live my life better than I do—except nobody understands what it's like to plot strategy against the father of my children. And nobody ever considers what all this cleverness might do to Beth and Cindy!"

I wanted to embrace Alix, to comfort and reassure her, but we were still in the heart of Clayton's business district. Maybe it was best to hold my fire until we reached the car. We could talk—or argue—while we drove home.

Spiraling slowly down an exit ramp in the parking garage, I rested my hand on Alix's thigh. "Sweetheart, I think I know how you feel, but you're not in control of this thing. As long as Charles is willing to play dirty, all you can do is respond in kind. The approach he's taken simply doesn't permit the luxury of a dignified reaction. After all—a custody battle isn't your idea. You've only asked for a fair deal."

"Charles won't *give* me a fair deal."

"Hard as it must be for good old Chuck to accept, that decision isn't in his hands, Alix. If push comes to shove, it'll be made by a judge, after a lot of preliminary negotiation."

"By a judge who knows Charles in his professional capacity. What are the odds I won't lose my children in the ugliest, most public way?"

"With good legal counsel, it needn't get near the trial stage. You know that."

"Don't you see, Lynn? I have to decide this as if it will! I have to think 'worst-case scenario.' I have to consider what an all-out custody fight would do to my daughters."

My voice was harder than I intended when I said, "And if you quietly hand them over to Charles? What will *that* do to them, Alix? Maybe it would be better if they saw a strong woman putting everything on the line for them. And—in the unlikely event that you do end up in court—there's no doubt that Charles will be exposed for the bastard that he is."

"I'm not so sure the girls need to see that," she said in an uncommonly caustic tone.

I gritted my teeth. "What's the use of *feminism* if a woman like you just sits passively while some asshole fucks her over?"

"*Jesus Christ*!" Alix shouted. "It's not like that at all! I haven't given up! I'm just trying to find a way to sustain relationships with everyone I care about. Screw it, man—I'm not a goddamned juggler!"

"Baby, baby," I said softly, "I didn't mean to insult you—I'm just so crazed."

"Lynn. If I hate how Charles is treating me, how can I behave the same way?"

"I don't know," I growled. "But I can't stand this, Alix. He's turning your own best impulses into weapons. He knows he can win because you're too decent to fight on his level. Think about it, hon. Nice guys don't just finish last—they get trampled in the rush."

I was certain I was right, sure about the importance of making an uncompromising stand on behalf of the girls. But the more I thought about everything Alix said, the more clearly I perceived the true dimensions of her struggle. And once I fully understood how many separate demands she was trying to satisfy, I was humbled. For the first time, I recognized that Alix was not only a far better person than I was—she was far finer than I *aspired* to be.

Because I was perfectly content to hate her husband, and I confidently expected to hate him till my dying day. But no matter how much I despised Charles, Alix *would* always care about him. She'd care about him if he forced her to fight to the bitter end. She'd care about him if he beat her in court. And whether I liked it or not, Dunnevan would be mixed up in our lives until the children were grown. Because Beth and Cindy needed the father they believed in—the knight in shining armor that Alix had married. Even if the knight had long since fallen from his horse, and his armor was past all repair.

CHAPTER TWENTY-EIGHT

I was at my desk in the studio when the phone rang. "Lynn," Alix said, a thin thread of desperation weaving through her words, "are you alone now?"

"Yeah, honey. What's up?"

"I just need to talk for a minute, but I don't want to interrupt anything important."

"You're not. I've closed the shop long enough to eat lunch. Is something going on?"

"Kind of. Charles just called and raked me over the coals for an hour. I tried not to let him know how badly he's upset me, but I'm pretty down right now."

I tossed my sandwich in the trash can. "Hold on, baby. I'm coming home right away."

"Oh, Lynn, I don't want you to close early! I only meant to take a second of your time."

I'd heard relief in her voice and I wasn't going to leave her hanging. "That's okay. It's been a slow day," I lied.

Covering clay barrels, clearing cash from the till, locking up had never taken so long. Racing home, I wished for teleportation. The road to our house was narrow and famous for its dangerous curves. Every other week a tow truck was hauling somebody's car out of a tough spot along the route.

"Slow *down*, woman!" I cautioned myself. "You're going to end up in the woods like all those *other* idiots!" But I couldn't take my own advice—my foot was way too heavy on the gas and still the drive seemed to take forever. I parked my car alongside Alix's and dashed indoors.

The house was unnaturally quiet. I found Alix huddled under a quilt on the couch—limp, drained of energy, a deathbed image by Edvard Munch. Sol had curled beside her in a vain attempt to provide comfort. Against his dark fur, her face was as white as paper.

I knelt and slipped both arms around Alix. At my touch, she began to shake uncontrollably. I held her until the trembling subsided, offering reassurance at a level that words don't reach. Then I kissed her forehead and left long enough to make hot chocolate. When I returned, we cuddled under the quilt, discussing Charles. What else?

"I was feeling so good this morning," Alix told me. "For the first time since you had the piano delivered, I could really feel control coming back to my hands. It was *wonderful*, Lynn! I practiced for a long time, trying to take myself seriously again. A new piece I've been composing was just beginning to shape up when the phone rang."

She sighed, setting down her mug. "I almost didn't answer it. I knew it could be Charles, or my parents, and I didn't want to speak with any of them. But then I thought it might be you so I picked up."

"Poor baby. I'll buy an answering machine as soon as possible. Until then, let's work out some kind of signal so you know it's me."

"Thank you, Lynn," she said, with a tremor in her voice. "Unfortunately, Charles was on the phone. He started out calmly enough, but he was raving by the time I hung up."

I recognized the pattern. "Why did he call?"

"To tell me he's through waiting for my decision. He wants me to sign his agreement so we can begin legal proceedings right away."

"Don't let him railroad you, Alix. Take some control—give yourself time to think."

"He really does know how to manipulate me," she admitted. "In fifteen minutes he can depress me so thoroughly that I can't function for a week."

"Remember what the good doctor says about depression, darling? That it's anger turned inward because you're afraid to release it in the proper direction. You're so certain Charles has all the power you can't use your own constructively."

"He *does* have all the power."

"I don't agree with that, Alix. And neither does your lawyer. His primary strength is his ability to make you doubt yourself."

Her face crumpled. "He called me a monster, Lynn! A bad influence on our children! He said if I cared for them, I'd end the marriage quietly and go far away so they'd never have to know the truth about me."

"Wouldn't that be convenient for Charles? You simply vanish and he secures all your property. Then he tells the girls some poisonous story about you. Because victors always write the history books—" I stopped in mid-stream, something elusive nagging at the back of my mind. "*Why* is Chuck in such a hurry all of a sudden?"

"I don't know, Lynn. He just kept telling me how horribly I'd hurt him and insisting he won't be able to get on with his life until he puts this to rest. He said he needs 'closure.'"

"Bullshit! Something's up, Alix. I don't know what it is, but I can feel it! Charles needs to rush you for some specific reason. Your mission is to resist and see what happens next."

She shook her head dispiritedly.

"I'm *telling* you, darling," I said, pumped up with an irrational certainty, "Charles is under some kind of pressure. If you can spin this out, it might break your way."

"You may be right, Lynn, but I don't think I have the stamina. If I sign the agreement now, we'll be free at last." She looked at me levelly. "This constant stress isn't exactly helping *our* relationship."

She was right, of course. But so was I. Gripping her hands urgently, I said, "Listen, Alix! I have good instincts. I *know* I'm right about this—I just *know* it. Play it out, don't force it, see how it unfolds."

"The world is ruled by letting things take their course," she intoned. "It cannot be ruled by interfering."

"Exactly! Nicely put."

"It's not original," Alix said dryly. "It's Lao Tzu—basic Taoism."

I was impressed. "I bow to your superior wisdom."

"But in this case that's not really practical."

"What's so fucking practical about deeding everything over to Charles?"

"It would be done with! We'd have peace!"

"At what price, sweetheart?"

Alix looked like the proverbial deer in the headlights, and I knew I'd better try a different approach. Suddenly, I remembered a lowbrow equivalent of Lao Tzu's maxim that might both reinforce my argument and amuse her. I put an arm around her shoulder. "Okay, Alix, stop me if you've heard this before. It's an old joke—or, maybe it's more like a parable…There are a million versions of it, but the ending's always the same…

"In ancient times, a man is sentenced to death for some offense, but he makes an appeal to his king. He asks to delay the execution for one year, during which time he swears he can teach the king's favorite horse to sing. If he succeeds, the king must set him free."

Alix looked interested, at least, so I continued. "Well, the king's intrigued by the claim, and he agrees to the bargain. One day, the convict's friend visit hims in the royal dungeon. When they talk about the arrangement, the friend says, '*What*? Are you *crazy*? You can't teach a horse to *sing*!' But the convict replies,

'*Anything* can happen in a year, my friend. The king may die. The horse may die. *I* may die. Or, who knows? The horse *may* learn to sing.'"

Alix laughed softly, her face less agitated now, more pensive.

"Just try to relax, honey," I pleaded. "Nothing else will happen today—you don't have to make the decision this instant. Next week we meet with the lawyer again. You can ask what Andrea thinks about the sudden push from Charles. And tomorrow you'll see Dr. Harrold. Maybe she'll have some bright ideas."

Alix nodded assent, glad to be done with the argument, at least for a while. I reclined on the couch, pulling her close against me under the quilt, rocking her gently. But inwardly I was cursing Dunnevan, designing a voodoo doll in his likeness and inflicting all manner of insult upon it. Which was certainly preferable to reviewing my own actions—far better than wondering whether I'd had a right to get involved with Alix, no matter how enticing I found her. No matter how eagerly she'd responded. No matter how much we loved one another.

* * *

There was something sheepish about Alix when she emerged from the therapist's office the next afternoon. I managed to keep my cool until we hit the street. But then, sensing a victory, I pounced. "So, what did she say?"

"Quit dancing on the sidewalk, you goof!"

"Nonresponsive," I pointed out.

"She said I should 'cultivate my anger.'"

"Amen, sister!" I shouted jubilantly, not caring when pedestrians stared.

"But I don't *feel* angry, Lynn. I feel *guilty*. No matter what anyone says, I understand what Charles expected of me and I know what I promised him. I can't help feeling I've violated a sacred trust—that I deserve the consequences of my actions."

We'd arrived at Alix's car by then. She unlocked her door and slid behind the wheel, not sorry, I could see, to have a break in our conversation.

"Let me drive," I suggested, reaching for her keys. "You forget to talk when you do."

We traded sides and I adjusted the rearview mirror, trying to decide how much to say. As I fumbled for change to pay the parking fee, I reminded Alix of the most critical thing on my list: "Charles has failed *you* a few times."

"I know that. But I have to answer for my own behavior. I'm talking about a commitment I thought I was capable of keeping. By my own calculations, I've fallen short. That's what bothers me."

"Christ, woman! What impossible standard are you trying to satisfy?"

"'To have and to hold from this day forward? For better or for worse?'"

I rolled my eyes. "Think how antiquated that vow is, Alix! Maybe it seemed reasonable when people died before thirty, but today it's totally unrealistic."

"That's too easy. Besides, how can you believe I'll be faithful to you when you've watched me betray Charles?"

I raised her hand to my lips. "In the first place, I haven't asked for any assurances. Pardon the clichés, but there are no guarantees in life, and you can't take a promise to the bank." Still clasping her hand in mine, I held it to my heart. "I want everything you have to offer for as long as it's genuine, sweetheart. But if we reach a point where you can no longer give fully and freely, what reason is there for staying together?"

Backing out of the parking slot, I said, "As hard as it was when Sarah left, I sure as hell didn't want her to stay. There's such a thing as pride, after all. If you don't want to be with Charles, if he knows that, how could he bear having you around?"

"He refuses to believe I don't love him anymore. He'll go to his grave thinking I was just confused—that you were a temporary aberration."

"That alone would make *me* mad enough to kill him, babe. It trivializes your decisions and it trivializes *you*." Merging with traffic, I asked, "Why can't you get angry at that asshole? You can sure let me have it when you think I'm wrong."

"Vell, accordink to Frau Doktor, eet all goes beck to mein Papa. Dr. Harrold says he taught me that expressing anger toward men was not only futile, it would get me into even more trouble."

I'd thought much the same, but only said, "Sounds logical."

"Sure. On paper. Every once in a while, I can almost hold on to the theory. Mostly, though, anger just seems like a cheap way out, like a rationalization for my own shortcomings."

"Alix, I've never *known* a better person. What do you want from yourself? Perfection?"

"But of course."

"Sorry—we're all sold out," I shot back. "Seriously, woman, give yourself a break every now and then. And quit letting Chuckie use your incredible decency against you."

She threw me a sideways glance. "I'm beginning to wonder why I'm paying a therapist for the same advice I can get so much closer to home."

"And so much *cheaper*. Change of subject: You're feeling better about Dr. Harrold, aren't you? You seem to like her much more than you did in the beginning."

"I do," Alix confirmed. "We laugh a lot lately, and I've learned some important things from her. But I'm still not open to *all* her methods—I'll never be able to pound on a pile of pillows with a plastic bat. At least, not on command."

"Patience, my dear, patience. The higher levels are attained but slowly."

Alix giggled, but she wasn't done explaining her altered perspective about the therapist. "I think it just took us time to find a workable method. Once I realized that everything Dr. Harrold said was aimed at helping me cope, I began to relax."

"Tell me what that means."

"At first, when she'd ask me to consider Charles's point of view, it sounded like she thought his position was more valid than mine. So I'd get defensive and shut down. Now I know it's not a question of her choosing sides—that's not her job. It's just a technique to enlarge my understanding of a situation. If I can see the whole picture and factor in all the information, I'll make better decisions for myself and for the girls."

Alix sounded tired now, as she always did after a therapy session. I knew the best way in the world to help her disengage. I slipped a cassette into the tape player and we rode the rest of the way home with Meg Christian.

CHAPTER TWENTY-NINE

The night of Deb Ransom's opening, I was in a holiday mood. Tension had become such a daily reality that I welcomed this diversion with an enthusiasm all out of proportion to the event. But Alix was feeling shy and tentative. She'd met few of my friends, and none in large groups. The extent of her anxiety became apparent when she tried to choose an outfit to wear to the reception. Her options were limited, of course—most of her clothing was impounded in the bedroom she'd once shared with Charles. And I was six inches taller. Nothing I owned would work for her.

After watching Alix sort through our closet three times, I said, "Want some advice?"

"Hours ago, you goof."

"Go as you are—you couldn't improve on it."

Glancing down at her nude body, Alix laughed. "How to make friends and influence people."

"Especially the former," I agreed. "But seriously, love, the things you wore for the student recital would be fine. And you look wonderful in them."

"Not too girly?"

"Not for a lipstick lesbian."

Alix rapped me smartly on the top of my head. "Look who's talking," she said as she reached behind me to unbraid my hair. "Leave it loose tonight, okay, Lynn? It's beautiful any way you fix it, but I like it down best of all."

I sat on the edge of our bed combing out the tangles, while Alix stepped into black slacks and buttoned her shirt. She fastened an elaborate buckle around her small waist. Silver hoops swung at her ears and shiny hair curved neatly about her face.

"Jesus! I'm not sure I want to expose you to the ravening hordes. You might get a better offer."

Alix took my face in her hands and kissed me meltingly. "Darling, don't you know it's not *possible* to tempt the woman who has everything?"

* * *

A veteran of too many mediocre exhibitions, I approach opening nights with caution. Nothing's more awkward than chatting with an artist whose output is second-rate. So it was a pleasure to respond to Deb's show with sincere enthusiasm. Her recent work had gathered force and brilliance. Each large canvas was a patchwork of jewel-like hues, the colors divided by an irregular black grid. These new paintings obviously had their origins in the stained glass she designed professionally.

"Deb, my dear, your gainful employment is showing," I teased her.

"Laugh if you must, but it supports my habit."

"Looks to me like your habit's supporting itself quite nicely." Because already a gratifying number of unobtrusive stickers punctuated the descriptive placards, each one proclaiming that the work had been sold.

"High time too," said my old friend.

"Maybe I could commission a miniature. I can't afford the real thing."

A voice from behind interjected a suggestion. "Buy one of her lithographs—same great designs at popular prices."

"Barb!" I cried, embracing my former teacher. "I didn't know you were coming!"

We pulled back to examine one another. She'd changed very little since my college days. Everything about Barb was generously cut. She had the largest hands and the widest grin I've ever seen on a woman.

"God, *you* look *great*!" she told me. "What's the secret?"

I pulled Alix closer. "Dare I say 'Love'?"

"Well, it suits you. Tell me about it."

"If we do, we'll owe you a consultation fee."

"That sounds interesting. I'll waive my usual charges."

To Alix, I offered a quick refresher: "Barbara managed to keep her children after her divorce. She can tell you about it."

I'd just begun to outline Alix's legal situation when a group of colleagues dragged me off to support their position in a heated debate. From the other side of the gallery, I could see Alix deep in conversation with Barbara Chase, looking animated and involved. I let myself relax and be drawn into controversy—the standard wrangle about the future of modernism—reveling in that purely intellectual exercise. What a luxury to argue about something so inconsequential for a change! But before the discussion degenerated into backbiting, I rejoined Alix.

She seemed thoughtful and at ease. I guessed my old friend was having an impact on her. "Join us after the reception, Barb. We're taking Deb and Susan for dinner at *Femme Seule*."

A smile spread across that broad, freckled face. "Nothing I'd like better."

Outside of Mattie's kitchen, *La Femme Seule* is my favorite dining spot in the whole world. The name's both appropriate and ironic—single women are seldom alone in that environment. Whether I'm celebrating or recuperating, it's a fabulous place to meet old friends and make new ones, to linger long over good conversation and great food. Some of my happiest dreams have contained flashes of *Femme Seule*.

Full of fruit and cheese from the reception, the five of us ate lightly, but we spent our laughter lavishly. I hadn't felt so carefree in months. It was late when Deb and Suze shoved back their chairs and left, claiming exhaustion. We watched them walk out arm in arm still glowing over the success of Deb's show.

After their departure, the mood at our table grew more serious. "Sounds like you two are in a pretty tough spot."

"Yeah, Barb. You know how it goes—her husband loves her so much he doesn't mind destroying her to prove it."

Barb laughed, and that wide-open, wonderful sound caused heads to turn in our direction. "God, this is all hideously familiar. It's bringing back things I haven't thought about for years."

Leaning closer to Alix, Barb said. "When I told Paul that I wanted a divorce, the first thing he did was close our bank accounts and cancel my credit card. I was outraged. I can remember yelling, 'How can you do this and still claim to care about me?' And do you know what he said?" Barb leaned back in her chair, rolling blue eyes upward. "I quote: 'That was *business*—it had nothing to do with *love*.'"

We shared a moment of sardonic amusement. "I've never understood how guys can compartmentalize like that," I raged. "Maybe you should do a container series about *them*, Barb."

"Not a chance. I can't put that much energy into men. My work is strictly about the female experi—"

Alix rapped a spoon sharply against her goblet. "Excuse me, you all? You've left me behind."

"Sorry, sweetheart. Barbara works primarily in hand-cast paper and she's produced an extended body of embossed paper containers. You should see them, Alix! They're just beautiful—airy, ephemeral. All white, flowing curves and subtle openings—"

"Kinda like disposable Nevelson…"

"Cut the crap, Barb! You'd never let me get away with downplaying my work like that."

"You taught her too well, it seems," Alix said slyly.

"Indeed. A mistake I've rarely repeated."

I sat unperturbed while the two of them tried to get a rise out of me. Watching Barb's big hands in motion, it was hard to believe them capable of such delicate work. But she was the best.

It was Barbara Chase who'd transformed me from student to artist, strengthening my skills and honing my critical capacity.

Her graduate courses had pushed me past old limitations. She had a low-key way of making me feel I'd let her down, been too easily pleased by my own cleverness. Time and again, she'd sent me back to the drawing board, bewildered but determined to satisfy her exacting standards. And ultimately I had.

Under Barb's careful tutelage, I'd developed focus, commitment and control. She'd begun as my mentor then become my friend. We'd been very close during the period when she and Janet broke up. Painful though that process had been, a deep connection still existed between the two women. Lately I'd lost touch with both of them. As soon as there was a lull in the conversation, I asked, "What's new with Janet?"

"Not much. Loves San Francisco, hates her job, Jamie keeps growing—she says he's taller than she is now. She'll be with me for Christmas—come visit us. You can catch up with each other then."

Alix had seized her spoon again. I wrested it from her fingers and placed it out of her reach. "Janet was Barbara's lover at the time that she divorced Paul."

"And for some years afterward," added Barb, resting her chin on one hand. "A peculiar, impulsive creature, my Janet. I still miss her every day."

"Why not?" I said. "You two had a pretty special relationship." I saw that Alix was curious, but too polite to ask. "We'd always considered Janet a delicate flower. Finally, she bailed—she just couldn't take the pressure."

"That happens to a lot of us, you know," Barb sighed. "I guess it's not surprising. Look how high the divorce rate is—and *straight* folks have the benefit of social approval."

She picked up her water glass and drank deeply. "Janet's whole family was breathing down our necks, watching Jamie for the slightest sign that he'd been warped by living with two women. Finally it was just easier for Jan to get the hell out. I could have gone with her, I suppose, but I have roots here. And I'm not really the California type."

Alix nodded sympathetically. "It must have been a difficult decision."

"Yeah. But in a lot of ways it was the right choice. I don't have many regrets about it now. We'd already done everything we could for each other."

"*Repeatedly*," I threw in.

"Well, crudeness!" Barbara chided me. "I had something rather different in mind. What I'm trying to say, Alix, is that Jan and I had come to the end of the line. We'd hit a point where we weren't growing any more. Both of us felt trapped by the patterns we'd established as a couple and neither of us could find a way to move beyond them while remaining together."

Bolder now, Alix asked, "Could you be more specific?"

"Ahh…Jan had lost interest in monogamy—"

I laughed. "*That's* a tasteful way to put it."

"—and *I* was more and more involved in activism, making speeches at gay pride events, advocating for gay students on campus…you get the picture. My increased visibility was only going to intensify the pressure from Janet's family. But by then, I wasn't willing to back down. I'd become a dyke in the fullest sense."

"What does that mean?" Alix wanted to know.

Barb smiled. "I'd finally accepted myself, wholeheartedly and without reservation. I'd worked through the coy phase. The one where you tell yourself you're not *really* a lesbian? You just 'happened' to fall in love with another woman? Kind of like it was an accident, rather than an expression of your identity."

Alix shifted in her chair just then and I saw something flit across her face—a moment of startled recognition—that sent a ripple of dismay through every molecule of my body. I hadn't realized she was struggling with definitions. That kind of equivocation could only complicate matters for her. At the same time, compassion mingled with my concern. We were walking a hard road that mostly wound through hostile territory. Why *wouldn't* she be skittish, why *wouldn't* she hope for a special exemption? Still, until Alix embraced the label, our relationship would be as vulnerable as one of Barbara's hollow boxes. Soon, very soon, we'd have to confront this.

Just then though, Alix's attention was elsewhere. "How in the world did you and Janet manage to keep your children?"

Barbara grimaced. "For Janet, it was easy. Her husband was a hippie type who'd gone with the flow. Mack was nowhere to be found. For me it was a different matter—I had to fight for my kids every step of the way."

Alix sighed heavily. "How did you stand that? I've spent most of my life trying to avoid conflict."

"That's a battle in itself," I said. Not for the first time.

"Of course it is," Barb agreed. Then she shrugged. "I suppose I saw it as a question of survival for both the twins and myself—they needed me and I needed them. I'd always been the more involved parent and I wasn't about to surrender the children. Their father was mostly going through the motions—something about machismo, I think. Still, I had to be prepared to counter everything he did. If I'd dropped my guard for a minute, Paul could have ended up with custody."

Barb grinned. "Fortunately—like most women—I knew my husband much better than he knew me. It wasn't difficult to stay a few steps ahead of him…" She laughed wryly before saying, "These days, the kids are such obnoxious little shits, I wonder why I fought so hard. Believe me, teenagers are pains in the rear!"

"I guess I'm a bit dense," Alix said. "I still can't see what weapons we have at our disposal."

"Well, brains and determination don't hurt. I'm tough and I'm a strategic thinker. I used everything that came to hand. Paul and I taught at the same university back then. Plenty of people there liked me. I knew some of them would support me when we got down to the crunch, and I made sure Paul knew it too."

I shot a look at Alix. She was shaking her head and I knew what she was thinking: Charles had already won that round. No one was backing her—not her family, not her old friends. But Barb's next comment had some potential, I thought. She said, "Then I wound Paul's cloak of liberalism around him so tightly that he couldn't make a single homophobic comment without compromising his own integrity."

I considered her point. Charles was unquestionably a bigot, but I wondered whether he was willing to go on record as one. Maybe he'd view that as a political liability? It was certainly something to keep in mind as we prepared for battle…

"And *this* was fun, Alix. I reminded Paul—delicately, of course—that certain of his colleagues would question his masculinity if he went public with our private business. They'd wonder why he hadn't been able to satisfy me, when they'd been so eager to try, poor fellows."

There was an impish glint in Barb's eye when she said, "Finally, whenever I thought Paul was about to suggest a courtroom fight, I'd beat him to the punch. And, naturally, he didn't want the expense, or the exposure—not really. In the long run, he was simply outmaneuvered. I hadn't given him anything to hang on to."

"The whole thing's such a farce!" I spat. "Precious few men want the daily reality of raising children. They mostly just want to scare the piss out of women!"

Barb nodded. "It goes without saying."

Alix had begun to droop. "We have such different personalities, Barb. I'm not sure I can use the same approaches that worked for you. And I'm almost overwhelmed by the ironies—I don't have a hope in hell of keeping my *girls* but the law generously concedes my right to some *real estate*, about which I couldn't care less."

Barbara's blue eyes grew even rounder and one heavy palm slapped down on the table. "For heaven's sake, Lynn! What have you been doing with your time?"

"Arguing this point, to no avail."

"Listen, sweetie," Barb said, "you can't take that attitude. We won't *let* you. It's an act of self-respect to claim what's rightfully yours—those things you've worked hard to earn. Anything less is the sickest kind of self-denial. We've all been programmed to prove that we're 'good women' by asking for nothing, but you're way too smart to fall into that trap."

She drained her glass and set it down solidly. "What's more, you have to protect your own interests. What if you and Lynn don't last? Plenty of women who care just as deeply can't handle the stress. So suddenly you're thirty-nine or forty-five and absolutely empty-handed? That's bullshit!"

We'd been browbeating Alix long enough. I saw withdrawal in her eyes, but Barb was still in go-mode. "If Charles had dumped you for some cute young thing, would *he* have walked away from all the material goods?"

"No, of course not. But all I really want is custody. I don't have the energy to fight for silver-plate when I've already lost my daughters."

Barb fixed Alix with an intense gaze. "I don't have a very serious face, so I'm telling you, hon: this is my earnest look. You *can't* give up so easily—you've *got* to fight for your girls for two reasons. First, they need to see that men can't push women around or split us off from one another. That lesson will serve them well throughout life. And, second, they need to know you care that much. In the final analysis, our children are sometimes all we have."

My dear Barbara, so seldom tearful, was soggy around the edges. "When Janet and I broke up, I was amazed by the support I got from the twins. They were still heartbreakingly young, yet they had love and advice and insights to offer me. All at once I realized my kids would be the most continuous presence in my life. I'm awfully glad I had them before I became a dyke."

"Shhhh, Barb!" I whispered melodramatically. "You could be shot on sight for saying that!" Turning to Alix, I said, "The hard-core crowd considers that treasonous!"

But, "Truth before everything," Barb argued.

"I guess that's the heart of the issue…" Alix said slowly "…how do I resolve this problem, while keeping my integrity intact?"

I covered her hand with mine. "Love, you haven't lied yet. You've been honest with yourself and with me and with Charles. Can't you see some way to tip the odds in your favor? To stay out of situations where you'd have to lie?"

"Not short of signing Charles's agreement, no."

Barb stood and began to search for her keys in an oversized bag. "Maybe I'm the original cockeyed optimist," she said, as she rummaged around, "but it's an article of faith with me that there's always an answer if I look long enough. I'm kind of superstitious about it, as a matter of fact. If I need a pair of brown socks, but can only find one in the dryer, I keep searching for a mate. And more often than not, I'll find it stuck in a shirtsleeve, or trapped inside a towel. Sometimes I think sheer force of will makes that sock materialize."

She finally located her key ring and slipped into her jacket. "I hate to leave, but I have to work tomorrow." Barb hugged us both, then directed her parting words at Alix. "You've already given up everything, baby. So what could you lose by fighting?"

* * *

Alix waited until we were in bed before asking a plaintive question. "Lynn? Doesn't *anyone* stay together? You and Sarah, Barb and Jan, Mattie and Diana—*nobody* seems able to make this work."

I rolled onto my back and folded my arms behind my head. "It's like Barb said tonight, Alix. There's so much external pressure that lots of people crack. The strain can ruin an otherwise good relationship. People move on, and sometimes they misplace the blame."

"I'm scared, Lynn."

"I get that, hon, but think about it like this—you've spent years coping with an equally difficult situation. The same system that causes gay people to split up can force straight couples to stick together." I propped myself up on one elbow and leaned over to kiss her. "If you hadn't had children, would you have stayed with Charles so long?"

"No," she answered, without hesitation.

"And you seem reasonably happy with me, yes?"

"Deliriously...except for all the bloody stress."

"Okay. So it's not that there's some superior bond in heterosexuality. It's just that society applauds you for preserving a miserable marriage."

Nuzzling her neck, I admitted to some fears of my own. "I guess swimming against the current is always a risky business.

There are bound to be casualties, and there's no guarantee that we won't be among them. But I get the feeling that Mattie and Diana could have gone on forever in a better world. And Deb has been with Susan longer than you were with Charles."

Suddenly, Alix was atop me, soft, warm and seductive. She ran her tongue down the length of my throat, then lower still. "I'll admit," she murmured, "there are a few *rewards*, along with the risks."

"They're just not as well-publicized," I whispered, surrendering myself gladly to her talented fingers.

CHAPTER THIRTY

That fall, Charles traveled so often we couldn't keep up with his schedule. His absences grew longer and his posture of offended morality took on an expedient cast. When he was home, he made it as difficult as he could for Alix to see the children. But when he needed to leave town, Charles became much more cooperative. The girls regularly arrived at our place with bulging backpacks and toys galore. Their fresh, bright bedroom began to look lived in. Just like it should.

Although I knew we were being used and manipulated, I welcomed those interludes with Cindy and Beth, which added so much richness to our lives. And I had the idea that Charles was eroding his claim to a superior legal position. How seriously could he argue my influence was harmful when he'd entrusted his daughters to my care on so many occasions? I began to keep my *own* records.

* * *

Out of the blue one Sunday, when we were all at the dinner table playing Go Fish, Beth raised guileless eyes. "Lynn, why don't you like boys?"

I managed to swallow my iced tea without choking. As calmly as possible, I said, "I *do* like boys, Beth. You met my nephews, Peter and Duncan, when they came from California for a visit. You know I like them a lot."

But Beth was insistent. "My *daddy* says you don't like boys."

So Charles had found a way to stir the pot even while away—how the hell was I supposed to handle this? I looked at Alix, sending a telepathic plea for rescue. But her answering gaze said that raising children would include plenty of challenging moments. Apparently this one was all mine.

I put my cards down. "Come here, Beth." She scrambled off her chair and climbed into my lap. I wrapped my arms around her, rocking slightly, searching for words that would mean something to a preschooler.

"I don't think your dad was talking about *little boys*, baby. I think he meant I don't like grown-up men. But that's not exactly true. Sometimes I don't like how guys *act*, but there are men I like very much. My friend, Nico, for instance. And Sven—remember, I took you and Cindy to see where he works? And Daniel, the glassblower, who has the studio next to mine in town."

"Do you like my *daddy*?"

There it was. I took a deep breath. "We aren't really friends, Beth," I said, hoping to leave it at that.

"But why won't you let my daddy come here?"

"Did I ever tell you he couldn't?"

"He *said* you wouldn't let him," she answered with a sharp note of accusation in her voice.

I sighed. There was no point in trying to sidestep this. "He's probably right, honey." I tipped Beth's head so that we were facing each other. "Listen, Little Bits, I don't know if I can explain this to you—it's pretty grown-up stuff—but I'll try. You know your mama and daddy are getting a divorce, don't you?"

Beth sniffled. "I don't *want* them to."

"I understand that, sweetheart, but they aren't happy together anymore. They hurt each other's feelings when they're together."

"Sometimes my mama cries," Beth confided.

"That's right. And your mom's my special friend, so I don't want her to be unhappy. If your dad came here, your mom would have sad times in *my* house too."

Her dark eyes filled with tears and her chest began to heave. "*I! Want! My! Daddy!*" Beth wailed.

I tried one last approach. "Honey, you have fun with your dad at *his* house, and fun with your mom *here*. Isn't that better than having lots of unhappy days with them both at home?"

Cindy, who hadn't seemed to be paying attention, looked up from the colorful pattern of cards she'd arranged on the tabletop. Before Beth could answer, she spoke. "Daddy says maybe we can all get a great big house and live together."

Alix dropped her iced tea. Her glass shattered and dozens of jagged shards formed a starburst on the pine floor, glistening in a spreading amber pool. Grateful for any interruption, I stood up and set Beth back on her chair. "Stay right there, punkin. Don't touch the glass." Then Alix and I raced for paper towels.

In the kitchen, we tried to exchange quick reactions, but found we were nearly incapable of speech. Settling for semi-hysteria, we clung together, laughing and snorting.

"My *god*!" I exclaimed.

"*Imagine*!" Alix gasped. She wiped streaming eyes with a wadded towel then tossed it over her shoulder in a display of abandon. "I give up! You've been right all along—the man's a lunatic!"

Then, afraid to leave the children exposed to that shattered glass any longer, Alix broke away. I followed her into the dining room and we began to mop up the mess.

* * *

At times that fall I felt we lived in a pressure cooker. The stress was so relentless that it became harder and harder to recover. The smallest increase in heat might blow us sky-high. We needed to let off steam, yet didn't dare leave town. Because Charles might do *anything* in our absence.

I came home one chilly night to find Alix at our kitchen table, scribbling lists. "Something's got to give," she announced, lifting her face for a kiss. "We're having a party. A big one—a whole weekend's worth."

"What's the occasion?"

"Your birthday, love." She riffled the pages of a cookbook. "We'll have just enough time to get everything done."

"What's to do?"

"I thought you'd never ask." Marking a place in the book, she set it aside and stepped into my arms. "You have to make some porcelain bowls to hold condiments for my world famous chicken curry."

"Alix, if there's one thing we have no shortage of, it's bowls."

"No, I mean something really special—"

"*Please*! You *wound* me!"

"Listen, goof. I want you to make a *set*, as souvenirs for your friends. Everyone will leave with a gift to commemorate our first party together." She shuffled through her papers and came up with a roster. "Is this everybody you'd want?"

I read through her notes with real appreciation—Alix had been paying attention. Reaching for her pencil, I added one name and crossed out two others. "I think *I* could handle Sarah and Greer now, but the rest of our guests might not know what to make of their presence here."

"I can understand that," Alix said. "And I guess I'd rather get to know them without a crowd of onlookers." She squinted at my handwriting. "Who's Claire Sandoval?"

"Another eccentric from my college days. I think you'll enjoy her. She weaves luscious stuff from fibers she spins herself."

"I'll need her address. And, Lynn? There's one more thing."

"Yes?"

"In your spare time, design a fabulous invitation."

I bowed deeply. "To hear is to obey."

* * *

Alix's eagerness for this gathering was contagious. I couldn't miss a correlation between Dunnevan's increased travel and her growing expansiveness. The longer Chuckie boy was away, doing whatever he was doing, the more open and alive Alix became. Sometimes I could almost ignore the bubble and hiss of that pressure cooker.

After a lot of thought, I set paper, scissors and spray adhesive on my drawing table, then sorted through photographs of good friends. When I opened one envelope, a few shots of Sarah tumbled out and I flinched a little. I guess you never really get over being judged second best—even when you've found the woman of your dreams. Dropping those photos in the trash, I brushed them from my mind.

Soon I was immersed in the process of creating our invitation. After hours of cutting, rearranging and discarding, I finally had a layout that satisfied me. For thirty minutes. Then I returned to my work, peeled up the pieces and began again. And again. Alix humored me for three days before gently reminding me that we'd actually need time to mail the finished product.

Still not wholly satisfied, I sent the pasteup to the firm that prepares promotional materials for my exhibitions. A few days later the job was ready. Too impatient to wait out the lazy rhythms of our little post office, I drove into St. Louis to collect the artwork. When the printer slid that black-and-white design from its protective sleeve, even I was surprised by its strength.

All halftones and irrelevancies had dropped out, leaving an appealingly ragged perimeter. Rich abstract images flowed into one another—Susan's classic profile was carved like marble against the boldness of Debra's sweater. The dark mass of Alix's hair merged with the shadow of Mattie's guitar. Barb Chase was silhouetted against the windows in her studio. This was more than an illustration. It was a montage of memories. I could hardly wait to be back at my drawing table pasting in text for the invitation.

CHAPTER THIRTY-ONE

Few things are as beautiful as well-thrown porcelain, and few arts are as difficult to perfect. Some clay bodies can be bullied into submission, but porcelain requires delicacy—an obeisance from the potter entirely in keeping with its singular presence. I'd never ceased to marvel that something as malleable as cream cheese could endure for millennia, if first exposed to heat. And, properly handled, porcelain has a quality of inevitability. "Of *course*," you feel, "what *else*?" But achieving that state is far from simple.

For the moment, I'd abandoned stoneware for the lure of porcelain perfection. White ideas kept rising to the surface of my mind long after I'd completed the set of bowls for our party. I threw piece after piece until my clay barrels were empty, then milled another big batch of the ivory-colored stuff. My sketchbook was full of new designs—forms that would push Sven Jarlsberg's inventiveness to the limit—and I was eager to start on that series of pots. Was the fresh porcelain ready? I lifted plastic sheeting to examine it. Nope—still too wet. I wouldn't be able to put it on the wheel for several days.

I considered my next move. Mix some glazes? Load a bisque firing into the electric kiln? Change the display in the shop window? Pay a few bills? I wasn't in the mood for any of those tasks, yet they all needed to be done.

On the other hand, a devilish little voice whispered, there are lots of loose ends to wrap up at the house before people arrive for the party...

What the hell—it was my birthday! I closed the shop and drove home hours early.

The phone was ringing when I walked through the front door. I picked up the receiver and found myself speaking to Cal Edwards. My heart sank. Alix's father would ruin our celebration. It never failed. No doubt the sky was about to fall—we'd just been too busy to look up. I set the phone down, harder than was politic, and called for Alix. Then I went upstairs, hoping to wash away my irritation along with the clay dust.

Crashing and banging noises greeted me as I stepped out of the shower. They were coming from below, and I thought I heard a voice raised in anger as well. Terrified, I grabbed a towel to wrap my body on the fly. I took the steps three at a time. Hitting the bottom, I whipped around the corner, then raced through the house.

The kitchen was in chaos. Whisks and wooden spoons sailed through the air then clattered to the tile floor. Broken pottery and glass lay everywhere. Cookbooks had been hurled. The telephone receiver—dangling from its cord like a dead weight—screeched a distress signal. In the center of the maelstrom, Alix whirled. Cursing. Kicking. Flinging.

She was *finally* angry. Gloriously, furiously, *appropriately* angry. And it was a wonderful, transformative sight. I didn't care what the cause was—the release had been so long in coming. I sheltered in the doorway, arms folded across my chest, while jars of spices exploded against one wall, leaving a residue as colorful as abstract art. Alix hardly knew I was there. At last, her energy depleted, she came to a halt, looking a little dazed.

I picked my way gingerly through the shards and took her in my arms. We stood amid the debris, shaking, laughing, kissing, until I said, "So…what's new?"

Alix shrugged incredulous shoulders. "How can I *tell* you this?" She bent to pick up a broken saucer, turning it in her hands as if it were an ancient artifact. "My father called with yet another proposal. It was his happy task to inform me that Charles will agree to joint custody and an equal division of property, if I'll sign a new contract he and Dad have prepared."

After everything I'd learned, I shouldn't have been scandalized—but I was. "Your *father's* in on this? Helping *Charles*?"

"*Oh*, yes. He's probably been masterminding the whole fucking thing from Day One."

I let go of her and tightened my towel savagely, afraid to guess the cost of this latest offer. "What's the catch?"

"Just a tiny little concession."

"Don't torture me, Alix! What are you supposed to give up now?"

"Oh, Christ," she said through clenched teeth, "what do you *think*?"

"Surely not me?"

"But, of course, Lynn. If I'll swear never to see you again, not only will Charles come through with custody, alimony and property, but as an extra, added incentive, Daddy will buy me a new house in the city of my choice."

No doubt the damp towel had something to do with the chill I felt. "Are you tempted?" I asked softly. After all, her children were at stake.

"Not! Even! Slightly!" Her brown eyes were blazing. "I'm so mad I could spit! I just have insufficient range!"

"What did you tell your dad?"

"I knew the fastest way to get him off the phone was to ask for a copy of the document. He'll mail it to me, but there's not a chance in hell I'll sign it!" She spread her arms and I stepped into her embrace.

I'd heard a new strength and certainty in her voice. It seemed that Alix had crossed some critical line, that at last we shared a common vision of our plight. Quite a birthday gift, I thought. And I couldn't help smiling as I realized that I had Charles to thank for it. Perhaps for the first time, I genuinely believed Alix and I would survive the endless assaults on our relationship. But there was no time to discuss anything in depth just then.

Playfully slapping her rear, I said, "Looks like you've only set us back two or three hours, babe. I've got to dry my hair and get dressed, but then we'd better break out the shovels."

Alix looked around the kitchen, seeming to take in the destruction for the first time. A look of horror spread over her face. "Oh, my *god*, Lynn! I'm *so sorry*! Your beautiful pots! The books! I just felt crazy…I wasn't thinking about what I was doing…"

"Not to worry, darling," I said, handing her a broom. "I can always throw new pots—and I'm not sorry to have an excuse to make some things just for *us*. Besides, given the circumstances, I wouldn't have cared if you'd smashed every damned thing I own."

Alix canted her head at me, a glorious grin replacing her penitent expression. Gesturing broadly at the devastation, she asked, "Is this what they mean by a *breakthrough*?"

* * *

Maybe we'd reached the saturation point with depression. Nothing could bring us down for the remainder of that afternoon. We sang while we restored the kitchen as best we could, and joked throughout our final preparations for the weekend. When we were finished, Alix collapsed on the couch.

"I'm too *tired* for company," she moaned. "Whose idea *was* this?"

"Ve haf vays of meking you party," I rasped in a sinister voice, tickling her lightly.

"Stop, you beast! I've got to lie down or die."

"That bad, hmmm?" I pushed Alix into a horizontal position and began to massage her neck and shoulders. By the time Mattie rapped on our front door, we were so relaxed, we were almost liquid. Nevertheless, we leaped up to greet her, delighted that she'd been the first to arrive.

Mattie hadn't seen this house yet. I took her on the grand tour, while Alix went to check on the simmering curry. Upstairs in my office, Mattie paused to pay tribute to a framed photograph that hung over my desk. Though I'd never met Diana Kingston, an image she'd captured one cold winter day was the only introduction necessary.

Shot with maximum depth of field that recorded every detail of light and texture, it read as an allegory. A young boy knelt alongside the crumpled and bloody carcass of a deer, tear-streaked face resting against the up-thrusting barrel of a rifle. His free hand tentatively explored the doe's lifeless flank and his look of startled remorse verged on recognition. I never glanced at the print without wondering which choice that child had made—"manhood" or humanity?

"That's *her*, that's my Diana," Mattie said softly, running a tender finger the length of the frame. "Not an easy image to live with, is it?"

"Keeps me honest."

Mattie turned those remarkable eyes on me. "Oh, she'd have *liked* that, Lynn—knowing that she's still doing her job."

Footsteps thudded on the wooden staircase then Deb Ransom burst into the room and embraced me. "Greetings, oh fair one. I bear a message from your lady love."

"Wash your mouth out with soap!" I said. "'Lady' is a four-letter word! An imposition of the patriarchy! A tool of the oppressor, designed to inhibit free—"

Deb interrupted, with upraised hand. "Let me rephrase... That fine-looking, feminist woman says you should get your sweet ass downstairs and introduce her to some recent arrivals."

I laughed with pleasure as the three of us linked arms and made our way to the first floor.

Sleeping bags had already begun to accumulate in a corner of our living room. The multicolored heap was topped off by Solly, who plainly resented having to relocate whenever a new arrival added her overnight gear to the stack. Women's voices were weaving a continuous tapestry of narrative and hilarity. In the background, Cris Williamson's circular rhythms underscored the festive mood, and the rich, warm aroma of curry filtered through our house. I couldn't remember a better birthday.

Twelve women sat cross-legged on an India print cloth to eat dinner. Small colorful towels were spread across our laps, serving as napkins. A huge platter of pineapple, melon, grapes and strawberries formed a rapidly dwindling centerpiece. We passed rice and curry, raisins and peanuts, sautéed onions and sieved eggs around the circle. Spirits were running so high that only a meal as fine as Alix's curry could have stilled the conversation—my friends take their eating seriously. We consumed embarrassing amounts of food that evening, then followed the meal with ice cream and cake. Rachel, groaning, insisted she'd never be able to move again. But Susan made a liar out of her by turning on irresistible dance music.

What is it about parties? They have a dynamic all their own. I've been to impromptu successes and meticulously planned flops. You just can't predict them. This one *worked*, some intangible chemistry fueling our gaiety. Alix was sparkling that night, freed at last from self-imposed constraints. And she'd begun to carve out a place in the group, to make connections all her own with my old friends. On my way to the kitchen for more wine, I heard Barb Chase commiserating with her.

"Why don't we have *Charles* committed? He was willing to do that to *you*. And it only takes three signatures."

"I'll sign," said Bree.

"Count *me* in," Mattie called from the kitchen.

I paused in the doorway. "Hell, I think we oughta just shoot the son of a bitch and be done with it."

"Too messy," vetoed Deb. "How 'bout cee-ment booties?"

"Too painless," insisted Alix.

"Would you consider terminal dentistry?"

"Stop!" Claire shuddered. "You just activated every one of my nerve endings."

"*I* kind of *like* the idea," Alix said, saluting me with her wineglass.

Raising my own goblet in response, I continued into the kitchen. Alix was doing fine without me.

* * *

When I returned with a new bottle of zinfandel, a pile of packages had materialized on the living room floor. Looking at that bright jumble of ribbons and wrapping paper, I protested. "You guys! You weren't supposed to bring presents!"

Mattie took my hand and pulled me down next to her. "You don't get to call all the shots, Lynn. Start opening."

Faced with that stack, I had no idea where to begin. "Do ours first," demanded Deb, as she tossed me a flexible bundle. "We bought these from a pair of crazy sisters at an equal rights rally last month."

I tore the wrapper and two screen-printed T-shirts dropped into my lap. I displayed the first one so everybody could see it. The crowd hooted with appreciation. We were all used to having red Stop ERA signs waved in our faces by rabid opponents of women's rights. Their leader—*our* arch-enemy Phyllis Schlafly—had appropriated the conventional stop sign image, using it with devastating effect. But the design on my T-shirt reclaimed the traffic emblem for *our* team. White letters on a red octagon read Schtop Schlafly.

"That's for days when you feel shy and retiring," Susan said. "The *other* one's for your more confrontational moods."

I shook out the second shirt, holding it up for inspection. Centered in the same stop sign design were the words Phuck Phyllis.

"Yeah, but who'd *want* to?" Niki laughed.

"No volunteers here," Rachel assured us.

"Courage, you all," Mattie drawled. "It might do her some good."

"Are you willing to take her on?"

Mattie ducked her gray head. "Sorry, my arthritis is kickin' up real bad. I think one of you younger gals ought to take a shot at it."

The jokes just got raunchier until I hollered, "Enough, everybody! I have important business to attend to here. What's next?"

Claire reached into the pile of presents and extracted a box containing a set of her hand-woven placemats and napkins. I fingered their rich textures and smiled with pleasure. "These are to die for, Claire! We'll treasure them."

Then someone shoved a heavy carton toward me. It was wrapped in newspaper and knotted with a big twine bow that somehow carried the unique stamp of Mattie's hand. "Nothing if not classy," she murmured with an ironic lift of one shoulder. Whatever this was, it would be amazing. I raised the flaps of the box. Inside, protected by cardboard dividers, were pint jars of wild honey and homemade preserves.

"Quick, Alix!" I whispered. "Hide this, or there'll be nothing left after breakfast!"

"Selfish twit!" Deb yelled. "Give us back our T-shirts!"

Barb raised an admonishing hand, saying, "Children, children! Calm yourselves." Then she tossed a long, narrow package at me. It felt absolutely weightless. "For your first Christmas tree together."

Eight miniature boxes crafted from thick, creamy paper. Embossed and elegant. Each strung on a fine gold cord. "My god," I breathed reverently, as I inspected the extraordinary craftsmanship, "these belong under glass."

"Not a chance!" said Alix, rescuing them from me. "They'll be gorgeous on our tree, Barb!"

I worked my way through the remaining gifts, touched to tears by the kindness of my friends. The last present was from Alix, who winked as she placed a thin, flat square in my hands. "There's more to come when we're alone," she murmured.

I studied the wrapping paper, a puzzled expression on my face. Alix had made no attempt to disguise the gift—I was holding a record album. But I couldn't begin to guess what she'd bought me. I had a habit of acquiring every feminist release the second it hit the stores. I knew I already owned everything current. Alix laughed at my bewilderment. "*Open* it, goof."

I slit the tape and slid the album from the shiny, patterned gift wrap. There, encased in plastic film, was a fresh copy of Gilberto's old album, *The Shadow of Your Smile.*

"Where in the world did you *find* this?" I demanded, hugging Alix with delight.

"I have my sources," she said demurely.

"Come on, babe, tell me."

"Nope."

"Did it cost you an arm and a leg?"

"Only your firstborn child," she giggled. "Boy, will *that* guy be surprised!"

I drew her close enough to whisper, "This is wonderful, darling. I want to dance to it later, but right now, will you and Mattie play for us?"

She dimpled. "Anything you'd like. It's your birthday, after all."

I handed over both guitar cases. Taking the lead, Alix strummed idly for a moment. The circle quieted. Only Mattie had heard her play before. She thought for a moment before breaking into a lighthearted rendition of "Single Girl," a song we'd all learned from Mary Travers and adopted as our anthem. Mattie laughed at the selection, joining in almost instantaneously. Before long, my irrepressible friends would suggest their own rowdy variations on the theme, but for now Alix and Mattie claimed our undivided attention.

* * *

The party was still in full swing well after midnight when I heard Solly's soft complaint on the front porch. I let him inside, and saw that his black fur was frosted with dew, each whisker beaded with moisture. Shutting the door behind me, I stepped alone into a fog so dense the world seemed to end at my wooden steps. We were cut adrift, sailing a swirling sea. A sense of peace enveloped me as I envisioned all my friends floating into eternity together, with love and laughter our freight. Hugging the thought to myself, I slipped quietly back indoors and returned to the celebration.

* * *

By the time I awoke the next morning, it was freezing cold. The mist had crystallized, bejeweling every branch and blade. In the shadows, the landscape was white-on-white, a monochrome wonderment. Sol, his dark body bounding through the yard, was an incongruity in that still and ghostly wilderness. But the sun was rising now and wherever the light of dawn struck, pink fire glowed in the ice.

I couldn't resist the magical scene. Dashing upstairs, I dressed for the weather. The early risers joined me for a spontaneous hike through the vast, glittering valley. On the far side, we stood arm in arm at the quarry's edge, gazing into its gleaming depths. I'm not sure that Alix even knew she'd begun to sing there. Emotion just turned to music, her mouth opened, and pure, effortless beauty poured out. Swaying side to side, the rest of us were hushed and joyous. All the way home, I felt like we'd been touched by something sacred.

Even the most determined of sleepers had roused themselves before we returned. Best of all, the late crew had acquainted themselves with our kitchen. Dannie was at the stove cooking omelets to order, while Vaughn kept up with the demand for toasted English muffins. And some degenerate had mixed several pitchers of Bloody Marys. It looked like another fine day.

The last of our guests left late Sunday. Alix and I waved goodbye long past the time they could see us then returned to the still house. We cleaned up a little, gathering empty glasses that we'd overlooked earlier and sweeping crumbs from the kitchen floor. But soon, I crashed on the couch, with Sol resting on my stomach. Alix sat cross-legged on the floor near us. She opened her guitar case and began to pick away in a desultory fashion. I knew her well enough now to realize that this was her own form of centering, a way of seeking inner calm and stable truths.

I studied her as she played. She was lost in thought, her head bent over drifting hands. In the lamplight, she looked tired. Too many late nights, I thought, and too much stress. Every trace of her summer tan was gone now. Those long lashes cast fluttering shadows on pale cheeks. The first faint signs of aging had begun to etch her face. I noticed a nearly invisible line where her dimple so often flashed and saw the slightest droop to that fine skin. None of that mattered, nor ever would. She was beautiful beyond telling. My heart's desire.

Suddenly her eyes snapped open and sought mine. Without prelude, Alix said, "Everyone here this weekend was a lesbian, right?"

"Yes," I answered steadily, not at all surprised that her interior conflict had finally surfaced.

"But they're all so different from one another, Lynn."

"Of course they are, darling. Look at the two of us."

Alix lifted the leather strap over her head and unlatched her guitar case. "Be patient with me for a few minutes," she requested as she shut the instrument away. "I need to talk about this at a pretty elementary level."

"You're really struggling with labels and stereotypes right now, aren't you?"

Alix nodded wearily. "Yeah, I am. Everybody 'knows' what lesbians look like, and how they act."

"Sure. I play that game myself. In the grocery store, I'll spot a woman ahead of me in line. She might have six kids in tow, but if she has a body like Mattie's, a haircut like Rachel's and a key ring clipped to her belt loop, I'll think, 'You may have fooled *yourself*, lady, but you can't fool *me*.'"

Alix laughed. "I know just what you mean."

"Well," I said, "that's fun, but it's really a silly, presumptuous pastime—and it's hardly what you'd call an ironclad method. Consider Sarah, for example. Or Claire. On that basis, no one would ever single *them* out as dykes."

"God, no!" Alix agreed. "Sarah looks like a runway model. Claire looks like Alice in Wonderland playing grown-up."

"And Bree looks like everyone's idea of the eternal maternal."

"But, Lynn, a lot of lesbians *do* fit the stereotype."

"I know, baby. That's one of the first things that attracted me to you."

Her mouth dropped open. Initial attempts at speech were unsuccessful. Finally Alix managed to frame the question: "You could tell just by *looking* at me?"

"No, love. I could *hope* just by looking at you."

"Am I really a lesbian, Lynn? Do you believe that about me? Do you trust it?"

I thought I understood her question. "If you mean, do I fear that someday you'll revert and dump me for a man, I'll answer honestly: I allow for that possibility. But I'd be surprised if that happened. I believe that you love not only *me* in particular, but *women* as a class. I think that Mattie exerts a stronger pull on you, say, than Charles ever did."

Those pallid cheeks flushed. "You're a shade more perceptive than you need to be, damn it."

"It's okay, love. Not only do I understand, but there's a kind of confirmation there, if you think about it. A reassurance that this *is* the right place for you. You didn't just 'happen' to fall in love with one woman, one time."

"But if you're a lesbian, and Sarah is too, and Vaughn is for sure, yet you're all so different, what can that label possibly represent?"

"Oh, Christ—diversity with a focused commitment, for a quick response. There are books and books, you know. I don't have all the answers, just my own working dogma."

Alix still looked earnest and perplexed. "But despite all that variation, Lynn, there *is* something different about dykes—something that makes them stand out from other women—"

I waited expectantly, only raising my eyebrows a little, only a little tense.

Fumbling for the right words, Alix continued. "I don't know how to pinpoint it exactly, or what to call it, but there's something about the way lesbians *move*. There's a freedom in it, or a naturalness—" She threw up her hands. "Am I making any sense at all?"

"Perfect sense. There's research that suggests we're more comfortable with physicality than straight women are, and that we use our bodies more confidently. I think those expansive movements are pretty powerful clues. They're probably one of the ways lesbians pick each other out in crowds—to the everlasting bewilderment of heterosexuals."

"You use those words so easily," Alix mused. "Lesbian, we, us, our…I wonder if they'll ever belong to me like they do to you. I wonder if I'll ever wear them as well." She raised searching eyes to mine. "I wonder if I'll ever really *know*."

"The absolute truth about yourself? Once and for all?"

Alix nodded.

"Some of us do. Dannie says there was never a question—she's always and only loved women. Claire says she can't imagine being with a guy. For myself, though, there was a matter of choice. I've occasionally—*very* occasionally—met a man who moved me. But I just can't imagine committing myself to someone who absorbed the idea of innate superiority with his mother's milk. I think that would ruin the most promising relationship. A long time ago, I closed that door without regret."

"What would you do if you fell off the wagon?"

"If I had an affair with a man? Assuming, of course, that *you* were unavailable to me? I suppose I'd manage to forgive myself. I almost never do things I can't justify. But I *want* this for myself," I explained, kissing Alix's eyelids. "I'm far happier living in a female framework than in the male-dominated world. As a lesbian, I may have to confront a hostile public, but at least I don't do violence to my own integrity."

Alix stood suddenly, stretching and yawning. "This is fascinating…and I know I started the conversation…but I'm tired, woman. Take me to bed."

"You'll never have to ask twice," I promised her.

* * *

A printed copy of Dunnevan's latest custody proposal arrived two days later. Alix set it by my plate at the dinner table, so I could review it when I got home from work. Instead, after glancing at the heading, I tucked the fat packet back into its envelope, unread. I couldn't bear to look at it. Didn't want to see the cool legal language that would excise me from Alix's life if she changed her mind. Because all she had to do to secure a claim on the children was sign her name on the line by that colorful little flag. A few strokes of a pen and I'd be history.

I handed the envelope to Alix and she set it out of sight on the chair beside her. "Any second thoughts?" I asked, just to be sure. After all, she was so accustomed to letting the men in her life run the show.

"None," she said firmly, as she picked up her wineglass.

"You'll need to forward that thing to Andrea Fasteau."

"I'll put a copy in the mail tomorrow with instructions to decline the offer."

Alix smiled warmly over her goblet, but I'd been swamped by a sudden wave of guilt and fear. I was remembering what I might cost her. Wondering how I'd forgive myself if she lost her beloved daughters. Trying to imagine how I'd survive losing her.

Alix had felt my mood shift into low gear. "*Trust* me, Lynn," she said, reaching across the table to squeeze my hand. "You have to trust me."

CHAPTER THIRTY-TWO

"Can I help?" Alix asked as I dressed before dawn one Saturday morning.

"Only if you're a glutton for punishment. I warn you, there's nothing fun about loading an outdoor kiln. And on a winter day, it's sheer drudgery."

"I want to see how it works," she insisted.

"Sucker! Little do you know that you're about to become slave labor."

"I'm used to it," Alix cracked. "I've been a housewife for years, you know."

"Bundle up, then. This will take several hours, even with both of us working."

So we drove into town together and opened my studio. The day before, I'd transported two batches of bisqueware. Those pots were already loaded into the kiln near our house. Now I needed to pack the pieces that hadn't fit into the station wagon on the earlier trips. But each pot had to be carefully wrapped to protect the delicate glazes during the drive. Before I began that process, I handed Alix a bucket and showed her how to mix fresh kiln wash.

"What's it for?"

"Sometimes a glaze will run more than you expect. But kiln wash keeps the pots from sticking to the shelves when that happens. You haven't lived till you've had to chip a piece you love off a thirty-dollar shelf. As often as not, both are trashed."

After we finished those preparations, we filled every spare inch of my car with heavy crates, the bucket of kiln wash and a small bag of moist clay. As always, heading homeward I cursed the distance between the shop and the firing site, a necessary but frustrating evil.

Just past our house there was a narrow, corrugated lane. I guided the car down it slowly, wincing at each bump, worrying about every clink in the crates behind us. Someday, I thought for the thousandth time, I need to have this path paved. Suddenly, I had an epiphany: Business was booming! I could actually afford to do that!

The wide clearing was old, familiar territory to me, so I set to work immediately. But Alix had to explore a little first. She completed a circuit around my sizable downdraft kiln before asking, "Did you build this thing by yourself?"

"Only partly. That was my original plan when I moved here. I was going to exhaust myself so thoroughly that I couldn't even *think* about my broken heart. But that was my first experience constructing a stoneware kiln." I shook my head, amazed by my own ignorance. "Soon, I realized that I'd radically underestimated the demands. I'd had no idea how long it was going to take—or how hard it was going to be—to build this thing solo."

"No doubt," said Alix, glancing at its impressive proportions, at the long arch of the roof.

"Then I had a bright idea. I got in touch with Nico Vivaldi, the ceramics instructor at the community college where Sarah used to teach. You remember him—you've met him once or twice at my studio?"

Alix nodded. He'd spent a little time messing around at my clay tables with Cindy and Beth when their visits overlapped.

And he was hard to forget—an immensely tall, strong, attractive Italian guy.

"I told Nico I could guarantee his students an invaluable learning experience. He thought it was an awesome opportunity, so he offered extra credit to anyone who'd help me complete the kiln. A whole gang of kids came to work and the thing was done in no time. If you take a close look when you're inside it, you'll see they carved their names into the firebrick so I'd never forget."

Alix laughed. "You're not dumb."

"Ah, a woman with remarkable powers of perception," I replied. Then I turned up the collar of her jacket and tightened my own muffler. The wind was howling and the temperature seemed to be dropping by the minute. Time to quit playing around. I asked Alix to unpack the pots, sorting them by height. While she unwound newspaper and set each piece on a low wall of railroad ties, I began to paint heavy shelves with thick, white kiln wash.

It was wonderful to have someone helping. Alix asked intelligent questions and observed analytically. Soon she could predict my needs. And she was a tireless worker. The furnace had never been loaded so quickly. When we finished, we ducked outside into spitting snow. Better work fast! I thought.

I began to stack firebrick in the entrance, sealing the chamber. After the opening was completely blocked, I handed Alix a pinch of soft clay and showed her how to roll it into a tiny snake. "We have to chink between the bricks in the 'door,'" I explained. "Wherever there's a gap, no matter how small, we stuff in a little coil of clay to keep the heat from escaping."

"Sort of like a log cabin?"

"Exactly," I agreed.

Chinking is best done by people with infinite patience and a limited need for stimulation. I am neither. Once again, Alix helped me make short work of a dreary task. Still our fingers were stiff and unresponsive by the time I lit the gas burners and adjusted the fuel mix.

I stood for a moment in the bitter wind, one arm around Alix's waist, offering a silent invocation to the kiln gods. Pottery is an unforgiving art form, made up of many separate stages, none of which can be rushed. At each step along the way, irreparable errors are possible. If the clay body isn't properly composed, it won't throw well. If a pot is perfectly thrown, it may be damaged as it dries. Even if it dries successfully, there are no guarantees that it won't crack in the bisque kiln. And you can invest a lot of care in a piece at every earlier stage then lose it in the final glaze firing. Sometimes I envied painters like Deb, who could simply rework an unsatisfactory section of a canvas. There are no "do-overs" in ceramics, no way to repair your errors. Perfect control is your best defense against the costly waste of time and materials.

Alix broke into my reflective stillness. "I'm cold, babe. Let's get in the car."

"Good idea. Maybe that's why I keep you around."

But once I was behind the wheel, Alix pointed at the kiln. "What's happening in there now? In simple terms."

"Christ, woman. I went to college for six years to learn the answer to that question. And I've been a professional for a decade, yet I'm always surprised when I unload a firing. Now *you* want the wisdom of centuries in twenty-five words or less?"

"Give it your best shot," she ordered. "And remember—I'm counting."

"Okay, here goes: The pots heat gradually until they reach maturity. Clay particles become so hot they fuse into a tough, nonporous, granite-like substance. Hence the name 'stoneware.'"

"Very good!" Alix applauded, having ticked off my words as I spoke.

"And not nearly complete enough. Brevity has its drawbacks, sweetheart. For instance, you still know nothing about 'quartz inversion,' but that's a critical period when pots can crack as the heat intensifies. And you don't have a clue about the cooling process."

I stopped there, afraid to bore her, but knowing I'd omitted dozens of crucial details. Most importantly, I hadn't even hinted at my elation when I've mastered every factor, from the first charcoal sketch to the last reduction in the firing. Opening a kiln can feel like Christmas morning.

I turned my attention from the slowly-warming structure to Alix. Her face was smudged and rosy. Her hands were marbled with cold. I shifted the car into reverse. "Enough of this nonsense. Let's go fix breakfast. I'm starving."

We'd just peeled off our coats and made our way to the kitchen, when the phone began to ring. Alix and I looked at each other in dismay. With the girls at Charles's house, we couldn't ignore it. But it wasn't even eight on a Saturday morning. Anyone we'd *want* to hear from would still be asleep.

I lifted the receiver and found myself listening to the diffident Southern murmurings of Lianna Edwards. "She's right here," I responded, handing over the phone.

Alix wrinkled her nose and slumped against a wall, kicking off her boots as she answered. "Hi, Mom. What's up?"

I opened the refrigerator and pulled out ingredients for my killer banana-pistachio pancakes. As I was setting eggs and milk on the counter, Alix stretched the phone cord to its furthest reaches. She tugged on my sleeve, waving a notepad under my nose.

They want me to go home for Thanksgiving! her frantic scribble read.

"Jesus," I groaned softly, "can't you say no?"

I've always gone, she wrote.

"Shit—" I whispered, pulling her close "—I want to be with you for the holidays." I began to explore her free ear with my tongue.

Alix shimmied deliciously in my arms, making no effort to pull away. In a deceptively ordinary voice she managed to say, "Well, Mama, Lynn and I were thinking of inviting you and Daddy to come *here* this year."

I struck the back of my wrist against my forehead, feigning horror, but I was actually impressed by this frontal assault.

Don't worry! Alix scrawled for my benefit. *They won't come.*

I turned her loose and went back to my recipe. Busy chopping pistachios, I lost track of the discussion for a few minutes. Then I realized that Alix was sounding progressively more strained, a sure sign that Caldecott Edwards had joined the conversation on an extension. I dusted my hands and went to her again. Sitting on a countertop, I held Alix to me while she fended off her father's attack. I could hear some of his comments, and it was simplicity itself to fill in the gaps. He had no intention of ever entering my house, or for that matter, any *other* pervert's home. That was that.

Alix kept her cool. In fact, she sounded so calm even her mother couldn't have guessed that tears were streaming down her cheeks now. "Well, Daddy," she said, matching his drawl, "do you intend to entertain perverts in your own home?"

Cal's agitated reply thundered through the phone. "I do *not*! Don't you *dare* bring that person down here! Do you *understand me*, daughter?"

"I wasn't referring to Lynn, Dad. I was talking about *myself*."

"*You're* not a pervert, *sugar*!" Lianna wailed.

"You're goddamned *right* I'm not," Alix shouted back. "I'm a lesbian, and proud of it! And if you want to spend time with me in the future, you'd better figure out the difference!"

When she slammed down the phone, I tried to cradle her in my arms. But Alix broke away, full of angry energy. Perched on the countertop, I crossed my legs and laid low while she crashed cabinet doors and banged plates onto the kitchen table. At last, I could contain my exuberance no longer. I let go of warm, bubbling laughter.

Alix stopped in her tracks. "Are you laughing at me?"

"Never, sweetheart. I'm laughing *for* you. That was magnificent!"

Alix collapsed against the counter, her anger spent. "Oh, my poor mother! She'll have a heart attack and it'll be all my fault."

"I don't know, Alix...maybe sweet Lianna just had her first *orgasm*. Because somebody finally told your dad where to *stick* it. And for that I do truly give thanks."

"Why, Lynn, darlin', how very, very crude of you," Alix drawled, barely suppressing a grin.

* * *

I rose quietly in the middle of that night and tiptoed downstairs, carrying jeans, a heavy sweater, hiking boots. In the living room, I dressed for the cold then left the sleeping house. Outdoors, I walked frozen ground under a freshening moon.

At my kiln, I pulled on asbestos gloves and withdrew a firebrick from the peephole. Peering into an orange glow, I waited for my eyes to adjust. In a moment, I was able to make out a row of tiny, heat-sensitive cones that I'd put in place to track the rising temperature. I was more than satisfied with what I saw. I had a feeling about this one—it was going to be a flawless firing.

CHAPTER THIRTY-THREE

Mattie, my dear—

How will you cope with this departure from the norm? I haven't got a single crisis to report to you—not one! This is just a note to bring you up to date. Things are uncharacteristically calm right now. Charles is away again—or am I being obvious? I don't have a clue what he's doing—and don't much care. All I know is that these quiet interludes restore our souls. Sometimes it's almost possible to forget he exists. The girls are with us now, as they always are when Chuckie's traveling. They're really enjoying the bedroom we've fixed up for them. What's more amazing is how comfortable *I* am after having added three people to my home, my routine, my life. Who'd have guessed?

Alix's divorce lawyer has recommended that she proceed at the most leisurely pace possible, using every conceivable excuse and delaying tactic to spin this thing out. Andrea's goal is twofold—to give Charles enough rope to hang himself, and to provide Alix with the maximum room to maneuver. One part of me keeps anticipating the next (inevitable) disaster. But mostly

I'm just reveling in this peace, trying hard to believe it's the shape of our future.

We've made a big change here: Alix has begun to manage my shop three days a week. (She's scheduled piano lessons on the other days—nearly all her students returned after the hiatus, a real tribute, I think). This new arrangement has tons of advantages. It frees me to work in the studio without interruption part of the time—very beneficial, as I've had to turn down some important opportunities just to keep all the balls in the air. And Alix has the kind of mathematical/analytical skills that so frequently coincide with musical ability. (Which, no surprise to you, *I* largely lack.)

She appears to enjoy working the business end and has already brought much-needed order to my world. Good news for customers, agents, suppliers, etc. And, of course, everyone who walks through the door loves her. I'm happy, happy, happy to spend more time producing, leaving the real-world stuff to her. So far, this seems like an inspired idea, and we may take it full time in the near future. Don't know why we didn't figure it out sooner.

In off hours, Alix has begun to compose music again, something she says she hasn't done for years. It's obviously an intensely private process, and so far she's keeping the results under wraps. I haven't heard a single note. But I know that she feels confident about the work—a good sign, since she's always her own worst critic.

I'm so damned *proud* of her, Mattie. When we fell in love, I didn't guess how rough this would be. Even my most pessimistic estimates were way short of the mark. Yet Alix has made it through everything thus far, just getting stronger and stronger under fire. She's learning to hold her own against her husband and family, which has had its amusing moments. I'll fill you in on the details next time we talk.

This morning for breakfast we baked baklava with the children (or 'blackalava,' as Beth calls it) using the last of your wild honey. It was excellent! Thought of you and the wonderful time we had at my party. We don't see each other enough, you know.

More later, my friend—I've got to run now...

Lynn

P. S. I almost forgot to mention Princess Esmeralda, the newest member of our household. She's a gerbil, and it goes without saying that Cindy named her. Esmeralda is a substitute for Gill and Finn, the goldfish who, sadly, reside with Charles. I wish you could see Solly—he crouches by Esmeralda's cage for hours, watching every move, just waiting for the moment when we slip up and leave the door unlatched...

* * *

The first thing I noticed when I stepped into our house one frosty night was the fabulous complex of smells that had made its way as far as the foyer—a spicy floral scent mingled with a wonderful roasted something. Chicken, maybe? With exotic herbs?

Alix was at the door to greet me. But before I'd had time to investigate further, she hustled me upstairs to shower. I was rinsing clay dust from my hair when an afterimage of her formed in my head. She'd been wearing that lipstick lesbian look again. Heels, because I'd barely had to bend my head for her kiss. A soft, thin sweater with a low neckline that just hinted at the tempting swell of her breasts. And hadn't I caught a flash of glittery earrings?

Something was going on—something that made me take extra care in the shower. Something that made me leave my hair swinging free. Something that made me turn away from my flannel shirt and favorite jeans hanging on a hook in the closet. Something that sent me downstairs in record time, dressed for a trip to the city, even though we were plainly dining in.

The next thing that caught my attention was the music—an intense, dramatic piano piece I couldn't identify. It stopped me in my tracks, filling the living room with explosive power. And just as it shifted into a flowing, lyrical passage, Alix reappeared. She was smiling, reaching for me, almost incandescent. I held her, speechless, bound by the music, rapt with love. When the room went silent, I pulled back to look at her.

"Holy god!" I said, gesturing at my tape player. "What *was* that."

"Just a little something I wrote," she said shyly. "In honor of us."

I felt my eyes widen. "That was *yours*, Alix? One of the compositions you've been keeping from me?"

She grinned. "No—it's one of the pieces I've been keeping *for* you."

"I'm honored," I said, with genuine fervor. "So why now? What's the occasion?"

"Think, Lynn, *think*," she challenged me.

I rolled the date around in my head for a moment, dismissing all the usual suspects. And then it hit me. "Oh, Christ! This would be the first anniversary…"

"…Of the night we met," she confirmed. "I'm very, very glad I decided to check out the Abbies, you know."

My heart hurt. "I'm embarrassed that I didn't remember, Alix."

"As well you should be. I guess you'll just have to make it up to me after dinner."

"Sweetheart, I promise I'll pay you back," I said. "With *interest*."

There were flowers and candles in the bedroom too. In my haste to dress, I hadn't even noticed. Alix turned on the stereo there, selecting something seductive and hypnotic. She made a ceremony of lighting those candles. Then, in keeping with my anniversary promise, *I* made a ceremony of undressing her. I slid that sweater off her shoulders, celebrating every inch of tender flesh, every curve and hollow, slowly revealing her, stroking her, warming her, leaving no part of her unkissed. I knew she was ready when she kicked her heels into a corner and reached for my belt buckle. I was strong enough, revved up enough, to carry her the short distance to our bed.

The music swelled and swirled around us, an enchantment like nothing I'd ever known. Entwined with Alix on tangled linen, I intensified my touch when the piano grew passionate and forced myself to pause at each rest. She shuddered and moaned and wound my hair around her hands and held me hard against her. Suddenly I realized that those were *her* fingers on the keyboard again, that we'd been making love in time with her own magic. "Oh, god, Alix!" I gasped. "Play it on *me*!"

And so her music flickered over me, shivered in my core and sparkled in my veins. It danced at my lips, cascaded through my spine and moved within me. When the final notes died away, it spilled me molten into the whirling universe. I lay limp in her arms, all our boundaries blurred, not sure I'd walk again. Forever after, I'd be at risk of spontaneous combustion when I heard that music. It seemed I'd only known the smallest part of Alix before, had only fully met her on this incendiary night.

After a long, peaceful silence, she whispered, "Happy anniversary, love."

An immeasurable period passed before I had the energy to respond. "What do you call *that* one, Alix?"

"You're gonna love it," she murmured in my ear. "I named it 'Westfalling.'"

CHAPTER THIRTY-FOUR

I was high on a ladder, wielding a paint roller, when I asked Alix the question: "What's Christmas all about for you?" She knew I didn't mean anything religious. We were both cheerful infidels. There'd be no advent calendars or crèches or church services for us—that was a given. Instead, I wanted to know what *mattered* to her about the holiday. What the girls would expect. How I should prepare.

Alix set her paintbrush on the edge of a can and looked around. The long attic room—soon to be a play space for the girls—was shaping up nicely. Everyone in the household was excited about it. Alix was motivated by a desire to protect me from the children's clutter, which had an astounding tendency to multiply, filling every nook and cranny of our house. Cindy couldn't wait because the room would include a sizeable art area. Beth was wild about the elaborate dollhouse we'd ordered. For Solly it was a new space to explore, with periodic patches of sunlight on the floor near the dormer windows. And I was thrilled mostly because the girls were.

"Can't believe we're almost done," Alix said to herself. Then she called up the ladder, "Come down and we'll talk about the holidays, Lynn."

"Do you have food?"

She patted her pockets. "A peppermint."

"Good enough." I shuffled down the ladder and she popped the candy into my mouth.

"About Christmas…" Alix sighed.

"Yes?"

"I guess I've been trying not to think about it. First of all, it means entering into negotiations with Charles. *Who* has the girls *when*? I'm not looking forward to that discussion—*or* to bouncing them around during the holidays."

I shrank from the thought of talking to Dunnevan, myself. "Here's a bizarre concept," I said. "Let Charles pick whatever dates he wants. As far as I'm concerned, it doesn't matter *when* we celebrate. December twenty-sixth? Fine by me. December twenty-ninth or January tenth? Okay too. Let's not give the man any power over our festivities."

"You *are* a dangerous radical," Alix said, but her smile was dazzling, so I knew she liked the idea. "All right. I'll talk with Charles and pin him down to some specifics."

I winced. That wouldn't be pleasant for her. Situation normal.

"There's another thing, Lynn…" Alix said, wiping a streak of paint from my cheek. "I'm guessing that Charles will overdo things for the girls this year, trying to be the big hero. And I'd rather not get into a competition with him. Let's keep things simple on our end."

I stretched a little. "Good idea. Why don't we finish here and talk more over lunch? We still haven't gotten to the heart of my question."

By the time we'd touched up the final spots, we were ravenous. We left our equipment sitting out—cleanup could wait. Downstairs, Alix heated turkey soup she'd made after Thanksgiving, and I set the table. Over lunch, I tried to explain my question.

"I've never once celebrated Christmas in my own home, Alix. I've traveled to be with relatives, or partied with friends, but I don't have any real holiday traditions. I don't even know what a Christmas with kids *looks* like."

"It looks however we want it to look, Lynn."

"Nice in theory, but I need your help getting started. Like… what are the most critical elements for the girls?"

"Ummm…anticipation, mystery, surprise," Alix said. "They love all the things that lead up to the event. Baking cookies from scratch. Seeing Santa at a department store in St. Louis. Decorating the tree. And we usually create some of the presents we give."

"Such as?" I asked, my curiosity piqued.

"Scented bath salts, no-cook fudge…whatever the girls are capable of making. Anything that helps them understand you don't have to spend a lot of money to give someone else pleasure."

"I'm totally onboard with that. We could make some clay ornaments to give away."

"Very cool."

"About the tree, Alix: Real? Artificial? Pine? Fir?"

"Real," she said instantly. "And I'm thinking…"

"Yeah?"

"You have all this land, Lynn. Why not buy a live tree, then plant it with the girls afterward?"

I knew what she hoped—that the tree would become an ongoing reminder of our first Christmas as a family. I leaned across the table and kissed her. "There's a *reason* I love you, Alix Dunnevan."

So the tree was a smallish thing, but lovely—a blue spruce that would outlive us all. Alix's collection of ornaments was out of reach, packed away in Charles's basement, and I had none. But I was happy to begin at the beginning. Except for a string of white lights, everything on our tree was handmade that year. Cindy and Beth pasted together dozens of ornaments, and kept making more as the season unfolded, until their creations crowded the branches. I added Barb Chase's elegant paper boxes, along with some delicate porcelain snowflakes and icicles that I'd crafted in my studio. Alix baked gingerbread till it was as hard as stoneware, then hung those aromatic cookies. And she fashioned a rustic star from grapevine she'd cut in the valley.

When she finished fastening it to the treetop, she studied the outcome critically. "Well, it's *unique* anyway."

I hugged her. "Just like we are."

Then the four of us stepped back to admire the results. We all agreed our tree was absolutely perfect.

Tins of holiday cookies were stacked in our kitchen, ready for guests who stopped by. The eggnog I'd made from an old family recipe was chilling in the fridge. A modest array of packages lay under the tree, and a few extra surprises were stashed in closets, waiting to be revealed at the last moment. Making a great show of secrecy, I helped the girls wrap presents they'd created for Alix. She helped them wrap little gifts for me.

Christmas was coming and I was crazy in love. Who could ask for anything more?

CHAPTER THIRTY-FIVE

We were all still in bed that Sunday morning when I heard a car spinning its wheels on snow in our driveway. Grabbing my robe, I peeked out the shuttered windows. "My god, Alix—get up! *Charles* is here!"

She shot from under the covers and began to tug on a pair of jeans. I ran downstairs, trying to plot my strategy. I'd made a private vow that Charles would never enter this house, but I hadn't expected him to appear unannounced on an icy morning while I was barely dressed. Before he could knock, I stepped onto the porch and stood blocking the entrance. He just shoved the door wide and pushed past me. I took a moment to straighten the wreath he'd brushed against while storming inside. Breathe deeply, I instructed myself. Keep your cool. Then I followed him into our living room.

Charles was standing there, staring contemptuously at the Christmas tree we'd decorated with such care only a few days earlier. When he heard me enter, he whirled around. "Where is my wife?"

"Alix will be down in a moment," I said coldly.

But Cindy and Beth beat her. Racing each other from the staircase, they tore across the floor, squealing, "Daddy! Daddy! Daddy!"

Charles dropped into a chair by our tree. He gathered up both girls, arranging them in a touching tableau on his knees. He whispered to them, stroked their hair and drew small treats from his pockets. I thought I might gag, but managed to hold my tongue. Alix would have to decide how to play this scene. When she finally appeared, I was standing in the center of the room, paralyzed, speechless, ill-at-ease. Dunnevan looked like he owned the place.

He rose to greet her, letting the children slide unceremoniously from his lap. "My dear," he said, reaching for Alix, "you look lovely, as always." And she did. Even in a faded sweatshirt. Even with sleep-tousled hair and drowsy eyes.

Alix didn't respond until she'd pulled free and seated herself on a distant, straight-backed chair. "What are you doing here, Charles?" she asked in a voice as frigid as the morning.

"I've come to visit you and the children."

I couldn't help myself, even with the girls present. "This is my house and you weren't invited. Don't make the same mistake twice."

Charles just ignored me. "Alix, I need to speak with you alone." He glanced around dismissively. "Is there some room we could use?"

I held my breath, restraining every impulse, hardly daring to hope she'd hang tough. Because I'd forgotten that *Charles* was every bit as attractive as Alix. Mr. GQ, himself. And in person, his magnetism was palpable, filling the room with irresistible power. You could actually feel him willing events to unfold as he chose.

Alix was pale, but her jaw was set. "No, Charles. You picked this time and place. If there's something you need to say, you can say it right here."

Charles obviously wasn't prepared for defiance. Now *he* was unsure of himself. He fussed with a pipe, trying to regroup. I decided to deprive him of his prop. "Excuse me, Mr. Dunnevan, but I don't permit smoking indoors."

His lips compressed as he jammed the unlit pipe into a leather pouch and shoved it back in his pocket. He looked pointedly at his daughters. "Alix, couldn't the girls go watch TV, or something?"

She nodded almost imperceptibly. I bent to Cindy. "Would you guys find Solly? Give him fresh food and water, then take him out back for a few minutes. You'll need coats and boots."

Beth jumped up immediately, but Cindy knew something important was going on. She looked a lot like Charles at that moment. Beautiful. Obstinate. Implacable.

Alix snapped her fingers. "Cynthia Nicole Dunnevan! Skedaddle! This is grown-up stuff."

As slowly as possible, Cindy crossed the living room and trudged upstairs. When we finally heard her calling for the cat, Charles began once more.

"Sweetheart," he said, failing to notice how Alix recoiled from the endearment, "you *know* I've never given up on our marriage. I believe in it. I believe we belong together. If I've done some unpleasant things recently, that was due to frustration and I sincerely regret any pain I've caused you. I love you very much."

Alix ran slender hands through rumpled hair. She seemed distracted, as if she were having trouble paying attention. I felt my shoulders begin to relax when she said, "I'm sorry, Charles, but it's really over. There's nothing left between us. I've tried to make that clear to you."

His fingers fumbled inside the pocket that held his pipe. When he spoke, his words were disarmingly gentle, intimate, as if I weren't a witness to the scene. "Alix. Darling. We can make things better. You'll see. We'll get some counseling and learn to work this out."

She shook her head slightly, barely concealing a yawn. "We should have done that years ago, Charles. I'm not interested anymore. Things have changed. *I've* changed."

"You can't have changed that much," he said, and an ominous tone crept into his voice. "You need me, Alix—you've *always* needed me. You'll never make it on your own."

Her laughter was genuine, welling up from some deep source. "Charles, I've been making it without you for one hell of a long time now. And you don't frighten me anymore."

Something panicky flickered in his indigo eyes. I couldn't let it pass unremarked. I leaned forward and plucked a clementine from a bowl on the coffee table. Tossing it lightly in the air, I said, "Perhaps it's you who needs Alix, Mr. Dunnevan?"

Charles froze for an instant, but quickly regrouped. "On the contrary, Lynn. I'm managing quite well, thank you."

He turned his attention to Alix again, deploying his trademark smile, the one that suggested they were all alone in the room. "I'm managing quite well indeed. As a matter of fact, darling, you're looking at the next lieutenant governor. Hawkins won't run again and the time's right for a new face. The party's been grooming me for the better part of a year. Your father's helped us mobilize an impressive network of first-time donors, with more to come after we go public. The campaign is completely designed and it's top-notch. I can't lose."

I felt like someone had just turned on floodlights. A hundred different details suddenly clicked into high resolution. All those mysterious trips, all those secret meetings. All Dunnevan's frantic attempts to wind things up with Alix—one way or another.

Because Charles had desperately needed to defuse the ticking time bomb we'd unwittingly introduced into his latest scheme. And he hadn't much cared how he accomplished his goal. Only success mattered, whether that meant seducing Alix or institutionalizing her or threatening or bribing her. Suddenly everything made sense. I shot a look in her direction. Did *she* see it too? But Alix wouldn't meet my eyes. *Couldn't* meet my eyes?

Confidence had begun to flow back into Charles. "You can be part of that, sweetheart. This is the kind of life you were raised for." His voice dropped into a confidential register. He was practically whispering when he said, "I'm on the fast track, Alix. And the sky's the limit!"

He didn't have to spell it out. After a term or two as lieutenant governor, he'd run for the top spot. Or maybe campaign for a US Senate seat. Whichever opportunity offered the shortest climb up the ladder at that moment in time. Fast forward a decade or so and Charles might even run for president. He was smart enough, handsome enough and—when it suited his purposes—charismatic enough to be a credible candidate. Especially in an era where style nearly always trumps substance. And hadn't Alix once told me that Charles never backed down after starting something?

I could imagine how relentlessly he'd pursue the ultimate prize. Charming voters at every photo op. Building name recognition. Steadily increasing his visibility. With expert handling, a signature "cause" or two and a little luck, he might well make it. Stranger things had happened. I could already see his chiseled face on thousands of waving posters at a nominating convention—older by then, of course, and more distinguished. I could visualize Dunnevan on *Meet the Press* and *Face the Nation*, debating weighty matters with all comers, positively oozing *gravitas*.

Alix had understood completely, had seen the bright path unfolding before him. Her eyes were suddenly sparkling with excitement and color had blossomed in her cheeks. "Well, *that's* a game changer," she breathed. "I'm stunned!"

Charles grinned triumphantly, while I stared at Alix in horror. "*Trust* me," she'd said. "Trust me." And I had. Now, every caution I'd heard about falling for straight women paraded through my mind, lit up like neon doom.

Alix's head was tipped on an angle, her dark eyes envisioning something far distant from this room, this life. The governor's mansion a few years from now. Or the halls of Congress. The White House, even. Herself as First Lady in the not too distant future. I could see her clever mind calculating, knew she was considering Dunnevan's offer, with all its implications. She was analyzing the whole picture, factoring in every data point, evaluating the best outcome for herself and the girls. Exactly as her therapist had *taught* her to do. Goddamn! I was going to be dumped again!

"Just think…" Alix said softly, "…if I came back to you, I'd have it all. The parties, the clothes, the comfort, the travel…"

An entire catalog of unsuspected desires. The little orange fell from my fingers, landing on pine floorboards with a sickening thud. I should have *guessed* the rich girl would return to her roots one day. How had I misunderstood her so completely?

"Absolutely," Charles assured Alix. "You'll have all of that. And—" he waved his hand, banishing our home, our little handcrafted Christmas tree "—naturally, a fine house."

"A grand new place on the river in Jeff City!" Alix crowed. "Plenty of room for entertaining! And I could live on the water again!"

Charles said, "Wherever you'd like, darling. Anything you want."

"It wouldn't be easy, though. We have a lot of unresolved issues—"

"I'll do whatever it takes, Alix."

"—but if we *were* able to work this out, Charles, I could live *exactly* the way my mother does."

"Exactly! Only more so. And, of course, the girls would meet all the best people."

Was I only imagining a dangerous edge in her voice when Alix said, "Just like *I* did?"

Charles answered without hesitation. "Yes, darling! Just like you did! Think about it!"

Alix tipped her chair against the wall, lacing slim fingers behind her head, staring at the ceiling. "I'm thinking, Charles. I'm thinking…" In the tantalizing pause while she reviewed his proposal, my heart stood still in my chest.

Finally, a breathtaking smile animated Alix's face. That dimple danced, as she said, "I can see it now. We'd be in the papers all the time—and on TV *too*! There are so *many* possibilities."

Dunnevan's smile grew even more brilliant, while every hope I had died. "That would be perfect! The filing deadline is three months away. We'll need to get you back in public view immediately, Alix—you've kept an awfully low profile since the girls were born. But this gives us time for tons of appearances and interviews before the formal announcement."

Still staring upward, Alix said, "That's doable. We could make *a lot* of headlines together, you and I." Her voice was dreamy, rich with anticipation.

"I've thought so too," Dunnevan agreed eagerly. "You'll be *such* an asset to the campaign, sweetheart!"

I wanted to flee the room, rend my clothes, tear my hair and do every wild, animal thing that grieving people were once allowed to do. But my feet seemed rooted to the spot. I couldn't take my eyes off Alix's beautiful, faithless face.

"I'll be glad to talk with any reporters you can round up," she assured Charles. "Because nobody knows you better than I do, babe." Then, looking directly at her husband, Alix said, "How's *this* for a headline? CANDIDATE SUES LESBIAN WIFE FOR CUSTODY. *That's* got a nice ring to it, don't you think? Or how about *this* one, darling? DUNNEVAN VS. GAYS AS HUNDREDS MARCH ON JEFF CITY."

Charles's triumphant face went ashen. "You wouldn't do that to me!" he gasped. "You couldn't, Alix! I'm the father of your children!"

"Try me," she said, her voice like granite. "I've got nothing to lose—you've seen to that."

Alix stood. Her chair fell back into place, striking the floor with a sharp, decisive clack. She seemed taller—powerful as some primordial goddess, and just as forbidding. "If you fight me for the girls, Charles, you can damn well kiss your political ambitions goodbye. Your campaign will never get off the ground."

She reached for my hand and I could breathe at last. "The minute you make trouble for us, Lynn and I will do outrageous things in public for the benefit of photographers. Won't we, love?"

"With a vengeance," I assured Charles, cheering inwardly. "I'm a *very* creative thinker, you know."

"You're crazy!" he hissed at Alix. "You should be locked up!"

"Too late. You missed your chance. Lock me up now and Lynn will sell our story to the sleaziest scandal sheet she can find—she'll have a ton of fun with that."

"Yeah, buddy!"

"*Please*, Alix," Charles choked out, "this opportunity means everything to me. I've worked so hard for it—I *deserve* it!"

"Whether you win the election is up to you, Charles, but you just lost custody of the children. You might as well settle for glory—it's all you're going to get. Play this any other way and I'll make your life a nightmare. I *can*, you know. I've learned how from a master."

Dunnevan was rigid with shock. "But this is blackmail!"

Alix laughed. "I *thought* you'd recognize it."

She handed Charles his coat, then cupped her palm under his elbow. As she steered him toward our front door, I heard her say more gently, "Have your lawyer call my lawyer. We'll work out a generous visitation plan. You'll be able to see the girls as often as you like. Of course, you'll be *awfully* busy in the capitol…"

Then she showed him onto the porch and said farewell.

I joined Alix at the threshold, still weak in the knees. Slipping an arm around her waist, I sent up silent hosannas, wondering why I'd doubted her, even for an instant. And knowing I'd never question her loyalty again. Tears of relief streamed down my face as we watched Charles clamber into his car and back viciously out of a tight spot.

When she turned to me, Alix was shaking from the stress of their encounter, but her face was alight. "We *did* it!" she exulted. "We *did* it! We beat him at his own game! We got the girls!"

"No, Alix. *You* did it! You did it all by yourself! And it was wondrous to behold."

* * *

Unchink the opening to a kiln and remove the crumbling firebrick. Transformations have taken place since you sealed the door some days before. While you've gone about the business of survival, fire and flux have done their work.

Mystery lies within that dark chamber. Miracles await the blind reach of your hand—or disasters. So much depends on the care devoted to each slightest act, on your ability to weigh, to balance, to envision grace.

All the rest may be attributed to the caprice of the kiln gods.